Joanna Toye worked on the production team of BBC Radio 4's *The Archers* for nine years and has written for *The Archers* and *Crossroads*. Her novelization of *Shula's Story*, based on *The Archers* is also published by Penguin/BBC Books.

Joanna Toye

DANGERFIELD

Series created by Don Shaw

PENGUIN BOOKS

BBC BOOKS

PENGUIN BOOKS
BBC BOOKS

Published by the Penguin Group and BBC Worldwide Ltd
Penguin Books Ltd, 27 Wrights Lane, London w8 5tz, England
Penguin Books USA Inc., 375 Hudson Street, New York, New York 10014, USA
Penguin Books Australia Ltd, Ringwood, Victoria, Australia
Penguin Books Canada Ltd, 10 Alcorn Avenue, Toronto, Ontario, Canada m4v 3b2
Penguin Books (NZ) Ltd, 182–190 Wairau Road, Auckland 10, New Zealand

Penguin Books Ltd, Registered Offices: Harmondsworth, Middlesex, England

First published 1996
1 3 5 7 9 10 8 6 4 2

🅱🅱🅲 ™ BBC used under licence

Set in 10/12pt Monotype Sabon
Typeset by Rowland Phototypesetting Ltd, Bury St Edmunds, Suffolk
Printed in England by Clays Ltd, St Ives plc

For my mother, who would have loved *Dangerfield*.

ACKNOWLEDGEMENTS

I would like to thank Doug Young at BBC Books and Andrew Cameron at Penguin for all their enthusiasm for this project. On the *Dangerfield* production team, thanks are due to the producers, Adrian Bate and Peter Wolfas, and to Jo Mainwaring and Linda Cordwell who got hold of scripts and tapes for me. Tim Prager, Keith Temple and Nick McCarty made their scripts available, as did the creator of *Dangerfield*, Don Shaw. His time, expertise and advice before I started made my task much easier, as did his policy of leaving me alone to get on with it, for which I am deeply grateful.

Joanna Toye, 1996

PART ONE

RUPTURE

Paul Dangerfield looked at his reflection in the mirror. His mouth, he noticed, was thin, thinner than usual, and there were deep lines etched on his forehead, a perpetual frown. How long had they been there? When had they arrived? He narrowed his eyes, as if squinting into a strong sun, or as if suddenly in pain. He was in pain. Not just the pain from the accident, his ribs and his shoulder, he could cope with that, but a deeper-seated hurt which he couldn't imagine would ever heal.

He sat down abruptly on the dressing-table stool in what he supposed he would come to refer as 'his' bedroom. It had been 'theirs' – his and Celia's. But Celia would never be here again. Today she would be buried in their little village church in the plot he had chosen under the sheltering elms.

He closed his eyes against what the day held and knew at once it was a mistake, for the same reason that lying down and trying to sleep was a mistake. As soon as his eyes closed on the brightness of the everyday world there was only one image imprinted there. Himself, at the wheel of the car, his son Marty in the back with the dog, and Celia beside him in the passenger seat, laughing at some absurd literary quiz programme which was being repeated on the radio.

They had been on their way back from a visit to Celia's parents in Kent. They'd only decided to go a few days earlier. The weather had turned warm, even for England in June, and Paul had been catching up with his post at the surgery at Wickton Road when Julia, the receptionist, had poked her head round the door.

'Can you see a rep?' she'd asked.

Paul pulled a reluctant face.

Reading his mind, which she had a worrying knack of doing, Julia added: 'It's Dr Mackenzie's half day, Dr Hamada has got his Mother and Baby clinic and Dr Stevens has been called out.'

Nick Mackenzie usually saw the reps; his tough, bantering manner weeded out the time-wasters pretty effectively. Shaaban – Dr Hamada – was, like Paul, of a more tolerant persuasion, and tended to make promises to reps which he couldn't really keep. Joanna Stevens was the newest recruit to the practice but Paul suspected that, like Nick, she would be more than capable of going a couple of rounds with a rep if necessary. However, today, none of these options was open and suddenly Paul couldn't bear it. Sunlight was filtering through the leaves of the lilac outside his window, dappling a glossy brochure advertising artificial limbs. Suddenly he knew he couldn't bear being cooped up for a moment longer on this particular day, especially if it meant having to listen to a sales pitch for anticoagulants.

'I'm sorry, Julia,' he said quickly. 'I'm picking my daughter up from school today. I really have got to be going.'

Julia's mouth moved in a silent 'Oh' of acknowledgement. Paul knew that she knew he was making excuses, so to add conviction to his story he stood up and reached for his car keys.

'I'll tell him to come back next week, then, shall I?' Julia suggested sweetly, enjoying the view from the moral high ground. 'Would Tuesday suit you?'

Unable to argue, Paul nodded resignedly. But he'd got what he wanted for today: an hour or two of freedom. He would pick Al up from school, sparing her a painstakingly slow journey on the school bus, and have a cup of tea at home before coming back into Warwick for evening surgery.

Al, who was thirteen, greeted him with a lack of enthusiasm bordering on coolness – an act, he knew, for the benefit of her friends. Once in the car, she greeted him properly with a hug and fresh demands for black jeans, a denim jacket and a choc-chip ice-cream. Paul gave in to the most easily fulfilled of these requests by stopping at the Italian ice-cream place near the castle and, leaving Warwick lying comatose in the sun, they drove the ten miles towards home, Al slurping happily.

When Paul and Celia had moved from London five years before, they had both been clear about wanting two things: space and greenery. Church House had been the first place they had looked at. Paul had loved the house on sight: Celia had been the one who had needed some convincing. Though the shell was sound and the warm Georgian brick exterior attractive, the previous owner had been a DIY freak of dubious taste and ability, and Celia's first reaction had been a non-negotiable 'no'. But with his usual quiet determination, Paul had persuaded her to take it on and between them they had transformed it, ripping away plasterboard and nylon carpets, replacing them with stripped floorboards and soft colours.

Paul pulled the car up on the gravel drive and, gazing out over the shimmering cornfields beyond the trembling greenery of the garden, he felt the familiar sense of peace at arriving home.

As he put his key in the lock and the front door swung open, he could hear voices from the kitchen. He suddenly remembered that Shaaban and his wife Amina were coming to supper, so Celia would be cooking. The other voice was that of Marty who was twelve.

'It's only us,' he shouted.

'Paul? Is anything wrong?' called Celia.

'Nope, everything's fine.'

Al dumped her bag in the hall and rifled through the post, tearing open a letter from her French penfriend. Paul

5

made his way towards the kitchen, and stood for a moment in the doorway.

Celia was trying to lift pastry into a flan ring and concentrate on a complicated story about Marty's friend Jason, a craft knife and the (with Jason, inevitable) visit to the headmaster. The sun caught the coppery highlights in her hair, bounced off the gleaming Aga, glowed on the pine cupboards. Suki the cat was stretched full length on the tiled floor, half in, half out of a shaft of sunlight, exuding contentment. Outside, Paul could see Boozie the dog lying in the shade, watching a butterfly. The whole scene gave Paul a sense of wellbeing you could have bottled.

'I had to escape from a rep,' he explained, coming into the kitchen as Celia looked up. 'Thought I'd pick up Al and take tea with my family before evening surgery. How are you?'

Celia turned her cheek for his kiss.

'Fine,' she said, absorbed. 'Better once I've got this in the Aga. Marty, put the kettle on?'

'Oh, I'll do it,' said Al, coming in to the kitchen and correctly anticipating Marty's whine of protest.

Paul smiled gratefully at his daughter. Like him, she would do anything to avoid a confrontation. Celia's only worry, he knew, was that Al was just too nice for her own good.

Paul stopped to tickle Suki behind the ears and sat down on a neighbouring chair. He stretched his long legs out in front of him and reached into his shirt pocket. He produced two tickets and laid them with a flourish on the table where Celia could see.

'Surprise,' he said. 'Stratford, Saturday night. You know I told you one of the actors came in last week, terrible sore throat; well, I didn't do anything really, just prescribed some antibiotics, but he dropped these in today. For *The Taming of the Shrew*.'

'Oh,' said Celia, surprised. 'That's nice.'

'Oh, perfect,' said Al, turning from the kettle. 'You know I told you Sophie wants me to go and stay over on Saturday night, try out her new hair-crimper? So if you can get rid of Brother of the Year here, you won't need a sitter.'

She moved swiftly out of range of Marty's lunge and started to get the mugs out.

'I'll be all right here by myself . . .' Marty began, but Celia interrupted.

'Um, that's not really the problem.'

'Problem?' Paul enquired.

'My mother rang at lunchtime. Asked us down to Kent. I knew it was your weekend off and we hadn't got anything planned – at least, I didn't know about the tickets – and it's been a while since we've seen them. Not since Christmas. So I said yes.'

'Oh, no way . . .'

'That's enough, Marty,' Paul cut in. 'If Mum's said we're going, we're going.'

He knew Celia felt increasingly guilty about her parents. She was their only child, and they felt that she lived a long way away. It was a nightmare journey, all the way to Kent, and the kids were inevitably bored when they got there, but Celia was right. It was time for their biannual visit.

'The thing is . . .' Al crossed the kitchen with two mugs in one hand and a full teapot in the other and put them down on the table. 'Soph needs me to be there. Her parents are going out and she hates being in the house on her own.' She began pouring the tea.

'If Al's not coming, I'm not coming!' insisted Marty, seizing his moment.

'Look, Marty, you don't decide what does and doesn't happen round here,' said Paul firmly. 'Al's got a previous engagement, she's got an excuse. You've got nothing else you need to do.'

'She doesn't *need* to go to Sophie's and talk about boys all night! It's not . . .'

'No, it's no fair, and I'm sorry, but that's the way it is. And . . .' Paul's voice tailed off as Marty jumped up, slopping tea on to the table, and rushed off upstairs.

'Wait for it,' said Al. 'Door slam, then Michael Jackson very loud indeed.'

Sure enough, they came. Paul sighed. So much for his perfect afternoon. He raised his eyebrows at Celia.

'I'll go up to him in a bit,' she said. Her hand rested lightly on Paul's shoulder as she carried the pastry case to the Aga. He raised his own hand and squeezed hers.

'We were doing fine till you got here,' she said with a smile.

'Well, I'm really glad I came home now,' said Paul wryly.

'Got to do my homework,' said Al. 'See ya.'

Celia and Paul exchanged glances. She straightened from the oven and turned to face him.

'What is it about you and Marty?' she asked. 'No one else can wind you up like he can without even trying.'

'Come and have your tea,' said Paul, pulling the mugs towards him across the table. 'Well, what's left of it.'

Celia wiped her hands on a tea-towel. She made to sit on the chair next to Paul's but he pulled her towards him and sat her on his lap. She looped her arms round his neck.

'What am I going to do with the pair of you?' she smiled.

'We'll be all right. As long as we've got you to referee.' Paul turned his head and kissed the soft inside of her elbow. 'Love you.'

Celia's face softened.

'Love you too,' she smiled. 'Look, I'm sorry about the tickets, Paul. Perhaps I could try and swop them.'

'Yes, why not?' Paul reached round her for his cooling

tea. 'Or I'll give them to Nick or Shaaban. Or Joanna, even.'

'But we will get to Stratford this season, I promise.'

'Of course.'

'Another time, that's all.'

'Sure.' Paul shrugged. 'Another time.'

Back in his bedroom on the day of the funeral, Paul rested his elbows on the polished wood of the dressing table and put his head in his hands. They wouldn't be going now, he thought bitterly.

Marty had had to cave in about the trip to his grand-parents in the end, though Paul had had to give ground too, in the shape of a new football shirt. But for all his occasional spats with Marty, Paul could see that he was a good kid, with none of the lip-curling insolence which he saw in the pre-teen children of some of his contemporaries. Marty loved tinkering about with all things mechanical and was forever disembowelling clocks and seized-up toasters and trying to get them to work again, but he also loved animals and plants and Boozie the dog and Suki the cat and his sister, even though it was dangerously unfashionable to do so. And he loved his mother. Not so long ago, Paul had found him curled up on the sofa with Celia reading him *Winnie the Pooh*. She had claimed that Marty had a touch of flu and Paul had shaken his head in disbelief. If he'd known what was coming for them all, he wouldn't have minded letting Marty hang on to his childhood. Now Paul wished passionately that he could have that moment back, and all the moments where he could see Celia in his mind's eye. He wished he could preserve that sense of security for Marty and he wished – he wished more than anything – that he hadn't teased him that day about being a Mummy's boy.

The visit to Kent had been good. Bill and Jenny, Celia's parents, had been in good shape. Paul had helped Bill to replace a pane in the greenhouse, they had been strawberry-picking, and had taken Marty to Dover Castle for the umpteenth time. Just a normal, happy, family weekend. They had eaten too much that Sunday lunchtime and had left later than they had intended, but as Sophie's mother had suggested that Al stay over on Sunday night as well, and go to school with Sophie on Monday, there was no real rush to get home.

The thunderstorm which had threatened all day held off until they had skirted London. Then, on a badly lit two-lane stretch of road, it burst down on them with a vengeance. The wind carried the rain in sheets, stinging against the windscreen of the car. Even on double speed, the wipers had trouble sloughing the water off, and Paul remembered Marty reminding him that, in India, car windscreen wipers had two speeds: normal and monsoon. He had half turned to acknowledge the remark, and, turning back, had caught Celia's eye and her special smile, the smile which said, eloquently and wordlessly: Thank you for taking time out for us this weekend, thank you for showing Marty that you care, thank you for being you. As Paul's brain registered all these things, and the unspoken question which was, 'And perhaps you might still have a little time for me, later, when we get home?' Marty spoke to him from the back. Paul didn't quite catch what he said, something about a sweet, and he half turned. In those few seconds he was not concentrating on the road, or, at least, not concentrating enough to see that the lorry in front had braked, hard, and that the distance between it and the front of their car was nothing like the distance he would need to stop on a wet, black road. He had recovered enough to twist the wheel, to try to swerve round the lorry, but as he did so, the lorry went into a skid, its tail end slewing to the left and its cab looming up sideways on in the very space which Paul had hoped would let them escape. In fact, in trying to take evasive action, Paul had succeeded only in ramming the passenger's side – Celia's side – hard into the lorry. Marty, in the back, had been lucky, because there had been nothing behind to cannon into them. The driver's side had been battered about – at least, that's what Paul later understood, for he'd lost consciousness – but the passenger's side had been pulverized.

When he came to, it was to find a paramedic putting a drip up. He moaned and shifted, licked his lips and tasted blood before passing out again. When he came round again in A&E, they didn't want to tell him anything about Celia, although he told them he was a doctor and not to bother fobbing him off: he was wise to all their delaying tactics and polite obfuscation. Instead they gave him countless X-rays, said they wouldn't strap up his ribs or his shoulder, thought he was mildly concussed. Marty, they told him, had got off lightly. Protected by his seatbelt, he had been thrown about a bit, had had a bang on the head and had suffered a bit from flying glass. His main problem was that he had remained conscious throughout, in a situation where both his parents were unconscious, injured and trapped and that had understandably traumatized him.

'What about Celia?' Paul kept asking. 'What about my wife?'

Finally the Senior Registrar came to see him in his little flowery-curtained cubicle. He pulled up a moulded brown plastic chair and sat down heavily. He told Paul that Celia's condition was critical. Paul knew exactly what that meant.

'I want to see her,' he said.

'Of course,' said the doctor. 'But we're doing all we can. You should get some rest. Or go and see your son.'

So Paul meekly did what was expected of him and went to see Marty, who had been given a sedative and was fast asleep. Paul touched his spiky hair on the clean hospital pillow. Then he went back and made another fuss about seeing Celia.

She was on a ventilator. Her face was a mess: she had been horribly cut. Two black eyes were already forming and her head was bandaged, but it was the extent of her internal injuries which was most worrying the medical team. They were keeping her under observation and the slightest fall in her blood pressure would mean an operation to see what was going on. There was also concern about the skull fracture she had sustained in case of bleeding into the brain. Paul stood by the bed, woozy from the painkillers, unable to take it all in. He touched her hand and said her name. There was not a flicker of recognition. He stayed for as long as they would let him, then went and, finally, slept.

In the morning, the consultant came to see him even before the tea trolley had been round. He was honest with Paul about the extent of Celia's injuries. There had, he said, been a marked deterioration in her condition during the night. He showed Paul the CAT scans. There was no brain-stem activity. He held out no false hopes. Paul knew what was expected of him. He explained that Al was being driven down that morning by a friend's mother. He wanted to wait till she arrived.

He went for a walk in the hospital grounds. It was a big, modern, teaching hospital outside Newbury, vastly different from the chaotic jumble of Victorian red brick and Portakabins which was Warwick County, where most of Paul's patients ended up. There were slabbed paths and beds of salvias, both in relentlessly straight lines. Last night's storm had had the usual effect of sweeping away all the foetid, wearying, warm air and the day was bright and blue with a new freshness and the promise of more warmth to come. Paul registered these things automatically; five minutes later he could not have described the route he took or the lab technician he passed on the path. After a very short time he felt exhausted – three ribs were broken and he could take only unsatisfying, shallow breaths – and sat down on a bench. From an open window he heard a clatter of pans and, though it was not yet ten, smelled a waft of lunch. He knew what he had to do.

He had never wanted to see Al so badly. Sophie's mother had offered to bring her down straightaway, when the police had phoned the previous night, but the hospital had said it could wait till morning. Even they, Paul surmised, had been unprepared for the change for the worse in Celia. Paul wandered back inside and sat and waited in the dayroom, with its red orthopaedic chairs and stern 'No Smoking' posters. He longed with a passion to be in their home which Celia had furnished with pale carpets and polished wood and big bowls of flowers. Anywhere but here, where the starkness of the furnishings served only to remind him of the ugliness of life.

He wanted so much to hug Al, and hold her tight, tight, when she arrived but his ribs didn't permit that: so he put his good arm round her and breathed in the clean smell of her hair. She had his blonde colouring but Celia's fine bone structure, whereas Marty had Celia's dark hair and his own squarer build. He told Al everything; there was no point in pretending. She was only thirteen, but she seemed much more than eighteen months older than Marty, she always had. Celia had always said when Al was tiny that she was three going on thirty. From the moment she could talk, conversations with her were like talking to an adult.

'I'd like to see Marty first,' said Al. 'I can't see him . . . after . . . and lie.'

They had agreed that Marty shouldn't be told about Celia yet.

Paul watched through the little porthole as Al hugged Marty and put out a gentle hand to his poor bruised face.

'I told Dad I didn't want to go,' he complained. 'And now look what's happened. Why hasn't Mum been to see me?'

'They're keeping her in bed,' said Al carefully. She had given a lot of thought to what she could and couldn't say.

'I could go and see her, then,' insisted Marty. 'She'll think I don't care.'

'Maybe later,' said Al with difficulty. 'Look, the nurse'll be back soon. They won't let me stay long. They say you need to rest.'

'I'm bored,' said Marty. 'I want to get up.'

'I'll come back and beat you at cards in a bit,' Al promised.

'Yeah, by cheating as usual.' Marty gave the familiar rejoinder but Al didn't defend herself.

'See you in a bit,' she whispered.

It was too soon to have the old, argumentative Marty back. She wasn't ready for him yet.

Celia Dangerfield was pronounced dead at 12.32 p.m. on Monday June 25th. The day before, Paul had been a happily married man, a GP and father of two. Now he was a widower, a single parent and an accident statistic.

Paul opened his eyes and blinked as he tried to refocus on his image in the mirror. Despite the lines and the dulled eyes, he was surprised to find himself looking as substantial as he did. Other people's robustness appalled him. The minutiae and trivia of everyday life which he'd observed on the drive back home from the hospital or as he went about the business of registering the death and dealing with the funeral arrangements, struck him as obscene, though of course there was no reason at all why other people shouldn't be getting on with their lives. But the sight of someone dragging a dustbin out or a mother forcing a reluctant toddler into a pushchair moved him beyond belief; tiny actions seemed to take on a huge tragic significance. He wanted to remonstrate with the mother, tell the dustbin-dragger not to bother. What did it matter if the rubbish went uncollected, if the bus was missed? Nothing mattered now. Nothing.

There was a tap on the door and Al appeared.

'Al,' he said. 'You don't have to knock. You've never knocked.'

'It's different now,' she said simply.

He nodded. Though he was wearing a dark suit and tie, he hadn't wanted her to wear black, so she was wearing white which was OK, she said, because it was the Chinese colour of mourning. Paul had no idea what Marty would wear, and minded that he minded. Marty hadn't asked for his advice; in fact, he hadn't said much at all after being told of Celia's death. Paul had registered this but hadn't had the resources to do anything about it.

'What's Marty doing?' he asked.

Al wandered over to the window.

'The car's here,' she said.

'Right,' said Paul. 'So where's Marty?'

Al turned from the window, her face streaked with tears.

'In his room. Crying,' she said. 'Oh, Dad.'

2

The funeral was a simple one, and small. It had to be, because the tiny village church could hold only about sixty people. Paul had been worried at first that Celia's parents would want her buried in their village churchyard in Kent, but they said that they felt it was more important for the children to be able to visit her grave. Paul was grateful for, and impressed by, their selflessness. They had come up for the funeral the day before, but had chosen to stay in a hotel rather than at Church House. They had come round for supper though, last night, supper cooked by Al.

Marty had dragged Bill off to look at his badge collection and Al had taken herself off to do the washing up. Paul and Jenny, Celia's mother, faced each other awkwardly across the low table in the sitting room, sipping their coffee to fill in the silence. Paul was waiting for the outburst: how he had killed their only daughter, how it must have been his fault, after all, he had been driving. It was what he believed himself; how could he expect Celia's parents to think differently? But when Jenny put down her coffee cup and spoke, it was not what he was expecting to hear.

'She was so happy with you, Paul,' she said. 'Only at the weekend she told me she couldn't believe it sometimes.'

Paul swallowed hard. Her gentleness, like an echo of Celia's, was harder to take than any amount of recrimination.

'I'm just . . . so, so sorry,' he began.

Jenny shook her head.

'You've got nothing to feel sorry for,' she said. 'You gave her everything she wanted. She had the perfect life.'

Paul wanted the funeral to be perfect too, just as Celia would have liked it. He wanted colour, and light, and music, lots of music. He had had the church filled with sweet-scented summer flowers, stocks and roses and delphiniums, massed in the dimpled brass vases. The vicar, who knew Celia from the Mothers' Union and Sunday School, was giving the address, and her friend Christine from the school PTA was reading one lesson, Paul the other. There was going to be Elgar and Bach and Delius and 'Onward Christian Soldiers', her favourite hymn.

The church was full but, as the mourners hung back to allow the family to proceed to the grave, Paul had never felt so alone in his life. He stood, one arm round Al, whose shoulders were shaking with sobs, the other round Marty, both of them rigid with the effort of not crying, and watched Celia's coffin lowered into the ground. Out of the corner of his eye he could see Jenny and Bill clinging to each other, openly weeping. His own parents were there too, standing stiffly erect. Apart from the most formal expression of sympathy, they had said nothing to him about Celia. Still, they had never shown him their feelings in forty years. They were hardly likely to start now.

'And so we commit to God the soul of our dear sister here departed, dust to dust, ashes to ashes . . .'

The vicar indicated to Paul that he should throw a handful of earth on to the coffin. Paul stooped to do so and was aware that Al and Marty had done the same.

'We come into this world alone and we leave it alone . . .'

Alone. For ever and ever, Amen.

Paul had never even seen it coming. He and Celia, who had talked about anything and everything, had never once discussed the possibility of either of them dying. What was that saying about the cobbler's family going ill-shod? He faced death and bereavement every day of his working life. He'd sat and held hands with husbands and daughters, wives and sons, after breaking the news of a terminal cancer, a brain haemorrhage, a car accident, even. He'd never thought he did any good, though many patients had said he had. Now he was even less inclined to believe them.

A few days after the funeral, Shaaban came to see him; kindly Shaaban, whom Paul had recruited to Wickton Road. Paul had never regretted the appointment and Shaaban's calm presence and tolerant attitude had saved the practice from disaster more than once. Celia had liked Shaaban. He came from an influential Egyptian family, from a background of privilege which had not equipped him particularly well for medical school in Britain in the fifties and still less so for life on the wards where, incredibly, he related, people had actually asked him if his colour came off in the bath or requested not to be seen by 'that darkie doctor'. Shaaban's saving grace had been his enormous dignity and great sense of humour which were no less useful at Wickton Road than they had been at Birmingham's General Hospital. He had enormous compassion, too. Paul had seen him weep for patients. But Shaaban knew that in Paul's situation there was nothing he could say which would mean anything.

'Words are of such little comfort at a time like this,' he said. 'It seems pointless even to try. But if *you* want to talk . . .'

Paul shook his head. He walked over to the drinks tray beside the fireplace and poured a finger of whisky into a glass. He saw Shaaban watching him.

'Not a good idea?' he remarked, indicating the decanter and glass. Shaaban had refused a drink.

'Paul, I haven't come to judge you.' Shaaban shrugged his shoulders and spread his hands. 'It's not my style. Look, if it helps you for now, there's no harm in it. Of course not.'

'I'm not going to get hooked on it, if that's what you're thinking.'

Paul came and sat down opposite his colleague.

'Show me an alcoholic who hasn't said that at some time in his life,' said Shaaban wryly. 'You'll be telling me next you've got it under control.'

Paul took a sip.

'Are all your consultations like this? You're not a GP, you're a mind-reader.'

Shaaban gave his little giggle which was so infectious.

'Paul, you've rumbled me at last. I'm actually a member of the Magic Circle.'

'Thanks, Shaaban.'

Shaaban looked at him, puzzled.

'For about thirty seconds there we were having a conversation, just like normal. We weren't talking about Celia, I wasn't even thinking about Celia . . .' Paul's voice tailed off.

'It will happen, Paul,' said Shaaban gently. 'Not yet, not for many, many months. But there will come a time when you realize that she is not part of your every thought. There'll be a time when you can pick yourself up and go forward. You won't always be stuck here.'

'What if I want to be, Shaaban?' said Paul suddenly. He leaned forward and put his glass down with a thud on the table between them. 'If I'd been a bit more careful, if I'd been paying more attention to the road, if I hadn't turned round to . . . well, Celia might still be here. Marty walks away with hardly a scratch, I'm knocked about a bit, Celia's killed. And I was the one doing the driving. How am I supposed to "go forward" with that little lot?'

'Paul.' Shaaban's tone contained the mildest of reproaches. 'You know, you've counselled enough people, just how unprofitable guilt can be. It was an accident.'

'Shaaban, for God's sake! Spare me the platitudes!' Paul jumped to his feet and paced tetchily round the back of the sofa. He turned to face Shaaban again. 'When I think of the times I've said that to people – they must have wanted to hit me! It just doesn't help! I'll never believe that it wasn't my fault!'

'I can't stop you from feeling what you're feeling, Paul,' said Shaaban mildly. 'You know as well as I do that guilt's all part of the process. I'm just asking you not to dwell on it more than usual because of the circumstances of Celia's death.'

Paul sighed. Absent-mindedly he picked up one of the silver-framed photographs of the four of them (well, five, counting Boozie) taken in the back garden last year, and put it back down on the piano. The rosewood surface was as lustrous as ever. Al must have been round with a duster.

'Shaaban,' he said. 'I'm sorry. It certainly isn't *your* fault.'

'No,' Shaaban replied. 'That's true. But I'd hate to feel you couldn't take it out on me. What are friends for?'

Over the next few months, Paul needed his friends. That first summer passed in a blur. He was persuaded to go on holiday with Celia's cousin and his wife and their three children, to a villa in Sardinia. Al and Marty seemed to enjoy themselves; which is to say that they lay by the pool with their Walkmans, played volleyball with the others on the beach, and disappeared each evening to hang around the local bar feeding lire into the Italian version of Space Invaders. For Paul the holiday was rather less successful. Away from everything which was familiar and thrown into the company of a couple, he was acutely aware of his aloneness. He took to walking along the beach on his own and spending hours sitting staring out to sea. Everything anyone said or did seemed to come back to Celia. He could not eat a plate of seafood without remembering previous holidays with her or hear the lilting language without remembering her trying to teach him

Italian during a long weekend in Venice when they were first engaged. He was glad to get home.

He didn't know what the answer was. The house was a constant reminder of her. Her photograph was everywhere. Her tapestry, half finished, still lay on the chair in the bedroom; her sheet music was opened on the piano. He couldn't bring himself to tidy any of it away. He spent a ghastly Sunday morning when both the children were out trying to parcel up her clothes. Nick Mackenzie's wife, Jean, had offered to do it for him, but he felt a perverse need to put himself through the pain he knew it would cause. After more cups of coffee than he could justify, he wearily climbed the stairs to their bedroom and opened the double doors of the wardrobe. Immediately he was hit by the scent of Celia. He put out a hand and touched the sleeve of a jacket, bringing it up to his face. Arpège. She'd always worn it, even as a student, when everyone else was wearing patchouli or musk. He swayed slightly. I can't do this, he thought. But I have to.

After that, he worked with a ferocious energy, stuffing clothes and shoes into black bin-liners, not even emptying the pockets, not looking at individual garments, knowing they would bring back memories. By noon, he had filled four sacks with clothes and one with shoes. He sank on to the bed and lay back, exhausted. He lay there for a while, thinking of absolutely nothing. Then he turned his head to look at the clock, and saw the chest of drawers. Oh, God, there was more. Her night things. Her cosmetics. Her underwear. It took him another hour and another three sacks. He didn't hear Al arrive home but she came upstairs and found him stuffing stockings into the last of the bags.

'Why didn't you tell me?' she said. 'I'd have helped.'

'It's done now,' he said briskly. 'Let's get some lunch.'

It wasn't done, because now he'd parcelled the stuff up, he didn't know what to do with it. He asked Julia at the surgery and she mentioned the women's refuge in Coventry which was always looking for clothes, and so next day he brought four sacks to work and loaded them into the back of Julia's car.

'They'll be awfully grateful,' she said.

Paul nodded. Part of him was repulsed and part of him wanted to smile at the vision of these poor, frightened, vulnerable women picking over Celia's clothes and trying them on for size.

'There might be some more,' he said. 'I don't know.'

But he never took the rest of the stuff. The shoes, the underwear and one bag of clothes which, though he hadn't been looking, he knew contained the red wool crêpe dress which Celia had worn last Christmas Day, which had been her Christmas present from him, he put up in the attic alongside the children's old toys and the chipped ewer and basin which Celia had been going to repair.

September came and the children went back to school. Paul felt relief. Now they had some structure, some routine back in their lives. He knew he hadn't been pulling his weight at the practice over the summer but Nick Mackenzie, the senior partner, who'd joined the practice as junior doctor to old Dr Rogers and had seen it expand to encompass first Paul, then Shaaban and, more recently, Joanna, assured him it hadn't been a problem. Lots of their patients were away, too, and it wasn't the time of year for coughs and colds and flu epidemics. But now it was September. Celia had been dead for nearly three months. Paul felt he ought to be beginning to operate normally (whatever that was) again.

With Al and Marty back at school, Paul felt weighed down by domestic responsibilities. They all had to have clean clothes, there had to be milk in the fridge for breakfast, and they couldn't go out and grab a pizza every night when there was homework to be done. Al had to choose her GCSE options this year. She told Paul she wanted to do French and either German or Latin. Which did he think would be best? Paul was at a loss. Celia, herself a linguist, would have been able to guide her. Paul hadn't a clue.

Some days he felt dizzy with it all. The alarm would go off at ten to seven and he would heave himself out of bed. He never felt as if he'd slept, even if he'd crashed out at ten-thirty. The deepest sleep did not refresh him, just made him feel more sluggish. Sometimes he thought that the nights where he was so strung up that he didn't sleep at all were actually preferable. Once he had given up trying to sleep, and gave in to his thoughts of Celia, he could be reconciled to being awake. It was quite pleasant, really, to have the sleeping house to the two of them. He could talk to Celia then, ask her if Al could go to that concert as long as Sophie's mum took and fetched them, or if she knew where Marty had left his football boots. She couldn't answer, of course, but he could see her smile, warm but faintly exasperated, as she always had been in the face of his helplessness. What did he expect her to do? Sometimes, frequently, he felt as though he were going mad.

Night-time wasn't the only time he saw Celia. There was one dreadful occasion, on the big roundabout outside town, where he actually saw her in her car, same numberplate and everything. He actually followed the car down the A46, followed when it pulled in for petrol, and saw a woman who looked nothing like Celia get out. And as he watched, the numberplate unscrambled itself into a sequence which was totally unfamiliar. Once he'd seen her in Sainsbury's. She was younger then, and had a younger Al and Marty with her – about the ages they had been when they first moved to Warwick. He knew it was Celia because they were putting Marty's favourite toffee yoghurts into the trolley. After the car experience he didn't try to follow her, or speak to her. He just stood, with his trolley blocking the aisle, watching the grace of her movements as she wheeled the trolley away, inclining her head to hear something the little girl was saying.

He told Nick about what he'd seen.

'It's perfectly normal,' Nick reassured him. 'It's your brain playing tricks. You *know* – rationally, you know – that Celia has gone. But emotionally you don't want to accept it. So you keep finding ways to prove to yourself that she's still around.'

'Yeah,' Paul sighed. 'I know all that – stages of grief and stuff. But how long is it going to go on?'

'You know the answer to that, as well.' Nick came and perched on the corner of Paul's desk. He picked up the photograph of Celia which had always been there and looked at it. 'It's a year at least, more likely two. And you can't duck any of it. You've just got to go through it.'

'How, Nick?' Paul's eyes searched his colleague's face desperately for the release he wanted. 'I don't feel as if I've got the strength to get through the day half the time.'

'Do you want us to get a locum in?'

'No!' Paul was vehement. 'It's only work, and Al and Marty, that's keeping me going at all.'

Nick smiled faintly.

'Then you've just answered your own question. How you get through it. You'll work your way through it, Paul, for Al and Marty. You'll do it because you have to.'

Then Nick took him to the pub and bought him a beer and a sandwich.

'Take the afternoon off,' he said.

'You just told me that work was the answer,' protested Paul.

Nick put a restraining hand on his arm and leaned closer.

'I don't want to get personal, Paul, but that's the third day running you've worn that shirt,' he said. 'Why don't you go home and get stuck in to a bit of housework?

Joanna's already offered to cover for you if we need her.'

Paul felt guilty about Joanna, too. She had only been with the practice three months when Celia died. When she had joined, Paul had promised to show her the ins and outs of the computer system over the summer and discuss the timing of her Well Woman clinic. All that had had to go on hold.

'That's decent of her,' he said. It was Joanna's half-day. 'We want to help, Paul,' said Nick. 'If you'll let us.'

'I don't see any of you offering to do my laundry.' Paul almost smiled. 'But OK, I can take a hint. I'll go home via the supermarket.'

Boozie thought it was his birthday when Paul got back at barely three o'clock. He lugged the shopping through to the kitchen, put the perishable stuff in the fridge and freezer, left the rest on the floor, and went to open the back door for the dog. Boozie ran out on to the terrace and immediately began worrying an old flip-flop he found under a chair. It had been a warm summer and the leaves were still a dull green, but the shadows were lengthening on the grass. The grass! If he'd cut it once since the accident, that was all. How was he going to keep on top of everything? The house, and the garden, and the washing and the ironing and the cooking and the shopping? Al was brilliant, but he couldn't expect her – and didn't want her – to take on the 'little mother' role. How had Celia coped with it all, and her supply teaching three days a week as well? The mountain of detail which seemed to make up family life overwhelmed him. He could not imagine ever returning to the situation which had always prevailed and which he had always taken for granted, whereby the right ingredients for a meal were planned, shopped for, cooked and served up on clean plates to children with shiny, shampooed hair, whose prep was done, whose school shirts were clean for the next day, who needed dinner money and money for the school trip and had to be reminded to take their art folder and clarinet and then there was the dog to be wormed . . .

Paul sat on the low wall, noticing as he did so that the trellis was coming off the back of the house and mentally adding it to his overwhelming list of tasks. He had two choices. He could give up and go under, or he could try to get to grips with things, at least domestically. Work, Nick kept telling him, could survive without his full attention, but the house and the children could not. So. He would get someone in a couple of times a week to deal with the housework and the ironing, which was what Jean and Julia had suggested all along. He could maybe even get someone in to see to the garden. That would leave him more time to concentrate on Al and Marty and, in time, on his own work again. It wasn't exactly progress, but it was the semblance of a plan. Slightly cheered despite himself, Paul did not even protest when Boozie brought him a disgusting old bone he'd unearthed from beneath the Michaelmas daisies and wiped it all over his trousers.

When Al and Marty came home, they found an unusual scene: Paul, sleeves rolled up, poring over a cookbook and trying to work out if the scales were properly calibrated.

Marty took one look at him and stumped upstairs, unimpressed, but Al came and read the cookbook over his shoulder.

'Spaghetti Bolognaise. Good for you, Dad.'

'Marty needn't worry. I can cook, you know,' said Paul. 'Don't really need a recipe. I used to live off this at university.'

'I wonder why that's not reassuring,' mused Al, giving the onions on the top of the Aga a prod with a wooden spoon. 'Want anything chopping?'

'No, it's all under control. Oh, you could empty the washing machine.'

'You've done a wash as well?'

Al crossed the kitchen and collected the big wicker basket Celia had used for the washing.

'Nick let me skive off. Right, one tin of tomatoes . . .'

Al opened the door of the machine.

'Dad . . .'

'Yup?' Paul was chopping mushrooms.

'What temperature did you do this on?'

'Hm? Fifty degrees, I think. I sorted all the whites into one pile, just like you're supposed to do . . .'

Al appeared before him, dangling a piece of blue cloth.

'All the whites, huh? And this navy-blue napkin?'

'Oh, you're joking.' Paul wheeled round to survey a pile of damp washing which gave a new meaning to the term blue-whiteness. 'Those are Marty's school shirts.'

'Never mind, Dad.' Al went to the fridge and fetched a carton of apple juice. 'You can only get better. By the way, I think your onions are burning.'

3

'That one!' cried Al.

'What, this one?'

It was a fortnight before Christmas, but Al always liked to get in early. Wincing as the pine needles pricked his flesh, Paul tugged the Christmas tree out from the bristling thicket stacked against the wall of the garden centre. He pulled it clear and banged it on the ground so that the branches, which had been compressed in transport, fell into the customary bottom-heavy shape.

'Yeah. Yeah, I like it,' declared Al.

Her eyes were bright and her cheeks red from the cold. She had crammed a bright green knitted hat over her blonde hair and her mittened hands peeped out from the sleeves of her duffle coat. She looked about six years old. Paul's heart gave a lurch. Their first Christmas without Celia. He was dreading it.

'What d'you think, Marty?' Al appealed to her brother.

Marty slouched over from the display of garden gnomes which he had been examining.

'S'OK, I suppose.'

As usual, Paul had to resist the urge to shake him. Marty was becoming, if that were possible, even less communicative. He still talked to Al, and sometimes she'd relay the gist of their conversation to Paul, but he hardly ever addressed a sentence to his father and when he did, his eyes never left the ground. The discovery, in October, that he had become a diabetic hadn't helped either. Paul had at first thought that the stomach cramps and sickness which Marty had been experiencing were bound up with not wanting to go to school, in the way that primary school children complain of a generalized 'tummy ache'. Paul had let it go for a week or so before describing his symptoms rather disparagingly to Joanna. She had immediately asked if Marty was drinking the same amount as usual. Paul knew what she was getting at straight away, and was ashamed that he hadn't thought of it, and was even more ashamed to admit that he didn't know whether or not Marty was exhibiting an increased thirst; he had never observed him closely enough to find out. But he was worried enough to phone the school and explain that he suspected that Marty was showing signs of diabetes: could he come and collect him at morning break and bring him back to the surgery so that he could run a simple urine test? Of course, in retrospect, that was the worst thing he could have done. Marty had emerged from a double history lesson to find his father waiting in the corridor, and was bustled away without explanation.

Once in the car, Paul told him his suspicions.

'I thought you'd decided I was just faking it to get out of school,' said Marty.

'If I gave you that impression, I'm sorry,' said Paul, stiffly, riddled with guilt and anxiety. 'But diabetes is a strong possibility and if it turns out to be the case, you don't want to leave it untreated for any longer than is necessary.'

'Oh, great. You reckon I've got some illness that's going to turn me into a freak, and just so I can get a taste of what it's going to feel like, you come and hoik me out of school in front of all the other kids. Thanks, Dad.'

Paul knew at once that he had handled things wrongly. He'd foolishly imagined that Marty would thank him for his concern, whereas all he could feel was exasperation at Marty's ingratitude. The urine test had proved conclusively that Marty was diabetic and Paul faced the unwelcome prospect of having to demonstrate to him how to do an insulin injection and to impress upon him the dangers of ignoring his condition. Maybe he had handled it badly, but, for whatever reason, the diabetes just seemed to put more distance between him and his son. It was Al who nagged Marty about his injections, because whenever Paul did, he got a sharp rebuke. Paul suspected that Marty would use the fact that he didn't ask against him but he didn't want to make an issue out of it. He knew, and he knew Marty knew, though nothing had ever been said, that Marty's diabetes was stress-induced and that it dated from the time of the crash.

'Come on, Dad, let's pay for it, then.' Al's voice brought Paul back to the present and he felt in his jacket pocket for his wallet.

'Ooh, we'll need a wreath too, for the front door. Mum always had a wreath.' Al was examining circlets of holly, ivy and trailing red ribbon.

'Mum always *made* a wreath,' said Marty, pointedly.

'Are you offering?' Al chose a largish one with wired-on fir cones. 'Get a life, Marty.'

Back at home, Al organized everything: a bucket covered in silver foil in which to wedge the tree, a white sheet to spread underneath it to catch the needles, the boxes of decorations down from the attic. Paul was glad he didn't have to clamber up there: he didn't want to see the bulging sacks of Celia's things which he had put there in the summer, and hoped he had stowed them well enough out of sight so that Al wouldn't see them either. Marty slumped on the sofa reading his Aston Villa magazine while Al and Paul wound tinsel around the branches, hung on the baubles and held their breath before switching on the lights.

Al clapped her hands in delight.

'Oh, look, Marty, isn't it gorgeous?'

Marty looked up and grunted. Paul shook his head at Al, meaning 'leave him alone'. He suspected that Marty was missing what he was missing, something which over the years had evolved into a family ritual. Celia had always sat at the piano after the Christmas tree lights had been switched on and played 'O, Tannenbaum' and carols. The children would sing off-key and she would smile secretly at Paul. Sometimes, even then, it had made him shiver. He had felt he hadn't deserved life to be this good.

Al went to make a pot of tea while Paul packed away the few decorations they had decided not to use. He could remember, not so long ago, the fierce squabble which would have broken out between Al and Marty over the honour of putting the angel on the top of the tree. He and Celia, both only children, had agreed that the constant arguing was the thing they found most wearisome about parenting, because neither of them had ever experienced it. Usually, they managed to come up with some compromise after a bit of quick thinking, such as Al putting the angel on top and Marty being allowed to switch the lights on, but Paul was always baffled by the things the two of them found worth arguing about. Now he would almost have welcomed a healthy disagreement between them in which he could appear as peace-maker. There was nothing like one of Marty's prolonged sulks to make you yearn for an argument to clear the air.

They were going to Kent for Christmas, to Celia's parents. His mother had asked them for Christmas Day, but only for form's sake, and had not seemed unduly put out when Paul had said that he felt his place was with Bill and Jenny.

Paul had been surprised by how much the prospect of Christmas had thrown him. There was nothing he could do about it, of course, but he felt that it had come at the wrong time. In the last couple of months he had almost felt that life had been returning to normal. After putting the word about in the village, he had been telephoned one day by a woman who introduced herself as Doreen. She had heard, she said, that he was looking for someone to help around the house: she wondered if she'd be suitable. From the name, he'd expected someone matronly in their fifties, but when she turned up she wore leggings and a leather jacket and couldn't have been more than thirty-five. She had four children, the eldest of whom was sixteen, she said, and two other jobs, one as a cleaner and the other behind the bar at the Legion on a Saturday lunchtime, but if she could help him out . . . In the spirit of adventure, Paul had agreed, and life now fell, he often said, into BD and AD – before and after Doreen. Once winter arrived, he didn't feel so guilty about the garden, and, after a brief bout of hacking things back, decided that everything else could wait until spring. His diabetes reluctantly under control, Marty got stuck back into his schoolwork and Al continued as she always had, with her friends and her tap class and her horse-riding.

Paul gradually found that he could attend to things at the practice without drifting off into a daydream about Celia or mentally running through the contents of the freezer. Maybe he had simply learned to work with only half his brain engaged. But at least he had taken back control of his life.

There was only one thing wrong. In delegating some of the domestic responsibility to Doreen, and in finding the portion which remained his responsibility easier to cope with, he actually found he had time on his hands. Al was frequently out, and Marty didn't seek his company, so he found himself alone in the sitting room in the evenings, flicking channels on the TV, or leafing through *General Practitioner* and feeling on edge.

He didn't mention this to Nick or Shaaban because he had a nasty feeling they might try to 'take him out of himself', even asking him round to their homes for dinner with, horror of horrors, a carefully chosen single woman, or suggesting he join an evening class in fly-tying or take up circuit training. Paul knew that he didn't want a social life, as such, and he didn't want to take up an activity in which he had no real interest just to fill in time. What he did fancy, and the realization came to him slowly, was doing something which was work-related, but which would extend his medical skills.

He remembered how impressed he'd been, in his brief moments of consciousness, by the paramedics at the scene of the crash. He'd travelled in ambulances with patients, of course, and had worked alongside ambulance crews during his A&E stint, but having been on the receiving end of their professionalism, he found himself with a new admiration for the emergency services. He knew he wasn't the type to train as a relief fireman or a special constable and couldn't quite see how he could fit in until, one night, chopping channels as usual, he came across a documentary about the work of a police surgeon. Something suddenly fell into place. Next day he made a few discreet calls, and by the end of the week, his mind was made up. He would get Christmas out of the way, and at the first partners' meeting of the New Year he would tell Nick, Shaaban and Joanna that, assuming he was considered suitable after training, he wanted to take on some 'outside work' as a police surgeon.

It would have been wonderful, Paul thought, to be able to say that their first Christmas without Celia was not as bad as he had expected. But it was exactly as he had expected. Everything felt like an absolute sham. When they sat down to lunch in the familiar dining room with Celia's parents, and Bill poured the wine, Paul actually had to stop himself saying, 'White for Celia', as if she were just in the kitchen, helping her mother, skimming the gravy and draining the sprouts. Al glanced across the table at him and looked quickly down at her lap. He saw her chewing her lip which meant that she was trying not to cry, but she couldn't quite manage it. She jumped up

33

from the table just as Jenny brought the turkey through. Paul went to follow her but Marty shook his head fiercely and Paul subsided into his seat. Al came back while Bill was still carving and slipped into her place. She picked up her cracker and held it out to Paul.

'Dad?'

She had splashed her face with cold water: her hair was wet at the front.

Paul stretched out a hand and pulled the cracker with her and it seemed to help. Then everyone pulled their crackers and they swapped jokes, and Marty traded his fortune-telling fish for Al's plastic key-ring. But not one of them bothered with the paper hats. They seemed too irreverent somehow.

The only good thing about Christmas, Paul reflected, as they drove back home, was that it was over. And in the New Year, with any luck, he would have the partners' approval for his outside work.

'OK, Dad, your time starts . . .' Al looked at her watch. 'Now. "Enumerate the differences between lacerations and incised wounds".'

'Oh, come on, Al.' Paul pulled the cork from a bottle of Sauvignon Blanc and poured himself a large glass. 'I've answered that question once today already.'

'OK, we'll go on to the next one. "Discuss the value of examining the hands of a victim of assault".'

It had been the day of the first part of his exams for his diploma in Medical Jurisprudence and Paul felt drained. After all the weeks of study, he had had two hours to answer twenty medical questions, plus an hour and three-quarters to write two essays on a further selection of topics such as the role of the coroner and the reliability of confession evidence.

The response to his decision to train as a police surgeon had been lukewarm, to say the least. Al had been positive, of course, but Marty had sneered something about playing Sherlock Holmes, while you could have cut the silence which fell at the partners' meeting with a scalpel.

Joanna had been the first to speak. She might have been the most recent recruit to the practice but she very much took the view that they were all equal partners with an equal say in how it was run.

'What about here? What about us?' she said directly.

'Well, there are two options,' said Paul. He had anticipated this. 'Either the practice can be paid direct by the Police Authority for my time, or I receive the payment and share it out among you for the extra workload which will be created.'

'Oh, so you admit we're all going to be working harder?' Joanna was as quick as a knife.

'Joanna, I'm not looking for an argument about this, I'm looking for a discussion,' pleaded Paul.

'Well, try not presenting us with a *fait accompli*,' she flashed back, wrapping her long grey cardigan round herself defensively.

'I don't think *fait accompli* is quite the right expression,' put in Shaaban gently. 'Paul is asking for our consent to his embarking on a course of action, which is quite proper.'

'Rubbish,' said Joanna. 'He's already made up his mind he's going to do it. He's obviously found out all about it and woe betide anyone who stops him.'

That was how it had started, and it had gone on in much the same vein for almost forty minutes. Partners' meetings never lasted more than half an hour. In the end they took a vote on it. Joanna voted against, and Nick and Shaaban for.

'Carried,' declared Nick. 'Sorry, Joanna. Good luck, Paul.'

Joanna looked furious as she swept out, her full skirt

brushing Paul's knees. Paul shrugged apologetically at the others.

'I don't want to cause trouble, honestly . . .' he began.

Nick, who relished the prospect of a fight with Joanna, whom he liked and respected as a colleague, but found slightly over-earnest, smiled impishly.

'Paul, you've made my day,' he said. 'At least it'll stop her going on about breast screening for a bit.'

Back in her room, Joanna sat at her battered Victorian desk with its green-shaded reading lamp and fumed. She couldn't say what she really wanted to, which was that because Paul was on his own, with two kids, everyone was going to give in to anything he wanted which he thought might make him feel better, because they felt sorry for him. She knew it was unreasonable, but she resented it deeply. When she had been in a similar situation, widowed, bereft, she had moved both home and job, and had come to live where nobody knew her, and she hadn't been able to trade on people's feelings because nobody had known her circumstances. In fact, far from courting sympathy, she had deliberately kept her situation quiet. Deep down she knew she was being unfair, because Paul didn't actually advertise his status, and if she had made hers public, then no doubt she would have attracted all the sympathy she felt she had missed out on. But it was too late now.

Detective Inspector Ken Jackson kissed the top of his wife's blonde head. She was engrossed in a magazine which she had spread among the breakfast dishes. It was the beginning of June, the Wednesday of a rainy week following a cold spring which was making people ask if summer had decided to miss out the Midlands this year.

'Now, look, I could be late. This pub raid I told you about, could be tonight or tomorrow, so don't cook me anything, OK?'

Yvette Jackson stretched her bare toes under the table. A few years ago, one year ago, even, she would have said disappointedly, 'Oh, but I got chops', or made sure she cooked something which could be heated up when he got in. She would certainly have known which pub it was they were targeting, because she used to listen when Ken talked about his job. Now she couldn't have told you if it was the White Horse or the Black Donkey, and she cared even less.

'OK,' she said absently.

Ken shrugged into his jacket and she tore her eyes away from the page ('There IS life after divorce – four readers tell THEIR story') to look at him. He hadn't changed that much since she'd married him. He hadn't run to fat, anyway, he was still as thin as a whippet, with a narrow, craggy face and curly brown hair which he wore long at the back, in compensation, she thought meanly, for the fact that it was thinning on top. No, he hadn't really changed at all. That was the trouble. It was just as it had always been: the job came first. She had had enough of it.

For years she had tried. What battles they had had, when they'd first been married; over the times he came in, over never being able to get in touch with him during the day, over the off-duty days when he 'just had to pop in' to the station to see how an enquiry was going without him. They'd been on holiday once, in Malta, and he'd bought a paper and found out there'd been a little lad abducted at a funfair on his patch. He'd wanted to get on the next plane home. On that occasion she had actually felt a curious surge of pride in him: he was dedicated, and he did a fantastic job. The police force were lucky to have him. But over the years, and especially after Tara was born, pride was replaced by resentment. She'd gone to parents' evenings alone, dealt with the toaster that caught fire and the bird that got down the chimney, and the time

Tara fell off the slide and had to have stitches. She'd tried to get Ken to see that, while she could cope on her own, she didn't feel she should have to – not all the time. She wanted him to give her and Tara as much time and energy as he gave the job, but it never happened, and gradually she stopped asking. Instead, she determined to find something which gave her as much of a kick as pulling in a villain did for Ken. She'd been temping off and on for years, but when Tara was thirteen she took a computer course at nightschool, then a book-keeping qualification and got herself a job at the head office of a firm making – of all things – lightbulbs. She'd moved across into marketing after eighteen months and now they had offered her a promotion, a sales job that would involve travelling.

Something told her that the time was right. Tara was about to finish her beauty therapy course at the tech and she'd already been for an interview for a job at a health farm in Surrey. She clearly wasn't going to hang around home for longer than she had to and Yvette didn't blame her; she felt the same herself. She wanted a new start. This wasn't just about the promotion at work. She wanted to leave Ken.

'T'ra,' said Ken, at the door.

'See you,' she replied, but her eyes were already back on her magazine. (' "My Toyboy Treasure – I never dreamt I could be so happy!" says Debbie, 46,' she read.)

Nicky Green, Ken's Detective Sergeant, who'd arrived at the Warwickshire force via Stafford and her home town of Gateshead, was waiting for him in his office, brandishing a fax.

'The news you've been waiting for,' she said.

'Andy wants me for the cricket team against Nuneaton nick?' asked Ken.

Nicky handed him the flimsy paper.

' "Appointment of new Police Surgeon",' he read. 'About time. Old Robbins is well past his sell-by date. Who's the lucky boy then?'

'A Paul Dangerfield, apparently,' said Nicky, saving Ken the bother of reading of the rest of it. 'I've checked in the phone book and he practises at Wickton Road. Went to school and university in Birmingham, it says.'

'Paul Dangerfield,' said Ken, sitting down. 'Well, fancy.'

'D'you know him?'

'He's had me in a headlock a good few times, yes,' said Ken drily.

'Sorry, Boss, you've lost me.' Nicky folded one long leg under her as she sat in the chair on the other side of Ken's desk. She pushed her bobbed auburn hair behind her ears and looked expectant.

'King Edwards, Birmingham,' said Ken, as if this would make everything become clear. 'Of course, he went to the paying one, Edgbaston. I went to the grammar, the one at Five Ways. It was where all us bright boys from Bartley Green wanted to go.'

'Boss, you're not really helping much.'

'Rugby,' said Ken, stating the obvious. 'His school used to play mine.'

Paul was actually doing a bit of gardening – some long overdue weeding – when he got the first call from the police on a Saturday evening about ten days later. The weather had turned fine at last but the weeds, profiting from the recent rain, were more visible than the plants.

'Someone called Keith Lardner on the phone for you, Dad,' Marty yelled from an upstairs window. The name didn't mean anything to Paul, until Lardner introduced himself as the custody sergeant at Warwick police. He wanted Paul to go to the station to pronounce a shoplifting suspect who was eight months pregnant fit for questioning.

'Sure,' said Paul, hoping he didn't sound as panicky as

he felt. He had somehow expected that he might get a sort of introductory tour of the police station, a handover from the police surgeon who was retiring, but he had been told there was nothing of the kind. He was in at the deep end. He loaded his bag into the Discovery which he'd bought with the police work in mind because he'd been tipped off that a 4-wheel drive might be a good idea for some of the more outlandish places he might get called to, and which was the only aspect of the job so far which had raised even a flicker of enthusiasm from Marty.

As he drove to the station he went over and over in his mind the things he was supposed to ask himself about 'fit for questioning' and any additional questions he should ask because of the pregnancy. Why had he thought this was such a good idea?

After Paul had seen the woman, who seemed perfectly healthy, and was about to leave, he felt a hand on his arm. He turned round to see a man of about his own age, but slighter than he was, who looked vaguely familiar.

'You don't remember, do you?' said Ken. 'I think our best showing was 18–15 to you. Usually you hammered us.'

Paul grinned sheepishly. 'I'm dreadful with names,' he said.

'Ken Jackson.' Ken held out his hand. 'Used to play you at rugby. Want to meet the team?'

So Ken had introduced him to Nicky with her soft Newcastle accent and cool Celtic looks, and to Keith Lardner, a cheerful Brummie and possibly the last man in the county to use Brylcreem. Then Ken took him into his office and poured him a whisky and they caught up on the last twenty years. Ken told him about how he'd joined the police cadets, married Yvette at twenty, and how they'd only had the one daughter, Tara, because Yvette had had 'complications'. Paul told him about Al and Marty and moving to Warwick from London and, finally, about Celia. Ken expressed sympathy but in a matter-of-fact way. Like all policemen, he lived in a hard world and nothing surprised him.

After Paul had gone home, they all hung over Keith's desk outside the custody area, eating the Quality Street he'd been given for his birthday the day before.

'What do you reckon, then, Keith, will our new doc make the grade?' asked Ken, chewing.

'Who cares, he's dead sexy,' said Nicky, fishing for her favourite.

Keith groaned.

'What's he got that I haven't?' he demanded.

'You mean, apart from a professional career, a socking great house no doubt, a spanking new 4-wheel drive and nice bedside manner?' asked Ken.

'Stuff all that,' said Nicky, popping an orange cream in her mouth. 'He's got a lovely bum.'

PART TWO

RECOVERY

(Four Years Later)

4

'Thanks, Boss.'

Nicky reached out for the first unappetizing coffee of the day which Ken was holding out to her. It was barely ten to eight but already, beyond the dusty venetian blinds of the canteen, the sun was high with the promise of a scorching day to come. Not that she'd see much of it; she'd be lucky if she got ten minutes on a park bench at lunchtime, even luckier if Gareth could get off at the same time. She sipped her coffee reflectively while Ken took a bite of his sausage sandwich. Somehow, he thought, he'd got to arrange to do a bit of shopping at a time when the shops were actually open. He'd been living off powdered milk at the flat for three days, and the heel of a large white loaf which he had been anticipating toasting for breakfast – having unaccountably missed supper – had been more green than white when he had removed it from its plastic bag.

'How does the doc do it, d'you reckon?' he asked, adding a dollop of brown sauce to his breakfast.

'Doctor Discovery, you mean?' queried Nicky. Lardner had come up with the nickname for Paul and it had stuck.

'Yeah. I mean, he's got two jobs, two kids . . .'

'Two incomes,' put in Nicky.

'Well, yeah, but he's got his life together, hasn't he? After all that happened. Must be coming up for five years since he lost his wife.'

Nicky nodded. Poor Ken. He'd been on his own for over three years now and he still couldn't handle it. His had been a typical police marriage, from the sound of it:

him working all hours, funny shifts, never at home. Yvette, his wife, had put up with it while their daughter Tara was little, but then she'd taken a couple of those courses for women returners and gone back to work. Nothing wrong with that, plenty of women did it. But from the way Ken told it, which he frequently did, Yvette had woken up one morning to find that she wasn't the person she had been, and there wasn't a place in the new Yvette's new life for Ken. She had managed without him all those years and had bitterly resented his not being there. Finally, it seemed, she had resented his being there equally bitterly. There was no one else; there was no one else she needed. Which, Nicky surmised, had made it harder for Ken. It was one thing to be dumped in favour of someone else, but it didn't do much for your confidence when your wife felt she was simply better off without you. Kind of knocked your self-esteem.

'I'm amazed he hasn't got married again.' Ken pushed his plate away.

For a copper, and beneath the cynical exterior, Ken was a romantic at heart. That was his trouble.

'Is that a hint, Boss?'

'You could do a lot worse, Nick.'

Nicky smiled to herself. What Ken didn't know was that she'd been seeing Gareth, a married DI from the Drugs Squad for two years, and was perfectly happy with the situation. No complications, none of that tedious wall-papering the stairwell at weekends, no having to put up with each other's relatives at Christmas, no having to cook for him every night. She knew she saw at least as much of him as his wife did – probably more. OK, when he went on holiday with his wife and kids she missed him, but what was that? Four weeks of the year? Five? And he was always so glad to get back . . .

'We'd better go and get some work done,' she said, standing up. 'But if the doc proposes to me over some drunk he's declaring fit for questioning, you'll be the first to know.'

'Is there any tea left?' asked Al, wandering into the kitchen.

'I don't know.' Paul was lost in thought. 'Right, keys . . . keys . . . bags . . .'

'Dad?' It was Marty this time. 'You seen my car manual?'

'No, Marty,' said Paul patiently. 'I haven't.'

It was a typical morning in the Dangerfield household. Ten to eight, and Paul was trying to remember everything he needed for the day, Marty was applying his usual delaying tactics to avoid school, and Al was calmly surveying the chaos with *Silas Marner* in her hand. It was the day of her English A-level.

'Car manual? I slung it in that heap outside,' offered Al helpfully.

'That heap' was a rusting Triumph Herald which Marty, who had passed his test last month, was trying to restore. Favouring his sister with the scowl which he had perfected over the years, Marty followed his father out on to the drive. Paul loaded his medical bag into the back of the Discovery and urged Boozie inside. Al appeared in the doorway.

'I'm going to get the Council to take it to the knacker's yard,' she said sweetly.

Marty thrust his unfinished piece of toast between her teeth to shut her up and clambered in beside his father. Al handed Paul his dictaphone.

'Thanks, Al,' he said, kissing her. 'Good luck with the exam.'

'Yeah.' Marty leaned out of the window and for a second Paul thought he was going to witness a moment of closeness between brother and sister. 'You should do really well after all that studying,' he added with heavy irony.

Paul raised his eyebrows at Al, started the engine and the car moved off.

The Wickton Road surgery was already busy – too busy, according to Joanna. She managed to corner both Nick and Shaaban before they took their first patients. There was a practice meeting later that morning but she didn't think it could wait.

'Look at us!' she said. 'Barely eight-thirty and we're rushed off our feet!'

Nick rolled his eyes. Joanna was a good doctor and, most of the time, a good colleague, but when she got going on the subject of Paul's outside work she was like a broken record. She hadn't agreed with him taking it on in the beginning and though she had had to give way, she had never given up.

'Joanna,' he said patiently. 'In terms of finance and kudos it's good for the practice.'

'Yes,' hissed Joanna, her intense violet eyes flashing, 'but because Paul is doing more and more police work we're taking on more and more of his patients. We're even doing his visits as well!'

'He pays you for it,' pointed out Shaaban mildly, indicating that Joanna should keep her voice down. Already they were attracting interested looks from a couple of patients in the waiting room.

When Paul had taken on his police surgeon commitment, they'd agreed that he should pay them each a proportion of the salary he would receive for the extra work they'd have to pick up.

Joanna sighed, feeling outnumbered and outmanoeuvred. Why did men always stick together?

'Well, I'd rather get paid less money and make sure this practice works properly,' she retorted. 'Paul should be a GP first and a police surgeon second.'

'Oh, come on, Joanna,' teased Shaaban. 'Paul likes helping to crack crime. A juicy murder is a little bit more interesting than the average chesty cough. Anyway, he's not called away that often.'

Julia, the head receptionist, approached with her usual look of apologetic 'it's out of my hands' helplessness.

'Dr Dangerfield's just rung in. Says he'll have to miss the meeting. He's had to go to the hospital on a police job.'

Joanna smiled heavily at the others. Good old Paul. Right on cue.

The drive to the hospital – slightly longer than the drive to the surgery – at least gave Paul the chance to reel off his shopping list on to the dictaphone. He was just adding oyster sauce (his cooking having progressed considerably in the last few years) as he pulled up into one of the reserved parking spaces and was met by Ken Jackson, whose hang-dog air was even more marked this morning. He started to brief Paul before he could even get out of the car.

'Bit close to home, this one,' he began. 'You know Nigel Spenser?'

'No,' said Paul, locking the door.

'One of the best uniforms we've got,' said Ken in explanation as they moved towards the hospital entrance. 'This guy Makin, the suspect, reckons that Nigel clobbered him when he arrested him this morning. Nigel's back at the nick,' he added, as he held open the swing door for Paul to pass through. 'He's in danger of being suspended.'

Ken continued as they made their way towards X-ray. Apparently Makin had been picked up at about six-thirty that morning with a TV and video in the boot of his car. Assuming that he was dealing with a burglary, Nigel Spenser had asked him to get out of his car. At this point, the stories began to diverge. Makin was alleging that Spenser had used 'undue force' in arresting him. Nigel disagreed.

'That sort of fairytale's par for the course these days,'

said Ken, dodging a technician with a crate of blood samples. 'But Nigel is at HQ tomorrow receiving a bravery award – the casino fire, you remember? Chief Constable, TV, you know . . . a whole black recruitment drive based on it.'

'Mm-hmm?' Paul raised a hand in greeting as they passed a chest consultant he knew.

'What I can't have,' continued Ken, 'is the Chief Constable singing Nigel's praises if he's suspended. I've got to get this sorted by tonight.'

Paul shot Ken one of the incredulous looks for which he was famed at the station.

'By tonight?'

Ken shrugged.

'Do your best, Paul.'

Before examining Makin, Paul went to have a look at the X-rays with the Registrar, Steve Withers.

'Somebody's given him a pretty good going over, haven't they?' said the doctor. 'A fractured rib and some pretty impressive bruising.' He pointed to the most deeply shadowed area. 'Looks like a direct blow.'

Paul considered. This one wasn't going to be straight-forward; not that any of them were, but the necessary time constraint which Ken was working under made it even more tricky. Paul would have to examine Makin and he knew he'd also have to examine Nigel for evidence of a struggle, and talk to Georgie Cudworth, the young WPC who'd been with Nigel when Makin was arrested, before he could offer Ken anything helpful. Either way, he doubted he'd get back to Wickton Road before ten-thirty. And he was due in court at half eleven.

He found Makin in a curtained-off cubicle in Casualty, biting his nails. He was about thirty, short and stocky, with tousled dark hair and light blue eyes that flickered over Paul as he took him in. Makin repeated his story for Paul's benefit.

'I was driving home this morning – and I got stopped by this black copper and this policewoman. And he just laid into me. Put me down to the floor.'

'Where were you coming from?' inquired Paul.

'I'd just been taking a TV and video to a mate,' replied Makin. 'He wasn't in, so I had to come home.'

'Bit of an odd time to be doing that, isn't it?' said Paul mildly.

'Yeah, well, he normally goes out about then. I just missed him.'

Paul nodded. The details of Makin's movements were not really his concern. His business was with his injuries.

'What did he beat you with?' asked Paul, examining the bruising.

'First, he hit me in the face with his fist,' Makin held his face up for Paul's inspection. The jaw was swollen and purplish. 'I went down, then he put the boot in and hit me with his truncheon.'

'Any idea why he did that?'

'I dunno. Ask *him*,' said Makin truculently.

'OK. Fair enough,' said Paul. His mobile trilled in his jacket pocket and he stepped outside to answer it. It was Julia, asking when he'd be back.

'Not long now,' he reassured her. 'If the others could just take a couple of my patients each . . . ?'

'Bye, Mrs Whitcombe. Bye-bye, Emily.' Joanna gave the two-year-old a little wave and retrieved her stethoscope, which she'd given her to play with while she talked to her mother, from the floor. She stuffed Mrs Whitcombe's notes back in their buff envelope, then pushed back her chair and stood up, stretching her arms and easing her shoulders. Her consulting room looked out on to Wickton Road, its austere Georgian frontages softened by the mellow local stone, and brightened at this time of year by geraniums, busy Lizzies and lobelia in hanging baskets and

51

window-boxes. She stood for a moment at the window, watching the shoppers, students and besuited businessmen pass. Apart from the extra workload – though, as Nick had pointed out, she was well paid for it – she wondered why she got so steamed up about Paul's outside work. She didn't like to think that she was sulking because she had been outvoted about him taking it on in the first place; after all, that had been four years ago. Even as a teenager she had been unable to sulk for that length of time. Sometimes she thought that she was guilty of taking her work too seriously, but then what could be more serious than people who were sick, or troubled, and who needed your time? Seven minutes – the time you were supposed to spend with a patient, on average – was short enough without having to squeeze in a couple of Paul's patients on top of her own allocation. At a time when patient care was supposed to be paramount, Joanna found it genuinely disturbing. What if one of them were too pressed, one day, to see a patient who really needed them? How ill did someone have to be to get a home visit on the days when Paul was in court or examining suspects? Why did Shaaban and Nick refuse to take her seriously? More irritated than ever, Joanna picked up the next set of patients' notes from her desk and went to the door.

'Mrs Simpson?' she called brightly. Mrs Simpson was seventy. She had diabetes and high blood pressure. Joanna could tell that her own blood pressure had risen while she'd been fuming about Paul and she stood impatiently while Mrs Simpson struggled to her feet – she was still at least two stone overweight, in Joanna's estimation – and wheezed towards her, her ankles puffy above her cream plastic shoes. Maybe there was something in what Shaaban had said. Maybe there was a glamour to what Paul did that Joanna resented. Maybe that was why he did it. But maybe he'd disagree. Well, if by a miracle he ever made it to a practice meeting, she could ask him.

'Come on in, Mrs Simpson,' she smiled. 'And how are you today?'

Over the years, Paul had found that young WPCs fell into one of two categories. They were either very assertive, almost loud-mouthed, or they were so shy and nervous-looking you couldn't imagine what they were doing in a job which involved walking the streets armed with nothing more than a torch, a truncheon and the training to talk yourself out of trouble. Both sorts, however, made equally good policewomen. Georgie Cudworth was of the latter persuasion.

'Be gentle with him,' joked Keith Lardner as Paul showed her into his room at the police station. Georgie turned a deep pink and Paul motioned her to sit down. She had a nasty bruise developing under her left cheekbone.

As Georgie told it, she and Nigel had stopped Makin on a 'suss'. He had got abusive, started calling her names and had lashed out with his fist.

'I went down,' she explained. 'Next thing I knew, he was down as well. Nigel . . . you know . . . got him down to arrest him.'

'Got him down or knocked him down?' asked Paul.

Cudworth shook her head in frustration.

'I don't know. I didn't see. I was still trying to recover. Then I saw Nigel handcuffing him on the deck,' she went on. 'Hands behind his back.'

'No further violence?' queried Paul.

'None,' said Georgie. Her look was open and direct. 'That was it.'

Nigel Spenser said the same. He looked a sorry figure, all six foot of him, seated in his socks, his boots having been taken away for forensic. His story corroborated Georgie's. He freely admitted hitting Makin with his fist to subdue him – and Nigel's swollen knuckles and Makin's bruised face confirmed this – but he absolutely denied either kicking him or hitting him with his truncheon while he was on the ground. He seemed totally bewildered by the whole thing.

'Look,' he said, 'I heard that Makin's got a broken rib. I didn't do that to him.'

'Somebody did,' said Paul, packing away his things. 'How did he get it?'

When he saw Ken afterwards, that was exactly the question Ken was asking. But Paul's examination couldn't put Nigel in the clear.

'It fits with Makin's story, Ken. Nigel admits hitting him and his knuckles are bruised.'

'What about the rib injury?' persisted Ken. 'Come on, Paul, I'm asking for your opinion. I'm not asking you to falsify the report.'

Paul shrugged. 'It could be consistent with the use of a police truncheon.'

Ken wasn't having any of it.

'So Makin's telling a good story.'

'I'm talking about the evidence, Ken,' Paul chided him.

'I just want to know if there's any indication – no matter how small – that he came by these injuries another way.'

Paul opened the door. At this rate he was going to be late for court as well as surgery.

'Get me another weapon,' he said.

Ken grimaced. Good job he'd had his breakfast in the end, because lunch was looking like a forgotten dream. So was the shopping for that matter. Anyway, that powdered milk was sprayed with vitamins, wasn't it? It couldn't be all that bad for you. He walked into the Incident Room and banged his hand on the table for quiet. Six attentive faces swivelled towards him. There was nothing more likely to rally an Incident Room than an accusation against another copper, and a mate.

'Right, listen,' he ordered, wearily. 'We've drawn a blank on the TV rental companies so we're going to have to do it the slow way. Double-check all the handlers, the manufacturers and the dealers and check every lost property list in the area for the TV and video that were found on Makin. And let's come up with something.'

By the time Paul had been to court and done a couple of house calls and a bereavement visit, it was time for afternoon surgery to begin. Julia had rescheduled some of his less urgent morning patients for the afternoon and for three hours he hardly had time to draw breath. By the time he ushered his last patient out, he felt totally exhausted.

He sank back into his chair, trying to gather the strength for the drive home and, when he got there, the unpacking of the shopping he had bought at various intervals during the day, chicken and dogfood, cornflakes and toilet paper from the supermarket, lemon grass and ginger from the specialist deli. Why had he picked tonight of all nights to ask Kate Durrani round for supper?

He thought back to their meeting in court earlier in the week, when she had been questioning him for the defence about the scars found on a three-year-old boy. She was always superb in court, elegant in her white stock and black gown, courteous and charming, but she was also able to go for the jugular when necessary; he'd seen it enough times and had been glad not to be on the receiving end of her incisive questions or her occasional flashes of irony. She'd only been in the area about six months, having moved from Bristol, but she seemed to have sensed a kindred spirit in him; another loner, perhaps, another outsider. Making her way in a profession as conservative as the law couldn't have been easy for a young, attractive Asian woman. Kate had told him once, as they grabbed a quick cup of tea during an adjournment, that she'd had to try nearly fifty firms before she could find one which would take her on to do her articles.

'I thought of changing my name to Kate Smith, to see

if that got me more interviews,' she grinned. She flicked back a strand of glossy dark hair from her face. 'Luckily, this tiny firm in Bristol, all legal aid work and unfashionable causes, took me on.'

Paul had found himself in a dilemma with Kate. He found her wildly attractive, funny, terrifyingly intelligent, and he thought she liked him. He had felt for weeks that he wanted to ask her out but something held him back and he knew what it was: sheer terror. It was years since he'd done this sort of thing. The one consolation about being older was that you were supposed to have more confidence, and in some things that was true. Paul could challenge the garage now about the repair bill to the car, and stand his ground when they tried to argue back. Practical things, work things, they were fine, but emotionally . . . the prospect of asking Kate out terrified him just as much now as it would have done when he was fifteen. That had been the most wonderful thing about meeting Celia.

They had met in the second term of Celia's second year at university in Birmingham, at a dreadful, drunken geographers' ball – in fancy dress, of all things. 'Come as a Country' the invitation had demanded. Paul had spotted her straight away. She had the most amazing costume: a spray-painted silver leotard – in which she was daringly bra-less (well, it *was* 1974) – with a skirt made out of what looked like banknotes. All evening he had watched her. She seemed to have come with a group of people but she didn't seem to be attached to anyone in particular. When he spotted her dancing with a burly medic called Alasdair who was in the year below him, Paul waylaid him at the bar and offered him a pint in exchange for her name. Alasdair bargained his way up to a pint for himself and his two mates, and told Paul she was a linguist called Celia Gibson, who also played the piano.

'She's supposed to be Argentina,' he said. 'She did

explain it to me but I sort of got a bit lost. Something to do with . . . I dunno, *argent* being "money" in French . . .'

Paul pressed a pint into his hand and disappeared. He had just spotted Celia sitting on her own.

'Argentina,' he said, materializing at her side.

She looked up, surprised.

'Very good,' she said. 'Or did someone tell you?'

'Of course not,' he replied. 'I've been puzzling over it all night. Can I sit down?'

Celia indicated assent by moving along on the velvet-covered bench.

'Paul Dangerfield,' he said, holding out his hand formally.

Celia twisted round to give him hers.

'Celia Gibson,' she said, with a smile. 'And you are?'

'I've just told you . . .' he began.

'Which *country* are you?' she persisted.

'Oh, I see. Can't you guess?'

She shook her head. He was wearing a dark sweater and trousers with a cream silk scarf wound round his neck.

'Something to do with the dark continent?' she hazarded.

'Ireland,' he grinned. 'I'm a pint of Guinness.'

'That's not a country,' she protested. 'It's a drink.'

'More a state of mind, really,' he said, fingering one of the counterfeit notes. 'Anyway, we can't all be artistic.'

Celia looked at him sceptically.

He picked her hand out of her lap and held it in both of his.

'Long fingers,' he said.

Celia smiled cynically.

'Do you ever watch those black-and-white films on TV on Sunday afternoons?' she asked.

Paul looked a bit sheepish.

'Well, yes, I do, actually,' he confessed. 'If they're on before the rugby,' he added quickly.

'Thought so,' said Celia crisply. 'Because I have to tell you, your chat-up lines are pathetic.'

Paul persisted anyway. She obviously thought he was a complete wally so he had nothing to lose.

'Who said anything about chatting up? It's basic anatomy. I bet you play the piano.'

'What else did Alasdair tell you?' She sighed, but in a way that told him she was pleased he'd bothered to find out.

They'd gone out together for the rest of his time at university, which was only six months (he was three years older than she was), and when it was time for him to leave he'd known he would have to ask her to marry him, because as well as being in love with her, he had felt so comfortable with her. He had known they could spend their lives together, and the marvellous thing about that, quite apart from the feeling of great good fortune, was that he would never again have to go through the dry-mouthed, sweaty-palmed panic of having to ask a girl to go out with him. Or so he had assumed.

Earlier in the week, while he dithered after court, Kate, being the sort of modern woman she was, had created the opportunity, by asking *him* if he'd got time for lunch. He hadn't of course, but it had meant that he had, rather falteringly, and making it sound an extremely uninviting prospect, been able to invite her for supper. And with her usual fresh directness, ignoring his stumbling explanations, she had accepted. Now it was time he went home and started cooking.

Then he caught sight of a Post-it note which had been stuck to his pile of post.

'Can I have a word before you go home?' it read. It was signed 'J'.

Paul's shoulders sagged. He knew perfectly well what it would be about, because Nick had called him on the mobile to warn him that Joanna was on the warpath again about his police work.

'So what's new?' Paul had said.

'Nothing,' Nick had replied. 'And nothing's going to change. You want to do it, and Shaaban and I support you. She has to accept a majority verdict. Won't stop her giving you a good drubbing, though.'

'You're quite looking forward to the prospect of me getting a good going over from Joanna, aren't you?' said Paul, hearing something mischievous in Nick's tone.

'If it means there might be a bit less earache for the rest of us, then, yes,' agreed Nick, whose attitude towards women tended towards the traditional, not to say the chauvinistic. Paul privately thought Nick was rather scared of Joanna. Paul wasn't scared of her: he just couldn't see the point of going round and round in circles. She had accepted the terms when he had begun his outside work four years before. What was the difference now?

'The difference is that we're a much busier practice!' she retorted, when he put the same question to her in her room five minutes later. 'We run clinics, we do more preventative work . . .'

'All of which was your idea,' put in Paul. 'And you don't see me complaining.'

'Because you're never here to shoulder any of the burden!' cried Joanna.

'Are you suggesting we reduce our patient services?' asked Paul.

'Of course not,' she snapped. 'I'm asking you to put in the time they require.'

'At the expense of my outside work.'

'For God's sake, Paul, you've had four years of playing cops and robbers, as well as being a GP and running a home and two children. You want a busy life – fine! But don't involve the rest of us. You may like running yourself ragged, but I don't!'

Paul sighed. There was some truth in what Joanna was

saying. He couldn't deny that he had taken up the police work to fill the enormous void left by Celia's death. But now – it was part of his life; he couldn't just give it up, and he didn't want to.

Paul felt completely cornered. The best thing to do would be to suggest a drink so that they could at least get on to neutral territory before resuming the discussion. But he couldn't do that, because Kate was coming to supper and he was late already. He'd phoned Al earlier to remind her that Kate was coming. Now he wanted just two things in life: to arrive at Church House before Kate did, and for Al to have tidied up.

'Look, I don't think we're going to get very far this evening,' he said to Joanna. 'Did you talk it through at the practice meeting?'

'Oh, yes,' she replied acidly. 'But we couldn't decide anything without you. And you were doing "outside work", weren't you?'

When Paul had gone, she sat at her desk, chewing her lip. She hadn't realized until she had said it that she might have uncovered another reason for her resentment of Paul's outside commitments: he crammed his life very full. And in comparison, hers was so very empty.

'Chicken Satay Tod Mon Pla', read Paul, 'otherwise known as Lady in Love, followed by Tom Yung Goong – spicy prawn soup with that Far Eastern favourite, lemon grass, served at the table in the traditional Thai pot.'

Kate giggled, her dark eyes beguiling over the rim of her wineglass.

'So you didn't go to any trouble, then?' she asked.

Paul had come a long way since his first attempts at cookery. At first he had just worked through Celia's cookery books, page after page, but when he got more confident he began experimenting and now he was open to every new food craze which came along. He'd been through his olives, capers and sun-dried tomatoes phase, bowed in the direction of Delia Smith's passion for limes, and was now exploring Thailand via its cuisine.

Marty was his usual uncommunicative self during supper but Al chatted happily to Kate about her plans to read French at university, asking her about cheap digs and places to eat in Bristol, which, along with Warwick, had offered her a place. Paul rather hoped that, whatever her grades, she would choose Warwick. Selfishly, he didn't want Al too far away. He was already dreading the house with just him and Marty in it. When they had finished, Al shooed them through to the sitting room and brought the coffee, then disappeared to wash up. Marty had long gone upstairs with some indescribable bits of engine and his precious car manual.

'Great kids you've got,' said Kate warmly, snuggling down into the sofa.

'They're all right,' said Paul modestly. At least he could say that about Al, and one out of two wasn't bad, under the circumstances.

'Well . . .' Kate began, only to be interrupted by the phone.

Paul answered it impatiently. It was Ken.

'I need you out here, Paul,' he said. 'It's urgent.'

Paul checked his irritation.

'Any chance of getting another police surgeon on this one?' he asked plaintively.

'Heath Farm, just off the M40,' said Ken in reply.

'OK, I'll be there.' Reluctantly, Paul took directions from Ken and turned to Kate as he hung up. 'I'm really sorry about this. But it isn't going to take very long. At least it's my side of town. Al and Marty will keep you company.'

He called Al through from the kitchen.

'Look after Kate for me, will you?' he asked. 'Police work.'

Al, who wanted to phone Fiona and Sophie about the exam, her French teacher about possible au pair jobs over the summer, and Nick Adamson for no reason at all except that he was drop-dead gorgeous, pinned on a smile. Perhaps if she did the first stint, Marty could come and take over in about half an hour. There was no way he was getting out of it.

Paul clambered for what seemed the hundredth time that day into the driving seat of the Discovery. His bag was in the back and the local OS map spread on the seat beside him. Heath Farm, Ken had said, just off the M40. As he drove, the image of poor Nigel Spenser, banished by the evening's activity of cooking and eating, suddenly appeared in Paul's mind. He didn't suppose Nigel would be getting much rest that night; he wondered what Ken had done about the bravery awards ceremony tomorrow. Probably nothing yet. Ken would wait until the very last moment before giving up hope on Nigel's behalf.

'The thing is, you see, Paul,' he had said. 'I know Makin's lying and I know Nigel's telling the truth.'

Paul didn't resent the fact that as soon as he was in the car, he had slipped back into work mode and that Kate had become a distant memory. He was used to it. After all, hadn't he been glad of it, in the beginning, when he had taken up the police work? He had relished leaping into the driving seat at any hour of the day or night, heading away from Church House, away from the memories of Celia. His police work had been the crutch which had helped him limp along when he could barely put one foot in front of the other; he was not ready to throw it away just yet. And the other thing, and equally important, was that he loved the work. He was grateful to it for the support it had given him: he could not cast it aside without regret. Anyway, it was part of him now. Kate, or anyone he got involved with, would have to accept that. He had just worked all this out in his mind (that was another reason he liked the work: all the driving gave him plenty of thinking time), when he reached his turning off the motorway. After a couple of hundred yards on an 'A' road, he found a track with a sign to 'Heath Farm' half-hidden in the hedge. The track wound round a corner and Paul was suddenly dazzled by the huge police arc-lights which had been set up. A police constable stepped out from the side of the track and, hearing who Paul was, waved him through.

The day might have been warm but the clear evening was chilly and Ken was hunched in his habitual leather jacket.

'Matthew Evans,' he informed Paul as they walked across the lawn towards the body. 'Sixty-six, lived alone. Sister popped by a few hours ago, found him dead in the garden. House broken into, rear window forced.' Ken grinned as they reached the body and stopped. 'And he's all yours.'

Paul grunted an ironic 'Thanks' as he stooped to examine the corpse. Ken seemed jolly pleased about something: pleased to be out here at an isolated farmhouse at ten o'clock at night with a dead body and a few SOCOs for company? Paul knew Ken was divorced and lived alone but, surely, even if he couldn't persuade anyone from the station to go out for a Chinese meal with him, a microwaved dinner and an evening in front of the TV was preferable to this?

Paul examined the body thoroughly but could find no signs of injury. As usual, he could only surmise as to the cause of death: the real cause of death would have to be established by a post-mortem conducted by the Home Office pathologist.

'Looks like a natural death – probably a heart attack,' he observed, straightening.

'Jim found some tablets in the house,' volunteered Nicky. 'Could be for a heart condition.'

Ken nodded. 'Go and get them, eh?' he asked.

'He's not got a lot of clothing on but it's been warm . . .' mused Paul. 'Rigor mortis is virtually complete and there's been a temperature drop of twenty degrees. I'd say he'd been dead at least twelve to sixteen hours.'

'About the first half of Nigel Spenser's shift,' said Ken in a satisfied tone.

Paul wrinkled his brow. Ken was a man obsessed. What on earth had a death at a farm in the middle of nowhere got to do with Nigel Spenser? Before he could ask, a uniformed constable approached them with what looked like a walking stick in a clear plastic bag.

'SOCOs finished with this, sir,' he said, handing the article to Ken. 'Says it's an African weapon. A knob-kerrie.'

Ken held the bag up and Paul saw a stick with a heavy, rounded end.

'Apparently Evans spent a lot of time in Africa,' he explained.

'How nice for him,' said Paul. The damp was beginning to seep through his shoes. If Ken was intent on conducting a cross between the 'Holiday Programme' and the 'Antiques Roadshow' for his delectation, he wished they could at least do it indoors.

'Found it in a hedge,' Ken went on, weighing the knob-kerrie in his hand. 'Let me tell you what I think. Evans was asleep last night when he heard a noise. He came downstairs, disturbed Makin, chased him out, clobbered him with this, dropped dead of a heart attack.'

Of course. The Nigel Spenser connection: Makin.

Paul reached for the weapon and felt its weight for himself. He had to admit that Ken's hypothesis could be right. It was heavier than a police truncheon, but it could certainly account for Makin's fractured rib.

'Guess what's missing from the house?' Ken was practically beaming.

'TV and a video?' hazarded Paul.

'Correct,' said Ken. 'So Makin, knowing he's left Evans here in God knows what state, makes the best of a bad job when he's picked up and disguises his injuries so we don't nick him. I like it.'

'So will Nigel Spenser,' agreed Paul.

'Oh, yes,' grinned Ken. 'I think Nigel Spenser's going to find his bravery award won't be the only thing he picks up tomorrow. I would imagine the drinks bill could be fairly large as well.'

The clock struck the half hour. Al, who had been chatting valiantly to Kate, had finally withdrawn into a magazine and Marty, who had been coerced by his sister into giving her some moral support downstairs, had come down on condition that he could bring his engine with him, which was currently reposing on the coffee table while he prodded it lovingly.

Kate yawned, no longer bothering to hide it. She'd got an early start tomorrow, a case conference before a domestic violence case and Paul might be hours yet.

'Look,' she said, struggling up out of the deep sofa cushions. 'You've been really kind but I think I'll be off.'

'Bye,' said Marty.

Al, with slightly more social poise, made a token protest, but agreed that 'not very long' in Paul's scheme of things could sometimes mean two or three hours.

'It's not really his fault,' she said defensively. 'He doesn't know how long it'll take till he gets there.'

'Don't worry, I understand,' smiled Kate. 'I've spent long enough at police stations to know the form.'

'Well, if you're sure . . .'

Al's hesitation was polite but she was already ushering Kate towards the front door.

'I'm sure. Tell your Dad thanks for supper. And I'll call him.'

'Of course. Nice to meet you. Bye.'

Al closed the front door with a sigh of relief and headed straight for the phone. As she was dialling Sophie's number – it was too late to ring her French teacher now, but she could always try Nick in a bit – Marty stuck his head round the door of her room, where she'd taken the cordless phone for a bit of privacy. She made a 'Scram' face at him and he held up his hands.

'I'm not stopping,' he said. 'But, hey, I think we saw her off, don't you?'

Al grinned and waved him away as she heard Sophie's voice.

'Soph? It's me. Sorry I couldn't ring before. What about that exam?'

Paul, driving back through the darkened lanes, dialled his home number on the mobile, only to get the engaged tone.

'Come on, Al,' he said to the darkness. 'Get off the phone.'

As he arrived at the crossroads at the end of their lane, he dipped his headlights as he saw another car coming towards him. He pulled to a halt to let it turn left, away towards Warwick, and realized as he sat there that it was Kate's. For a brief second he imagined pursuing her, then glanced at the dashboard clock. A quarter to eleven. Maybe not.

Back home, he let Boozie out and stood on the front step breathing in the smells of a summer night. They'd been cutting silage in the field across the road and the sweetest smell in the world, that of new-mown grass, made him want to take lungfuls of air and never, never stop.

'Come on, Boozie!' he called. 'Let's get to bed sometime tonight, shall we?'

Boozie skittered across the gravel and into the house. Paul closed and bolted the door on the limpid night, on Makin, on Nigel, on Ken, on Kate. Climbing the stairs he looked in on Al – still on the phone – and made cut-throat gestures to her. She nodded, but he knew it would make no difference.

'Night, Marty,' he called, over the din of guitar chords emanating from Marty's room. And, automatically, 'Turn that thing down!'

He went into his own room and, as always, just before he drew the curtains, looked out into the night and thought of Celia, wherever she was. His thoughts nowadays were fond – and final. She was never coming back. But he was going on. And he could, surprisingly, live with the prospect.

He eased off his shoes which had left, he noticed, clumps of wet grass all over the carpet, and went to brush his teeth.

5

'Are you around for supper tonight, Marty?'

Paul peeled the plastic wrapping off a tray of chicken breasts and laid them on the chopping board.

Deep in his car manual, Marty didn't reply. He was having a good half-term break: not only had he got long days to work on his beloved car, but Nick Mackenzie, who had been banned for six months for a drink driving offence, was employing him as a chauffeur to take him to his house calls. Having insured Marty for his car, Nick took the view that Marty might as well get the benefit, and justify the huge premium he had had to pay, by using it in the evenings and at weekends and school holidays. All Nick asked was that Marty paid for his own petrol and since, as Al frequently pointed out, Marty's generous allowance from Paul certainly wasn't spent on clothes, Marty could afford to go out several nights a week (Paul and homework permitting). Hence Paul's question, which he now repeated. Marty slammed his book shut and glared.

'Dad, will you stop going on at me!'

'I'm only asking.' Having removed the skin, Paul daubed the chicken with his special lemon and thyme marinade. The barbecue was already heating up and Kate was due any minute.

'Well, don't.' Marty stood up. 'Yes I am going out as it happens and no I don't know what time I'll be back and yes of course I'll be careful. OK?'

'Look.' Paul pointed at him with the tip of a knife. 'I was only asking. It's not a crime.'

'Oh, yeah? You're always "only asking". Who I'm with,

where I'm going . . . What's it to you? I don't ask you what you get up to with Kate, do I?'

Before Paul had a chance to reply he had gone, banging the door behind him. As Paul turned back to his chicken, Al, wearing an apron, came in through the back door.

'Did I hear the dulcet tones of a slight disagreement?' she asked. 'Mmm, that smells gorgeous.'

'Oh, just Marty being Marty,' sighed Paul. 'I can't help worrying, Al. Even if he's sensible, how do I know his friends aren't going to persuade him to have a drink, or drive too fast . . .'

'Well, maybe, but what can you do about it?' asked Al sensibly, mixing salad leaves in a big pottery bowl. 'You've got to let him make his own mistakes, I suppose.'

'And he's so snide about Kate . . .'

'He's probably just jealous,' soothed Al. 'Kate's great. I like her, anyway.'

Paul looked gratefully at his daughter.

'Why can't he be more like you, Al?' he asked.

'I think it's something to do with chromosomes,' grinned Al. 'If you'll go and check the barbecue, I'll listen for the door.'

Marty was still seething when he got into town. God, all he was doing was going out for a drink with a couple of mates. He wasn't even going to drink in the true pub sense of the word, only low-alcohol lager. I mean, how stupid did Dad think he was? He was hardly likely to risk losing the chance of a summer job with wheels thrown in for the odd pint, especially when he had an object lesson in drink driving right in front of him in the shape of Nick. He parked the car, scraping the tyres savagely against the kerb and made his way towards the pub. He hoped Kath would be there. He really liked Kath.

Kath was there, but so was that creep Terry Bradshaw, who stuck to her like glue all evening. Marty did manage to get her on her own for a bit, while Terry was on the pool table, and sort of managed to suggest that he could give her a lift home. But when they left the pub, there was Terry again, right behind Kath, determined not to miss out. Marty couldn't bear it.

'Me and Kath are going for a drive,' he blurted out.

'Sounds good to me,' said Terry, in a waft of beery breath. 'Where?'

Kath explained that Marty had promised to drive her past a badger sett he knew.

'Badgers?' said Terry in disbelief.

'It might be fun,' said Kath defensively. Marty knew she was trapped. She liked him, or he thought she did, but Terry was a bit older and smoother – brasher, in other words – and girls always liked older men, didn't they? So in the end, Terry invited himself along and Marty found himself driving both him and Kath up to Hilton's Farm, where, if you were lucky, you could see badgers by night in the copse.

Roger Keen's cottage was one of a pair on the track which led up to Hilton's place. If he had been listening, or watching from the window, as he sometimes did, he would have heard Marty, in Nick's Saab, drive past, splashing through the potholes. If he had been less pre-occupied, he would definitely have heard it, because there was never any traffic up that track after dark. Hilton never went out and the other cottage of the pair was unoccupied, and had been for years, ever since Hilton had laid off his other farmworker. Now he had done the same with Roger. Which meant that he and Moira and the baby would have to leave their cottage and go – where? Moira had said something about the council housing list but Roger hadn't really taken it in. The council houses in the village were all taken and he didn't want to go and live in some flat twenty floors above the ground. They couldn't put him in there. It was as bad as . . . well, being locked up. But Roger had no idea how else they were going to manage. Most of his waking thoughts were dominated by an all-absorbing hatred of Hilton for what he had done to him. Only that morning, seeing Roger watching him from the other side of the wall which protected the yard, Hilton had shouted at him to get lost, or he'd call the police. Hilton had no right to speak to him like that. As if he hated him. Roger hated Hilton, but that was right and proper. That was what he deserved. This evening, how-ever, Roger had other things to think about than his former employer. Moira was worried about the baby. Roger stood by helplessly as she moved the wailing infant – Sam was five months now – from one damp shoulder to another. He kept drawing his legs up to his little tummy which, Moira had read in one of her baby books, meant he was in pain. Suddenly she thrust Sam towards him. She was slight and small-boned, too weary to care that her dark hair was unbrushed and that her eyes were smudged with fatigue.

'I'm going to ring the doctor again.'

She caught Joanna just as she'd finished supper, which was, Joanna reflected, unusual: normally when you were on call, the phone rang as the first forkful went in. Moira explained that she, Roger and Sam were all patients of Dr Dangerfield, that she had seen him with Sam the day before and that he had given her drops for colic.

'But the baby's still crying,' she explained.

Joanna reached for her spritzer.

'It does sound as if you have a colicky baby, Mrs Keen,' she said. 'Has he got any other symptoms . . . vomiting, diarrhoea?'

'No, well, not really,' said Moira vaguely.

'Feverish?'

'No. I've given him the drops again . . .'

'Look.' Joanna had to make a decision, and this really

didn't sound as if it merited a night visit. 'If you're still worried, bring him in in the morning, but if he's not right in another couple of hours give me another ring.'

Moira glanced at Roger, who was gazing down lovingly at Sam. The baby actually seemed to have settled down a bit.

'And take some paracetamol for yourself,' smiled Joanna.

Moira knew she was being given the brush-off.

'Thank you, Doctor,' she said resignedly.

'Not at all . . .' said Joanna. 'Night night.'

Sam stirred and began to grizzle again.

'Oh, come on,' said Moira. 'I'll take him.'

Joanna picked up her drink and went through to the sitting room. Perhaps there'd be something mindless on television.

Edward Hilton took his twelve-bore from the gun cabinet which had been his father's and loaded the cartridges calmly. Many men would not have relished tramping about the dark, dewy fields at ten-thirty at night, after a hard day's work, but Edward Hilton was used to it. Sometimes he got a fox, more likely a rabbit or two. He couldn't do anything about the badgers, because they were protected by an Act of Parliament these days, which made them twice the problem to him that they had been. The local conservation group had spread the word that there was a sett on his land, which meant townies coming out by the carload to try and see them, sitting around at night in their immaculate thornproofs with their expensive cameras, borrowing his countryside, trespassing on his land. He might not be able to do anything about the badgers, but, Hilton reflected as he put a box of extra cartridges in his pocket, giving a couple of townies a fright was almost as satisfying. He thought he'd heard a car earlier on, so he wouldn't be surprised if he found he had some visitors tonight. There was no other reason for any traffic up past the farm. And the Keens never had anyone call. Not that they'd be there much longer, annoying him, disturbing his peace of mind.

He'd felt sorry for Roger Keen when he'd first met him. He'd seemed a decent enough bloke, though he jumped like a doe rabbit when you spoke to him, and could hardly stutter his thanks when Hilton had offered him the farmworker's job. It was only after he'd taken him on that he'd found out, from gossip in The Three Horseshoes, that Keen had some kind of mental illness, even though it was supposed to be 'controlled' by medication. After that, Hilton, not the most sympathetic of men, had watched him like a hawk, alert for any indication, any lapse of concentration or quirk of behaviour which might mean a recurrence. You couldn't be too careful. There were enough odd folk around these days without welcoming one on to your farm and working alongside him day in, day out. But for a long time there had been nothing. Then Keen's wife, Moira, had become pregnant and given birth to a little boy. It must have been about three months later that Hilton had come into the tractor shed and found Keen staring into the flame of the paraffin heater.

'Look!' he said. 'The Twelve Apostles.'

Hilton had humoured him and peered at the flame, determined from that very moment that Keen would have to go. Unfortunately his visions, and the voices he started to hear, didn't interfere with his work: he didn't forget to milk the cows, or give them their rations or hose the parlour down. But Hilton felt he had to watch him every minute of the day. He couldn't trust him any longer. He found himself checking up on tasks that Roger had been set to do. And as he said to his old friend George Griggs over a game of dominoes: 'Why have a dog and bark yourself?'

So, when the cows were turned out in mid-April, he'd

given Roger a month's notice. Said he wouldn't be needing him any longer. What he planned to do was get a contractor in for the silage and the haymaking and the bit of forage maize that he grew, and come the autumn, look for another man to help with the mucking-out when the cows were indoors. He'd got a story all worked out about needing to economize, but he hadn't needed it, because Keen hadn't seemed to take it in that he was being sacked. Six weeks later and he was still hanging around the farm, and now Hilton was going to have to go to the bother of getting a court order to evict them from the cottage, which wasn't good with a little kiddie involved, but what else could he do?

Only that morning, he'd felt someone watching him and had turned to find Keen at the gate.

'Go on! Get off!' he'd shouted. 'Clear off! I can't help you any more!' And then, when Keen didn't move: 'Go on or I'll get the police.'

Hilton wasn't a man who was easily frightened – he wasn't sensitive enough for that – but Roger Keen was starting to get him worried. The way he looked at him sometimes, with that far-away look on his face. And the way Keen had started to fight back, saying that Hilton couldn't sack him, he'd done nothing wrong, and how sorry he'd be if he did.

'I already have!' Hilton had snapped, but Roger had smiled a faint, curving smile which had unnerved him all the more.

Hilton snapped himself back to reality. He was going out to walk the farm, as he always did. He had his gun and plenty of cartridges. And if he came across Keen up to no good . . . well, it'd be the worse for him

But it wasn't Keen that he found. The yard was quiet: the padlock on the door of the henhouse was secure. Hilton set off round the fields, keeping close to the hedges, treading the familiar rutted paths. Then, in Badger Hollow, he saw it. A fire. It was one of two things. Badger lovers or badger baiters. Either way, they had no business on his land.

As he approached the rim of the hollow, he could see two figures lying on the grass. Worse still. A flaming courting couple.

'Come on! Off!' he shouted, his voice ringing back at him from the trees. 'Out of it!'

'Who are you?' came a lad's voice.

'I own this land.' Hilton advanced down the slope. 'And you are on it.'

'Oh, come on,' coaxed the lad. 'We're just here to look at the badgers.'

Hilton continued to advance. 'Come on, get out of it. Off!' He had the satisfaction of seeing the lad freeze when he saw the gun. The girl with him was still scrambling to her feet.

'Here,' said the lad, his voice less confident now. 'D'you mind not pointing that thing at me, please.'

'I'll point this thing at you till you're off my land! Now, come on, out of it!' Hilton waved the gun in the boy's face. Behind him the girl made little whimpering noises.

'Come on, Terry, please! Just do as he says,' she urged.

The boy took a step closer to Hilton. In the light of the fire, Hilton could see he was about eighteen or nineteen, with dark hair and a coarse, yet good-looking face. He was wearing jeans and a denim jacket, like they all did.

'Don't point it at me,' the boy said, 'or I'm going to take it off you. I mean it.' He had recovered his bravado now. But Hilton was confident that that was all it was.

'Come on!' he said roughly. 'Away!'

The boy raised his arms and grabbed the barrel of the gun.

'I said, don't point it!'

'No!' cried the girl. 'Terry, no!'

The two men grappled for control of the gun. The lad

75

was nearly forty years younger than Hilton, but he hadn't been toughened up by a lifetime of manual work. They struggled for a good few seconds, till Hilton felt his boots slip and heard the gun go off and was aware of a hot, bright pain in his left side; then he knew no more.

Marty was hunched in the driver's seat of the Saab with Primal Scream on full blast, trying to keep warm. Terry had no right to muscle in on his evening with Kath, and then to imply that he wasn't wanted and send him back to the car like a six-year-old. Bloody cheek. Marty had a good mind just to drive off and leave them to it. If it hadn't been for Kath . . . He was just brooding on how he would never be able to look her in the eye again, and wondering how many of his mates Terry would tell about the evening, and what he and Kath might be doing right at this moment, when he heard the shot. He sat up quickly, and turned off the cassette. Before he could get out of the car, Terry and Kath came stumbling towards him from the direction of the wood. Terry wrenched the back door of the car open and pushed Kath inside.

'What's going on?' demanded Marty.

'Some farmer's just taken a pot-shot at us,' gabbled Terry, scrambling in after her. 'Just drive!'

Roger heard the shot as well. He had just been raking the fire for the night. The baby seemed calmer now and Moira was dozing as she held him in her arms, her head drooping forward like a flower. A daffodil, perhaps. He went to the front door, which opened straight into the living room, and looked out at the night. Glancing back at Moira, who hadn't stirred, he reached for his gumboots and went out. He walked carefully across the field towards the farm, but skirted the dimly-lit yard, favouring the shadow of the wall. In the woods at the bottom of the sloping field at the back of the house he could see a fire burning. Cautiously he approached. Hilton lay where he had fallen, a gun by his side.

Wickton Road the next day was the usual seething mass of people, receptionists waving notes, the various doctors shepherding patients in or out of their consulting rooms, three phones going at once. Joanna caught Paul's eye.

'Mrs Keen rang me last night about her baby,' she explained. 'Said you'd treated him in surgery.'

'Yes, I did,' Paul agreed. 'Day before yesterday.'

'I agreed it sounded like colic,' Joanna went on. 'Do you want me to follow it up?'

Paul was tempted to say yes, knowing he had to be at court later that day, then he remembered.

'I've got her husband in, actually. I'll check.'

Joanna nodded curtly and called her next patient.

Roger Keen was a paranoid schizophrenic. He'd had everything over the years: been sectioned, had electric shock therapy, tried most of the known drugs ... He'd had his periods of remission, most recently about eighteen months ago, which is why he and Moira had decided to have the baby, but lately many of his symptoms had returned and Paul would have preferred him to be back on medication.

'Right, Roger,' he said, consulting his computer screen. 'Now, you haven't taken your Depixol for well over a month . . .'

Roger was a big-built, sandy-haired man of nearly forty, but seated in Paul's consulting room with his open, fresh face and bright eyes, he looked positively boyish.

'Yeah, well, it's out of our control, isn't it?' he said in his soft Warwickshire accent. 'Like destiny. Like me getting the sack.'

Paul knew Roger had worked at Hilton's Farm for the past two years.

'Why did Hilton sack you?' he enquired.

'He said I was threatening him.'

'Were you?' asked Paul gently.

'No!' said Roger vehemently.

Paul knew that Roger had been having counselling from Shaaban, who had a training in psychiatry. It might be worth having a word with him. But most of all he wished Roger had kept up his medication.

'How's the baby this morning?' he asked.

'He's stopped crying,' said Roger, eager to please. 'But he was slightly sick, and he passed some blood.'

A prickle of agitation ran over Paul's scalp.

'Fresh blood?' he asked. 'Diarrhoea?'

'Not really,' faltered Roger. 'My wife was asleep. I changed the nappy and there was the blood – well, not blood – like red jelly. It crossed my mind to bring him but he was sleeping . . .'

Paul didn't want to alarm him. The last thing he wanted to do was alarm him.

'All right,' he said confidently – more confidently than he could warrant. He excused himself and went to find Joanna.

Luckily he practically bumped into her in the corridor.

'Sounds like a possible intussusception. I'd better go,' he said briefly.

Joanna was insistent.

'No, no, I took the call. It's my responsibility.'

Paul shook his head slightly. Why did she get so defensive whenever she thought anyone was doing her a favour? Why didn't she ever allow anyone to help her? Sam Keen was his patient: he was the one who had come up with the colic diagnosis in the first place. So why was no one allowed to feel guilty but Joanna?

Still, this wasn't the time or place. Intussusception was a serious complaint – possibly life-threatening. He didn't envy Joanna having to go and tell Mrs Keen that her baby was very, very sick.

'All right,' he agreed. 'We'll cover.'

Joanna gave him an ironic look – it was unusual for him to be the one doing the covering – and left to get her bag.

She knew as soon as she felt the baby's stomach, with a worried Moira Keen chirruping at her elbow, that Paul's suspicion was correct. She lifted Sam out of the cot in one swift movement.

'What are you doing?' said Moira, alarmed.

By the time she had got off to sleep it had been nearly two, which is why Roger had left her to sleep in that morning. Used to rising early, getting up late always threw her, and she felt worse than if she'd had no sleep at all.

'I'm taking him to hospital,' said Joanna simply. 'I think you should come with me.'

All the way there, with Moira in the back of the car holding the baby, she cursed that she hadn't even thought of intussusception. Sure, it was rare but once she'd felt the lump in Sam's stomach just now, there could be no doubt. They'd have to operate as soon as they could. She was still tormenting herself when she arrived back at the surgery, having left Moira with Sam in intensive care.

'I should have gone out,' she said to Paul. 'I made an assumption.'

'If you had gone out you'd have seen a colicky baby. It obviously blew up during the night,' said Paul reasonably. Then almost to himself, still unsettled by his consultation with Roger Keen that morning, 'God, I wish I'd been on call.' Joanna looked at him questioningly and he added quickly, 'I mean, they're my patients.'

'I don't want any favours, Paul,' she snapped.

Paul sighed. So much for trying to make her feel better. With Joanna, you couldn't do right for doing wrong.

'Doctor,' called Julia, the phone receiver draped over her shoulder. 'It's the police.'

Paul took the phone. It was Ken Jackson. They'd found a body.

'Sorry, everybody,' he said, replacing the receiver. 'I've got to go.'

Julia raised her eyebrows at Mandy, the other receptionist, and together they began poring over the appointments book in the customary damage limitation exercise.

Nick, who had come through to collect some notes, beamed beneficently.

'Off you go and enjoy yourself!' he said, waving Paul away. Paul grinned gratefully, but before he could leave, Nick motioned him back and pulled him to one side. 'Your son, my chauffeur, I've had to let him go for the day,' he said. 'He doesn't seem very well. Do I detect a conspiracy here? Father and son in collusion?'

'It's nothing of the sort!' protested Paul.

Nick spread his hands and beamed. He always knew how to make the most of a moment. 'Be of good cheer,' he addressed the waiting room at large. 'The Blessed Saint Nicholas will cover for you all!'

The body was Hilton's. Ken had established his identity before Paul got there. All that remained for Paul to do was to certify death and to try to determine how long he'd been dead. Judging from the temperature drop, he estimated the time of death at around midnight the night before.

'Thanks, Paul.' Ken looked thoughtful. 'Now, it's a funny one, this. Badger sett nearby and they've lit a fire here, see, the ashes are still warm.' Paul gave a little nod of acknowledgement. 'How about he came across some badger baiters and they had a confrontation, so they killed him?'

It was a possibility. Anything was a possibility at this stage.

'It's not suicide, is it?' Paul agreed. 'He couldn't shoot himself like that, y'know, Ken.' The gunshot wound was in Hilton's left side, under the ribs. Paul looked around, noting the fire, the trampled grass. 'There's been a struggle, hasn't there? Any leads?'

'We're checking the gun for prints. The helicopter picked up a lot of sets of footprints in the dew early this morning. Four lots came from the farm but another set came from a cottage over the back. I'm off there next.'

'OK, Ken. Good luck.'

Roger raised the axe high above his head and, with a grunt of effort, let it fall. The log on the block in front of him flew apart, cleft neatly in two. Out of the corner of his eye he saw a car draw up at the side of the house. He raised the axe again. This ought to have been a good day, too, what with Hilton being dead – he had seen him, hadn't he, last night, lying there? But then he had got back from the doctor's to find a note pinned to the front door from Moira, saying she'd taken the baby to the hospital. Roger hadn't known what to do. He'd just come back from town on the morning bus, there wouldn't be another till two. So in the meantime he'd thought he'd chop a few logs. It still got chilly in the evenings even if the sun had been up all day. And when Moira got back from the hospital she'd want a bit of a warm.

He was aware that someone had come round the side of the house and was standing watching him. He propped the axe blade on the block and leaned on the handle.

'Are you here about Mr Hilton?' he asked.

Ken Jackson was taken aback. What was this, ESP?

'Why, what's happened to Mr Hilton?' he asked carefully, keeping an eye on Roger's beefy hands, folded around the axe.

'Well, it was inevitable, wasn't it?'

'What was?' asked Ken patiently.

If he'd known he was going to be confronted by the mad axeman, he'd have asked a couple of the lads to come with him.

'You know he's dead?' queried Roger.

'Yeah . . . I do,' said Ken. '*I* know he is. How did *you* know he is?'

Roger was beginning to lose patience. Why did everyone talk to him as if he was a child?

'I saw him. Last night in the hollow.'

'Did you tell anybody?' asked Ken, still choosing his words.

'No,' said Roger scornfully. He stooped and set another log on its end on the block. They were apple logs from the orchard, lovely sweet-smelling apple logs. Despite his years of training in disarmament and in negotiation, Ken couldn't help flinching as Roger raised the axe above his head. Then he brought it down savagely on the lifeless piece of wood. 'He really had it in for me!'

After Nick had told him to take the rest of the day off, Marty hadn't known what to do with himself. He went and sat by the river for a bit, brooding about last night. He was no longer so bothered about himself and Kath and Terry; what was really bugging him was that gunshot he'd heard. Fine, so it was pretty scary if the farmer had appeared and taken a shot at them like Terry had said, but Terry was tough, he wouldn't have been that frightened. Yet when he and Kath had come back to the car . . . Neither of them had said any more about it all the way home, despite Marty's questions. It didn't seem right, somehow. Maybe he should ring Kath. But she'd probably just think he was being a stupid kid. Finally, realizing that his backside was numb from the damp grass and that it was nearly two, he heaved himself up to get some chips or a sandwich or something. This diabetes was a right pain. Then he'd go back to Wickton Road and tell

Nick he was fine. He certainly wasn't going to feel any better sitting around thinking about things. He might as well be doing something. Anyway, Nick might say something to his Dad, then it'd be the third degree all evening.

Marty strolled past the castle towards the centre of town, easing his stiff legs, when he suddenly noticed a billboard outside a newsagent's. 'LOCAL FARMER SHOT DEAD' it said in big black letters. It was drizzling a bit by now and they had started to go all fuzzy at the edges. Marty went in and bought a paper.

'Edward Hilton, fifty-eight . . .' the article began. Marty didn't need to read the rest. He ran round the corner to where he knew there was a phone box and dialled Kath's number. Then he went back to the riverbank to wait for her.

She arrived after about twenty minutes, which was impressive because she lived on the far side of town, by the Science Park. She looked lovely, her dark hair caught back on one side in a bunch of plaited threads, exposing her smooth white cheek which Marty just wanted to bury his face against. She was wearing a long skirt and her violet Doc Martens and a lot of clinking silver jewellery.

'It was a complete accident,' she explained, looking him straight in the eyes. 'Terry didn't do anything. This bloke just appeared, and told us to get off his land. Terry got hold of the gun 'cos it was pointing right at us . . . I haven't even slept. I can't sleep. I tried to ring Terry this morning but he's just gone. I'm really scared, Marty . . .'

'But what about the police?' Marty broke in. 'I mean . . .'

Kath looked appalled.

'We can't tell the police, can we? It was an accident. But if we tell the police, they'll think we did it!'

Marty could see why she was scared. And he wasn't blameless. He might not have been there when Hilton got shot, but he'd only been a couple of hundred yards away. And whose bright idea had it been to go to the farm in the first place? That was trespass, wasn't it, for a start? And where the hell had Terry gone? Marty wasn't at all sure about Terry. He wouldn't have put it past him to try to offload the blame in some way – some way that got Marty deeper into it.

'We could talk to my Dad about it, maybe . . .' he started, but Kath grabbed his arm. He could feel her fingers, delicate and bony, but strong, through his shirt.

'No! Look, Terry has vanished, OK? So that's you and me, and we're in this together, so please, please . . . don't . . . it's for both of us. Marty, don't tell. Don't tell anybody.'

Then she jumped up and hurried away, and she didn't look back even when he called her.

Ken caught Paul on his mobile on his way back from court and told him that Roger Keen had been arrested on suspicion of murder. The other police surgeon, Andy Rawnsley, had declared him fit for questioning, but in searching the cottage they'd found an old prescription signed by Paul and Ken wondered if he could throw any light on the situation. Paul confirmed that Roger was his patient, and also explained to Ken, in case Roger hadn't, or hadn't made it clear enough, the situation with the baby.

'I've had to stand back from this one,' Paul explained to Shaaban when he got back to Wickton Road. 'It's too close to home. When was Roger Keen sectioned?'

Shaaban thought for a moment.

'Nineteen ninety,' he said after a pause. 'He was sent to the Granby Psychiatric Unit. I was against it.'

'Can you access his full psychiatric history?' asked Paul. 'They may need it for mitigating circumstances. I'm just hoping that his baby's illness wasn't a trigger.'

Then Joanna really would have something to feel guilty about. Paul glanced at his watch. He was supposed to be meeting Kate in . . . no, five minutes ago. Still, she practically *expected* him to be late. Paul knew he couldn't be part of the police inquiry into Roger's involvement in Hilton's murder, but Moira might be able to throw some light on things. She was bound to be at the hospital with the baby. Paul did a quick calculation and reckoned that, if Kate didn't mind him rushing off, he'd just about got time to get to the hospital and back before afternoon surgery.

Kate was waiting for him when he arrived, striking in her black court suit against the gaudy parasols of the little bistro she had suggested. Paul sat down on an uncomfortable wrought-iron chair and took off his sunglasses.

Kate pushed a cup of cappuccino across the table to him and smiled.

'Here, I got you this. I was just about to give up.'

Paul sipped his coffee. Most of the foam had evaporated but it was still warm, which was something.

'Yes, I'm sorry,' he said, wanting desperately to reach for her hand, slim and brown on the marble-topped table. But he knew he couldn't be seen holding hands, not in public in the middle of Warwick, not when she was employed half the time to pick holes in his evidence. It could shake the entire foundations of the British justice system. 'Can't stay long either,' he explained. 'I've got to go to the hospital.'

'Ah,' said Kate. 'Is that to the Keens? They've taken Roger down there to see the baby. Ken wasn't very thrilled but Nicky persuaded him. I've picked him up as duty solicitor,' she added, when Paul looked puzzled by her prescience. 'Is there anything you can tell me about the circumstances of Hilton's death?'

'No,' said Paul. 'Roger's my patient, you know.'

'So you can tell me about his case history,' persisted Kate, her dark chocolate eyes on his face.

Paul relented a little.

'He came to us after he was discharged from Granby,' he said. 'They think his trauma was sparked off by his relationship with his father, who seems to have been a rather violent and abusive man.'

'So it is possible, with provocation, he could have become involved in Hilton's death?'

Paul shrugged his shoulders imperceptibly. It was possible, but was it probable? That was what the police had to find out.

'The police think it's murder,' said Kate, reading his thoughts, 'and he's the prime suspect. So I need all the help his doctor can give.'

'Well, if the solicitor wants to talk to the doctor,' smiled Paul, 'she has to get her client's permission.'

'And how does she get that?' asked Kate facetiously.

'Well . . .' Paul answered in the same vein. 'The doctor could try and persuade him when he sees him at the hospital.'

Kate broke into a smile which lit up the mobile planes of her face.

'Thank you.' She got up. 'Oh, could the solicitor ask the doctor to phone her at home? If he's got a moment, that is?'

And, handing him one of her business cards, she walked off down the street. Paul grinned and slipped it into his wallet. He'd find a moment, she could be sure of that.

Paul found a pathetic sight when he arrived at the hospital. There was the baby, a mass of plastic tubing and sticking plaster. There was Moira, looking half crazed with worry. And there was Roger, looking utterly blank, handcuffed to a policeman. Paul had already checked with the consultant in charge. They had removed Sam's necrotic bowel but she wouldn't be drawn on his chances. All they could do was wait. Nicky was standing outside the baby's room.

'How's Roger behaving?' Paul asked her.

She offered him a mint.

'Very strangely. Is he mad?'

Just then Moira appeared in the doorway. She seemed to have shrunk with the worry of it all.

'I came to see the baby and to see if I can help Roger,' said Paul at once.

'The baby's not very well and neither is Roger and I don't think you can do anything,' said Moira flatly.

'I want his permission to talk to his solicitor,' explained Paul.

'What for?' Her tone was suddenly sharp. 'To make up for Dr Stevens's incompetence? She came here this morning, you know, to see me. It's no good coming *now*, is it?'

'Moira, I just want to help Roger . . .'

'I'm not going to let her get away with it,' Moira continued. 'And if you're trying to make it better . . .'

'I'm not trying to make it better,' reasoned Paul. 'I'm just trying to help Roger. If you've got a complaint against Dr Stevens . . .'

'She should have known!'

'If you've got a complaint against Dr Stevens,' repeated Paul, 'that's your right. I'm not pleading for her and I'm not trying to stop you.'

'You'd better not try,' said Moira bitterly. 'Now, if you'll excuse me, I'm going to the Ladies.'

Nicky grimaced at Paul.

'I have to tell you that Dr Rawnsley came, gave Roger some medication. Said he's fit to be detained. I've interviewed the wife and she says he was with her all night. But we'll have to take him back.'

Rawnsley must have given Roger some Largactil, Paul supposed. Great, he thought. Now he takes it.

The interview with Roger Keen was not one of the easiest Ken had ever conducted. Just before they'd begun, Nigel

Spenser had handed him the first forensic report, which had picked up no prints on the gun at all, not even the farmer's. The gun had been wiped. Does a psychotic wipe out evidence against himself? Ken wondered, as Roger was brought from the cells to the interview room along with that Asian solicitor woman who was far too bloody attractive not to be a distraction in these circumstances. And pretty hot at her job as well.

'Right, Roger.' Ken adopted what he thought was his most caring tone. 'What can you tell me about your relationship with Edward Hilton?'

'Ah well,' said Roger earnestly. 'You consult Nostradamus. Look at his prophecies.'

Wonderful. It was like interviewing Old Moore's Almanac.

'Why should I do that, Roger?' asked Ken, bemused.

'Oh, well,' said Roger airily. 'Everything's pre-planned. Fate takes control. Like you're just about to charge me with murder, and there's nothing I can do about it, is there?'

'D'you think he could be having us on?' he asked Keith Lardner after he'd suspended the interview forty wearisome minutes later and Roger was led back to his cell.

'Oh, I don't think, Ken.' Lardner glanced up from his Custody Register. 'You know that.'

'Look, Kath, read it!' Marty thrust a copy of the evening paper in front of Kath's nose. They were sitting in the car park at Kenilworth Castle. They had been supposed to be going for a drink, but neither of them could be bothered to get out of the car. 'All right, I'll read it to you!' He had read it enough times to himself, he practically knew it off by heart, but he read it out loud this time. 'OK, listen. "A man, believed to be a former farmworker of Mr Hilton's, has been arrested on suspicion of his murder and is helping the police with their enquiries." We've got to tell them, Kath.'

Kath was hunched up against the door. She didn't look at Marty but stared out of the window at the broken mass of the castle ruins.

'They can't find him guilty. What evidence would they have?'

'Look, Kath, we've got to tell them the truth.'

Kath spun round in her seat and a strand of her hair, now released from its plaits and prettily crinkled, brushed against his cheek.

'I've told you, they'll think we did it. They won't find this bloke guilty. I just know they won't, OK?'

Marty didn't reply. Together they sat and stared straight ahead with their terrible secret, watching the rain which had just started to fall.

After a sunny day, it had turned into a night just like the night of the crash, thought Marty as he drove home. The rain was coming down in torrents, just like before, and suddenly he was back in his Dad's car, on the way home from Granny and Grandad's, with Boozie slobbering on his bare knees, wanting one of the toffees Marty was unwrapping. Marty had asked his Dad if he wanted one, but there was a lot of noise, what with the wipers, and the car engine, and the de-mister, and the spray on the road, and his Dad had half turned to catch what he had been saying and so Marty had seen it first, the bright red lights of the lorry in front, braking, and then Mum had seen it and screamed 'Paul!' and then there'd been a screech and such a bang, a dreadful bang like a bomb.

They hadn't even let him see Mum in the hospital – not before she died. The hospital hadn't thought it was a good idea, and Dad had agreed. They hadn't let him see the body afterwards, either, but by then it was too late. She'd never heard him say how much he loved her, or beg her not to die. He just knew that if they'd let him see her while she was still alive, even when she was so terribly injured, it would have made a difference. He just knew.

He managed to avoid his Dad and Al next morning, by sticking his head under the pillow so he couldn't hear them calling him down to breakfast. For Christ's sake, it was the holidays, wasn't it? Why did Al have to pretend they were like some family in one of those story books he'd had as a kid, all checked tablecloths and rosy cheeks? They were a mess. Ever since Mum died, nothing had gone right. Al was just pretending. Well, he couldn't pretend. Not about that, any more, and not about Hilton.

He managed to roll out of bed by ten, though his legs felt as heavy as lead, and dragged himself to Wickton Road to meet Nick. The first house call he had to take him to was a flat in one of the elegant Regency crescents on the outskirts of Leamington. When they got there Marty lowered his head on to the steering wheel. He couldn't go on.

Nick, who had been half-way out, eased himself back into the car.

'Something really is bothering you, isn't it?' he enquired gently.

Marty nodded. And told him the whole thing.

'I'm really surprised,' Nick reflected finally, 'that you didn't tell your father. I thought you were really close after your mother died.' He paused for a moment, then went on. 'Your father was driving the car when it crashed, wasn't he? Don't you think there might be something in all that? I mean, deep down, something that stops you trusting your father?'

'I don't know,' said Marty dully. How could he tell Nick what he really thought, which was that surely his Dad must blame him, like Marty blamed himself, for offering that stupid sweet, which had made his Dad turn round in the first place . . .

Nick's voice stopped him from going over it, from seeing it replayed in his head for the umpteenth time.

'I'll tell you what I do know. I know you've got to tell the police about Hilton,' said Nick. 'And you've got to do it now.'

Paul rang the hospital as soon as he had a gap between patients to ask about Sam Keen. The sister said he'd had a good night and they were much more optimistic.

'I think we caught it just in time,' she said.

Then he rang Nicky at the station but she'd already checked with the hospital herself.

'Ken doesn't want Roger told yet,' she explained, not sounding entirely happy about it. 'Says he doesn't want him excited.'

Paul was called to the hospital himself not half an hour later, to examine a drunk driver who'd had an altercation with a lamppost. As he left, he bumped into Moira Keen.

'You look exhausted,' he said, concerned. 'Can I get you something to help you sleep?'

'No thanks.' Moira was chilly. She had slept in her clothes and her hair needed a wash, but she was impressively dignified. 'That's not why you're here, is it?'

'No,' said Paul, but didn't go into details. 'Look, I really do want to help Roger if I can.'

'Well, that's fairly straightforward.' Moira folded her arms. 'My baby will live but Roger will die. I mean, that's simple, isn't it?'

'What do you mean?' asked Paul. 'Roger's not going to die.'

Moira gave a thin smile.

'Don't you remember what happened to him last time he was sectioned? Don't you?'

Roger had made three ludicrously hamfisted attempts at suicide.

'Yes, I do,' he said gently, 'and he's not going to be sectioned again if I can help it.'

'I don't think I want any more help.' Moira Keen turned away, then said over her shoulder, 'Don't worry, Dr Stevens is safe, I shan't complain. I think I'm best left on my own to pick up the pieces.'

Paul was half-way back to the surgery, where he knew he'd got to make a start on two weeks' worth of paper-work, when Ken caught him on the mobile. Paul had never heard him so furious.

'OK, OK, look, calm down, Ken.' Paul pulled in to the side of the road. This did not sound like a conversation he could conduct while driving along, even in a ten-mile-an-hour queue past the roadworks by Warwick Castle.

When he heard what Ken had to say he could understand his fury.

'I'll be right there.'

He cursed to himself as he clicked the phone off and inched out to make a U-turn. What did Marty think he was playing at?

When Paul got to the station, Ken hauled him straight into his office. They'd told Roger that the baby was all right, and released him. Nicky had driven him over to the hospital herself. The poor blighter still didn't seem to have the slightest idea what was going on. He'd cried when they'd told him about Sam and tried to hug Lardner. It was great about the baby, but that still didn't make the previous thirty-six hours all right, did it?

'I mean, we arrest the bloke, we question him – how we question him! – and all along he's innocent. Meanwhile the lad we should have been questioning – this Terry Bradshaw character – has "gone away". There's blokes from three forces trying to track him down now. And all the time your own son knows what happened! I've got a good mind to nick him for wasting police time!' Ken ranted at Paul. 'He's got to learn about responsibility, preferably before he's old enough to draw his dole cheques, because by then, Paul, it's far too late. In the meantime, he shouldn't be running round loose and you'd better see it's taken care of!'

In his frustration Ken said more than he meant to, and said it more strongly. He could see Paul was stung, especially by the 'running round loose' bit, but, hell, it was said now. He saw Paul's eyes become dangerously light and his lips disappear almost into invisibility. He'd seen Paul like it only once before, when a suspect had spat at him.

'I intend to!' was all Paul said, before he left.

He drove straight home, hooting impatiently in the rush-hour traffic. Marty's door was closed but at least there wasn't any music coming from the other side, nor the beeping of one of his computer games. Paul burst in without knocking. Marty looked up, startled. He was sitting on the edge of his bed, threading new laces into his trainers.

'Why didn't you tell me?' demanded Paul. 'This Terry, did he threaten you?'

Marty shook his head.

'The girl, then? What was it, Marty? What stops you from talking to me?'

Marty looked at the floor.

'I thought I'd let you down.'

'Let me down?' Paul was incredulous. 'You've had the police on a wild-goose chase, nearly endangered a man's life – I'll say you've let me down!'

'You see!' Marty jumped up, stung into retaliation. 'How can I talk to you? I haven't talked to you since you killed . . . since Mum . . .' His voice was wavering with five years' worth of suppressed emotion.

Paul was shocked by what was dammed up inside Marty, and what it meant for them both. He took a step towards his son, holding out his hands.

'Marty . . . Marty, I'm sorry.'

Marty jumped back before Paul could touch him.

'Dad, please! Just get out, get out! Please, Dad . . . just go!'

Paul could see there was nothing he could salvage from the situation that evening.

'I'll talk to you later, all right?' he said quietly.

Marty flung himself angrily down on his bed, angry that he'd given so much of himself away and still not revealed what really bothered him: that it wasn't his father who was to blame for the crash, it was him.

He heard the door close quietly and Paul's steps recede down the stairs. He wiped away the hot tears with his fists and wondered if things would ever get better.

Paul went straight to the drinks tray and poured himself a large Scotch, earning himself a rebuke from Al, who hated him to drink. Just then the doorbell shrilled and he moved to get it, feeling just in the mood for a confrontation with a couple of Jehovah's Witnesses. It was Joanna. The first thing he noticed about her was that she was wearing a deep pink jacket, which really suited her. Usually she wore safe, dull colours such as navy or grey or cream. The bright fabric lifted the colour in her cheeks and made her eyes sparkle. Then he realized that it was a cold sparkle. She was furious.

'You went to see Mrs Keen behind my back and pleaded with her not to complain about me. Didn't you?'

Paul instinctively took a step back.

'Look, come inside . . .'

'Nick's just been round to see me and he told me that Mrs Keen isn't going to take out a formal complaint. Did you talk to her?'

'No, I didn't,' said Paul at once, then corrected himself.

'Well, yes I did, but only to see if I could help. I certainly didn't plead for you. I mean, they are my patients.'

Joanna thumped her fist in frustration on the door jamb.

'Yes – but Paul, when we cover for you, they become *our* responsibility. Just stop trying to do everything because you can't. Nobody can!'

As if Paul needed telling, with Al huffing about in the kitchen because he'd had a whisky and Marty going through his adolescent angst and Ken laying in to him . . . And now Joanna was doing the same.

'I just wanted to see if I could help,' he said ineffectually.

'I don't need any help.' Joanna turned and crunched across the gravel to her car. Paul followed her and grabbed her by the arm, turning her around to face him.

'Why?' he demanded.

'What?'

'Why can't anybody help you? I did it for *you*, Joanna.' There was a pause. She looked at him and he looked at her and neither seemed able to pull their eyes away. 'Look,' he said more gently, 'you didn't have to come round tonight. This could have waited till tomorrow, couldn't it?' Joanna gave no answer. She shrugged off his arm and opened the car door but he leaned across to stop her. 'You don't have to go,' he said.

He realized in that moment that he would have given anything for her to stay. He needed her that evening. He needed her quizzical look and her rare throaty laugh. He looked at her in mute appeal. She hesitated for a brief second before shaking her head. Then **she got** in the car and drove away.

6

It was not the best of times for Paul. Soon it would be the fifth anniversary of Celia's death. He looked back miserably over the time which had passed. What he hated most was that just when he was feeling that things had got better, that he was in control, something happened like this upset with Marty which seemed to send him right back to where he had started. Rationally he knew that this wasn't the case, and he knew his bouts of depression or despair – call it what you will – were not nearly as frequent nor as long-lasting as they had been in that first, dreadful year; but it still depressed him that they were happening at all. He sometimes felt that, when Celia had died, he had been flung into a deep, dark pit. The sides were steep and slippery, but he kept clawing his way up. Often he slid back down and had to start again. And when he did manage to get to the top, someone stamped on his fingers.

If Paul himself had not been so vulnerable emotionally, he might have been better able to cope with Marty. The conversation which they were going to have 'later' never happened, partly because Paul was busy both at the surgery and on police work, and partly because Marty contrived not to be in the house at the same time as his father. He spent a night with his mate Toby, and another with Jason, whom he didn't really get on with any longer, which showed how desperate he must have been to avoid Paul's company. But Marty's accusation that Paul had 'killed' Celia haunted the pair of them.

Nick was concerned about Marty, too. Marty was still driving Nick around after school and using the car in the evenings to take himself off to his various friends' houses. Nick was amazed that Marty hadn't spoken to Paul about what he knew of Hilton's death and Roger Keen's innocence.

'Don't talk to me about it,' said Paul, as he poured them a drink from a bottle of wine which a grateful patient had left for him. Nick took the view that the one consolation of being banned was that he could enjoy a drink or three with impunity. Paul, while not wishing to encourage Nick to even greater excesses, and aware that he had to drive home himself some time that evening, thought he would join him for just one.

Nick swilled the red wine round in his glass and took a sniff.

'Mm. Château Tesco 1995 and none the worse for that,' he proclaimed, taking a deep swig. 'Cheers.'

'Cheers,' said Paul glumly. He told Nick the gist of his confrontation with Marty, and the terrible thing which had been said.

Nick looked a bit sheepish.

'Ah, well, I might be to blame for that,' he admitted. 'It did occur to me afterwards that I might have given him a very convenient stick to beat you with.'

'You haven't been playing the amateur psychologist again, have you?' groaned Paul. Nick, who felt a bit threatened, Paul intuited, by Shaaban's impressive string of psychiatry qualifications, had in the past attempted to operate on the same level.

'Well, I might just have suggested that, since Marty's diabetes started up after the crash, and since you were driving at the time, there could just be a causal connection. Between Celia's death and him not trusting you, I mean.'

'Oh? And where does the diabetes fit in?' enquired Paul. God knew, Marty was stroppy enough as it was, without Nick giving him an excuse for it.

'That's a physical reaction, obviously, to the stress which the lack of trust caused.'

'Yes, thank you, Doctor,' said Paul, uncomfortably.

Nick shrugged.

'All right, it's just a theory. But so much of what we do is guesswork. And have you got a better one?'

Paul refilled Nick's glass which was already empty, and topped up his own. He sat down heavily in his creaking leather chair.

'No,' he said.

On the way home, he realized with a guilty start that he had not phoned Kate as she had requested. He hadn't seen her since their brief meeting at the bistro on the day of Roger Keen's arrest. When he got in he dialled her home number.

'This is Kate Durrani,' said her cool, clear voice. 'I'm sorry I'm not able to take your call at the moment, but please leave your name and number after the tone and I'll get back to you. Thanks for calling.' Paul held the receiver away from his ear while the three-note tone shrilled, then said: 'Kate, it's Paul. Sorry I haven't rung. Usual family crises. I wondered if you were free tomorrow night. Supper? Cinema? Something else? Can you call me back? Thanks.'

Then he went through to the kitchen to start supper. Marty was there, in the process of assembling himself a sandwich for which he had amassed most of the contents of the fridge. Al was out at some girlie get-together. Could this be the moment?

'We don't seem to have seen much of each other recently,' said Paul lightly.

'Nope.' Marty concentrated on his sandwich filling.

'Are you going to be around tonight?' The monster sandwich indicated otherwise but Paul had to start somewhere. 'We could have a knock-about at tennis.'

Marty looked up briefly. His face was unexpressive.

'Sorry. I'm going over to Toby's, help with his exhaust.'

Paul nodded assent. He didn't feel he could push it.

'Tomorrow night maybe?'

'Maybe.'

Too late, Paul realized that he'd asked Kate out tomorrow. Terrific!

It was about ten o'clock when she rang back, sounding full of beans and waking Paul from a stupor in front of the television.

'Great, let's do something,' she said, not remarking on the fact that it had taken him all this time to call her. 'I'll tell you what I fancy — well, it was Al's idea, really.'

'What?' asked Paul nervously.

'Laser. Or Quasar or whatever it's called. There's a place not too far away. You know, you have to blast each other with those gun things.'

'OK.' Paul affected an enthusiasm he didn't feel, but at least it was the sort of thing which might appeal to Marty. If he couldn't have Kate on his own, then they might as well make it a complete family outing. He arranged to pick Kate up at six the following evening and left notes for Al and Marty as he had to leave early the next day.

Someone else he'd hardly seen was Joanna, he thought next morning as he drove to work. The day after she had turned up at Church House to berate him for intervening with Mrs Keen on her behalf, or so she believed, she had driven her widowed father to Scotland to stay with his sister and had stayed a couple of days herself. She was due back at work today, and from the tin of shortbread reposing on Julia's desk which caught Paul's eye when he arrived, he deduced that she was in. Feeling that he had badly lost the initiative with Marty and determined not to let it happen at work as well, he popped his head round the door of her office. The few days away had done her good. She looked less drawn than usual, and she seemed, even in that brief time, to have relaxed.

'Hi,' said Paul.

'Oh, hello, Paul,' she said warmly. 'I think I owe you an apology.'

'Really?' This was better than he'd dared hope.

'There's nothing like a long solitary drive down the M6 to focus the mind,' she smiled. 'I'm sorry about the other day. I over-reacted.'

'I wasn't trying to interfere, honestly . . .' he began, but she held up her hand.

'Let's say no more about it,' she said, smiling.

Surprised, Paul felt he ought to say something. He'd worked with Joanna for five years and he didn't really know her at all.

'Well, um, you'll have to come over another evening and stay a bit longer,' he suggested.

'Great. How about tonight?'

'Er, no . . .' Paul was rather taken aback. 'I'd say tonight, but . . .' There was Kate tonight.

'Don't worry.' There seemed to be a tingle of disappointment in her voice. 'Any time you're free.'

Al greeted the idea of a trip to play laser games with delight, but all Paul got from Marty was his original note returned with 'No thanks' scribbled on the corner.

'Do you know what he's up to tonight?' Paul asked Al when she came down the stairs dressed for the evening in jeans and a new pink T-shirt.

'Sorry, Dad, no.' Al looked as if she wished she could make it better. 'He hasn't said anything to me.'

Marty waited till he heard the Discovery scrunch away down the drive, then he swung his legs off his bed and rooted on top of the wardrobe. He'd had plenty of time to think over the last few days but he felt he still needed more. He certainly wasn't about to go playing happy families with Dad and Al and that Kate, who was probably nearer his own age than his Dad's and always trying to be hip. Laser games. How old did she think he was, ten? He didn't know why Al went along with it, but then, assuming she got good grades, which she would of course, Al would be off to university in October, so she wouldn't be around much longer. And the thought of just him and his Dad in the house, alone, was too awful to think about.

Underneath his old cricket bat and Monopoly game, he found what he was looking for. His sleeping bag. He probably hadn't used it since Scout camp, but it would still be OK. Luckily you didn't grow out of sleeping bags. Marty re-rolled it rather more neatly and wedged it on top of his rucksack, which he had already packed with a change of clothes, his Jack Kerouac and his Jack Higgins and, of course, his insulin. Boozie scratched at the door and Marty let him in. Boozie promptly jumped on the bed, which was forbidden, and started sniffing around.

'You can't stay there, Boozie,' admonished Marty, then: 'Oh, why not. See you, boy.'

Paul wasn't too sure he liked the laser place. It seemed to consist of trying to creep around undetected in the dark while other people shot at you – just what had always put him off the Cadet Corps. However, Al and Kate seemed to think it was terrific, especially since they were spectacularly successful at zapping him.

'If Marty had turned up you would have been obliterated, vaporized, both of you!' Paul asserted when they broke for a drink, determined not to let them get away with it.

'Oh, really?' said Kate. 'I'll have a mineral water, please.'

'I'll get them,' offered Al. Then, turning to her father she added, 'But you're paying!'

'Why?' demanded Paul.

'Because you lost!'

Come back, Marty, all is forgiven, thought Paul, delving into his pocket.

Marty hadn't checked the trains or anything, even though he knew where he was going. He caught a local train to Birmingham, correctly supposing he'd have to get an InterCity from there and, possibly, after that, another local train. He was lucky. He got straight on a train to Birmingham where he was told that the next train, the six forty-one, would get him there at ten past ten. Perfect.

It had been perfect, that holiday, the last they had had with Mum, the year before she died. It was seaside just like it was supposed to be, little boats nodding up and down in the harbour, fishermen mending their nets on the quayside, seagulls wheeling overhead in search of lunch. Nearby there had been little coves where he and Al had played pirates and mucked about in rock pools and swum in the exciting, cold, clear water, floating on their backs and looking up at the picturebook sky.

He could no longer get close to his Dad, and what he'd said, about him killing Mum, which was not what he really believed at all, was hardly going to make things any better, even if they did 'talk' about it, which Dad seemed to think was such a good idea. Marty had his doubts. He worried that if they did talk, a load of other hurtful things which were best left unsaid might come out. Like how Dad preferred Al to him, and always had, how he felt his Dad was disappointed in him because he wasn't as quick at his schoolwork as Al had always been.

He had thought he was close to Al, but she was all wrapped up in her friends, and her A-levels, and going to university. She was leaving him behind. The only person he still felt close to was Mum, and he had thought that if he could get to Aberdovey, where they had all last been together as a family, then maybe somehow, he might be able to get that family feeling back. It sounded muddled enough even when he tried to explain it to himself, which is why he knew he could never have explained it to Dad, or even to Al, so there was no point leaving a note. But he didn't want them to worry. He'd ring when he got there.

When he did arrive, the train being three minutes early, or so the conductor told them smugly, he could smell the sea straight away. The light was beautiful, too, still pinkish, though darkening by the second. Marty walked to the front. Hopeful seagulls swooped around him in welcome. He leaned on the rail and took a deep breath. He'd been right to come.

After letting them beat him again ('That's just what he would say, isn't it, Al?') and feeling he had let himself be ganged up on by the two women for long enough, Paul drove the three of them home.

'Looks like Marty's back early,' observed Al, seeing Nick's Saab parked on the drive.

Or probably never went out, thought Paul. It would be typical of Marty to profit from their absence actually to spend an evening at home.

'I'll put the kettle on,' announced Al when they were inside.

Paul ushered Kate through to the sitting room, drew the curtains and switched on a lamp. There was no loud music from Marty's room. Perhaps he'd decided to do some homework and get his head down early for once.

Wherever Marty had spent the evening, it hadn't been in here. There was no detritus of Coke cans and crisp packets which were his usual mark of occupation.

'Sit down,' he urged Kate. But she came over to him, and stood close.

'I've got some news,' she said. 'I've been offered a job in Bristol.'

'Oh?' said Paul, trying to sound unsurprised. For goodness' sake, she'd only been here six months!

'I just wondered . . . what you thought about it.'

He took her elbow and guided her to the sofa, then sat down beside her.

'I don't know,' he said. 'Whatever's best for you, I suppose.'

'Yeah.' She nodded. 'Yeah. I mean I don't know really.'

Paul didn't know what else to say.

'Well, um, is it a good job?'

'Sort of. I think so. Yes.'

She looked at him searchingly but he was still lost for words. He had the feeling, though, that he was supposed to say something meaningful and significant. And he couldn't think how to start.

After Al had gone upstairs, they talked about safer things – like Marty.

'Thank God Al's stable,' reflected Paul.

'She's been very welcoming to me,' said Kate. 'I thought she might be protective of you.'

Paul leaned forward till their noses almost touched.

'Protect me from what?' he asked.

A wry smile twitched at the corner of Kate's mouth.

'Predatory women?' she asked.

'I don't think I want protecting from them,' murmured Paul, leaning fractionally forward to touch his lips to hers. His arms went round her before he could stop himself and she shifted slightly to ease her arms round his neck. But all the time Paul was kissing her all he could think of was that Marty would probably crash in at any minute on his way to the fridge.

After a while Kate whispered that she'd have to go.

'Do you have to?' Her slender body was unbearably arousing.

'I don't think this is the time or place,' she said softly. 'To be honest, I don't feel very comfortable . . . like this . . . here.'

Paul checked himself. He had been so carried away, so

in need of her, that he hadn't considered that Kate might feel awkward in what had been his and Celia's home.

'OK,' he said gently. 'But let's not leave it too long, hm?'

Kate had recovered her composure. She nodded, smiled and got up. Then she leaned down to kiss him on the lips.

'Sleep tight,' she said.

And he had, for the two hours till the phone woke him and he had to drag himself down to the police station where Ken – did the man never go home? – had in custody a dosser who'd been caught up in some sort of fire which they believed to be arson. By the time Paul got home at four-thirty he was too exhausted to undress again. He fell face down on the bed fully clothed, and went out like a light.

'Dad! Dad! Wake up!'

'Mm?'

Paul groaned as he registered, from the light in the room, that it must be morning already. Al was shaking his shoulder.

'Marty's gone!' she cried. 'I think he might have run away, I don't know. You shouldn't have shouted at him, Dad.'

Paul leaped to his feet, feeling giddy as the blood rushed to his head. He raced to Marty's room, as if by seeing for himself he could make him reappear. He opened the wardrobe and noted the empty hangers.

'His rucksack's gone, I checked,' said Al mutedly.

Paul turned to face her.

'Oh, God, Al . . . where's he gone?'

She shook her head and began to cry.

He managed to persuade Al to have a bit of breakfast, then got her to call Sophie to come over and be with her. She refused to leave the house in case Marty rang and he didn't want her to be on her own all day.

'Are you going to ring the police?' she demanded.

Paul promised to give Ken a ring but he knew what the answer would be. They could circulate Marty's description to neighbouring forces but the bottom line was that, at seventeen, he was considered to be an adult, and if he wanted to leave home, with or without telling Paul, there wasn't much anyone could do about it. Paul could see that he'd taken a good supply of insulin, so he couldn't be said to be at any particular risk to his health. It was brutal, but the sad fact was that hundreds, no probably thousands, of kids ran away from home each year and the police hadn't got the resources to hunt for them all. Paul remembered dimly that there was some sort of missing person's helpline to which he'd once referred a patient whose daughter had run away. He'd never thought he might need it himself.

Marty had found himself a decent B&B which was clean and comfy and, since it was away from the sea, cheaper than some. He'd taken all his savings – £250 – out of his building society account but he knew they wouldn't last long. He'd have to get a job. Still, nearly school holiday time, seaside resort – it couldn't be too hard. But first he'd better phone the old man.

Joanna answered when he got through to Wickton Road. She said Paul was with a patient. Typical.

'Can you just tell him there's no problem and I'll call him later,' said Marty. 'He'll understand.'

Joanna didn't know what to think about Paul. When she'd come back from Scotland, she'd been prepared to forgive and forget, but in the couple of days she'd been back, she was already feeling as if she'd never been away. The surgery was overworked and harassed from the moment it opened, and responsibility for that had to be down to Paul and his bloody police work. Plus – and she knew it was unreasonable because she was letting personal feelings cloud her professional judgement – she didn't think he really meant it about her coming over one evening. He'd just been fobbing her off. *And* she'd overheard Julia and Mandy saying that he was seeing someone called Kate. When he got the inevitable call from Ken Jackson near the end of morning surgery she enjoyed saying, pointedly, that she'd cover some of his visits for him, adding: 'Oh, by the way, Marty phoned.'

If she hadn't turned away so quickly she would have seen the mixture of relief and disappointment that he hadn't taken the call which suffused Paul's face.

At least Al was more cheerful when he got home.

'Sophie says he'll come back when he gets hungry,' she said blithely.

Paul wished he felt so sure. He sat down on the piano stool and idly pressed the keys. He didn't even know if the piano was still in tune. Celia's face looked back at him from one of the many photographs which cluttered its top. She was half turned to the camera, with the light catching her eyes and her chestnut hair thrown back. What would she have done about Marty? The question would never have arisen. If she'd been around, he would never have gone.

'You'd better get ready, if you're going.' Al's voice made him jump.

He'd forgotten. Last night, at the laser place, Kate had produced tickets for *King Lear* at Stratford. Tonight. He hoped he'd be able to stay awake. Still, at least it was a play about ungrateful daughters. Ungrateful sons would have been too much to take.

In the interval, they wandered out on to the terrace which overlooked the river, on which the swans were still sliding, shimmering against the dark water. They chatted for a bit about the play, and about work, then Kate laid her hand on his arm.

'Look, can we talk about us?' she said softly. 'Am I going to Bristol, or not? I mean, I miss Bristol. But the air's not as fresh as round here . . .'

As she was talking, Paul had another of those 'seeing Celia' experiences. There was a woman in the crowd who, from the back, had hair just like hers. As Paul stared at the back of her head, it was as if the woman turned, and suddenly it was Celia. She was looking at him full in the face, a look full of love but also of understanding and release. Another theatre-goer suddenly obscured Paul's line of vision and she was gone. He was aware that Kate was looking at him, waiting for a reply.

He reached out for her, sliding his fingers under her heavy hair and feeling her neck warm to his touch. Then he bent his head and kissed her.

'Don't go,' he said. 'I want you, Kate, so much.'

Next day was the anniversary of Celia's death.

'I'll tell you what,' he said to Al. 'I'm off after lunch. Let's go out and drink a toast to Mum.'

'I can't believe it's five years today,' said Al, shaking her head. They were both silent for a moment, remembering. Then Al added: 'Oh, Dad. Marty phoned last night. He said he was fine, he's got a place to stay.'

'Where?' asked Paul. He could be anywhere. Birmingham, Oxford, London . . .

'I don't know. He didn't say. But he's OK, that's the main thing.'

Kate saw her client to the door and motioned to one of the secretaries.

'Jackie, could you hold my calls for half an hour? Just take messages, would you, and say I'll call back this afternoon?'

She went back into her office and closed the door. She wandered over to the window which overlooked the hubbub of Warwick market. It was nice here, that was for sure. The other partners were really friendly, there was a good mix of work, she had just started to feel settled in her flat, and then there was Paul. Well, what about Paul? He was a lovely guy, and she found him desperately sexy, probably because he was so unaware of it, but, deep down, she had to admit that they had nothing in common. She sometimes felt that she had more to talk to Al about than to him, though the problem wasn't really to do with their ages, more to do with attitude. She suspected Paul had always been a pretty serious sort of bloke, even when he was younger. Whereas, perhaps as an antidote to the sort of work she did, Kate liked a laugh. When the day was done, she wanted to go out and enjoy herself. Paul was quieter, more reflective. In time, would it get on her nerves? And there were his children, who weren't a problem exactly, but who would always be there. And what with the crazy hours he worked . . . Still, life was always a compromise. Even so, it would be worth finding out a bit more about what was on offer in Bristol. It couldn't do any harm. Finally decided, she picked up the phone and dialled the number of her old firm.

'Colin?' she asked when she'd been put through. 'Hi, it's me. Now, listen, tell me more about this senior partnership you're dangling in front of me.'

Joanna finished watering her hanging baskets – they were such a fiddle, but they were worth it, bright against the rough white wall of the cottage – and wondered what to do with the rest of the evening. She could phone a girlfriend for a chat, but she didn't feel like going through the usual round of gossip about work and moaning about the lack of eligible men in the Midlands. Too depressing. Of course, there was one eligible man whom she knew.

What about giving Paul a ring? She could invite him over for a drink and perhaps, in a more social atmosphere, they might be able to have a sensible talk about his outside work and her new idea, which was to get a locum in to help out on an occasional basis, to relieve the pressure on the other partners. But when she dialled his number, all she got was the answering machine. She replaced the receiver quickly. He was probably out with this Kate person. He led such a complicated life. The phone call from Marty suddenly came back to her and she wondered if everything was all right between those two. They'd had their disagreements in the past, she knew. Still, it wasn't her concern.

After a supper of fish and chips (again), Marty found himself back on the seafront. It was about nine and the beach was deserted except for a couple of dog-walkers. He wondered how Boozie was and if he'd had the good sense to get off Marty's bed before Dad or Al could discover him. Maybe it was that which gave him the idea of phoning, but anyway he fished in his pocket for some change and dialled the number at home.

Paul was in the study, reading an article in the *BMJ* about 'Living Wills'. When he picked up the phone, all he could hear was silence.

'Marty?' he said urgently. 'Marty, is that you? Hello? Marty?'

At the sound of his Dad's voice, sounding so worried, Marty had to swallow very hard. He struggled to say something but the words just wouldn't come out. Sadly he replaced the receiver and went to stand with his hands on the harbour rail, watching the sun as it lowered itself gently into the sea.

7

Paul parked the Discovery as close to the side of the lane as the verge, frothing with cow parsley, would allow, reached over for his bag and got out. He picked his way along the edge of the field, then through the crop to the white taped area where the body had been found. The corn was not far off cutting, and it waved against his legs with little whispering sounds as he walked. He wondered idly about compensation. Could the farmer claim on his insurance for the loss of a crop owing to a dead body being found in it, and the subsequent police operation? Or would that qualify as an 'Act of God'?

Ken was standing over the body like a lion with its prey, supervising the photographer. When the body had been photographed from all angles, Paul was free to start his examination.

'Any idea what he was doing here?' he asked Ken, as he crouched down.

'Well, he doesn't exactly look like a rambler,' remarked Ken laconically, referring to the man's business suit and polished shoes. 'We're looking for his car.'

'There's no sign of head injury,' said Paul, feeling the skull. 'All right to turn him over?'

Ken gave him a hand. The man was in his mid-forties, well-built, probably a bit out of condition, with thinning, sandy hair. There was still no sign of any external injury.

Paul checked his watch. 'OK, I certify death at three twenty-seven.' As he took the body temperature, one of the constables shouted to Ken.

'We've found it, sir!'

Paul's examination told him that the man had been

dead for twenty-four hours at the most and probably less. When he had finished, he joined Ken and Nicky by the dead man's car.

'It looks like natural causes, but we'll have to wait for the PM,' he told Ken. 'Look, I've got to go. Afternoon surgery. I'm unpopular enough at Wickton Road.'

'OK, Paul.' Ken was sifting through a load of brochures from a briefcase in the back of the car. 'Insurance, pensions...' He looked up suddenly. 'Any news from Marty?'

'Nothing new. He spoke to Al, said he had somewhere to stay. And we weren't to worry. Easier said than done.'

'Makes me glad I had a daughter, even if I do only see her Christmas and birthdays. If then.'

Ken grimaced. He hardly ever spoke about his private life and Paul suddenly felt guilty that he paraded his own for all to see.

'Yeah, well, you never stop worrying about them, do you?' he said quickly.

'Nope. Anyway. On with the job. Better go and break the bad news to his missis. OK, Nicky?'

Funny how she always got the really good jobs, Nicky thought, as she drove with a uniformed officer to Little Bagot where, she knew, she would find a normal Friday afternoon unfolding at number 4, Clover Road, a normality which she was about to shatter for ever. She turned the dead man's business card which, like his home address, they had got from his wallet, over and over in her hands.

'William J. Burford, appointed representative Harcourt and Smith Assurance Marketing Group, King's St, Nottingham.'

Assurance Marketing. Well, at least he'd have left his family well provided for.

Clover Road was a modern cul-de-sac off the main village street. The houses were semi-detached, with gaily-painted garage doors and little rockeries in the front gardens. Number 4 had a willow sapling, too. Nicky's heart sank when she saw two kids, a boy and girl of about eight and ten, playing on the front drive. Next time she'd make sure Ken did this bit, for once.

Lesley Burford couldn't seem to take it in. Nicky had to repeat it about three times. Finally, she left her sitting in the front room and went to make some tea.

'A field?' Lesley kept saying.

'Yes,' said Nicky. 'We don't know why he was found there. They have to do – tests. The doctor thinks it might have been a heart attack.'

Lesley shook her head fiercely.

'It's not him, it can't be. He's in Nottingham. He rang me from his car. He's not coming back till tonight!'

Nicky put her hand over Lesley's.

'We contacted his head office in Nottingham and he never arrived last night. We found his car by the field. He could have been phoning from anywhere.'

Lesley collapsed in tears.

'No!' she kept saying, over and over.

'I'll call your doctor,' said Nicky.

Al smiled to herself as the train pulled out of Birmingham. It had suddenly all come together. She'd thought she could hear this peculiar screeching noise in the background on one of Marty's phone calls. Then she'd been dusting the piano, and caught sight of the photograph, the one from the last holiday they'd had with Mum. Aberdovey! Sea-gulls! Of course!

'I know where you are, Marty Dangerfield!' she'd suddenly realized.

And today she was going to bring him home.

Kate folded the letter and put it back in the envelope. The terms really were very generous. She had expected to have to negotiate, but her old firm in Bristol obviously wanted her back pretty badly. The money wasn't everything, of course, but things weren't exactly going brilliantly here with Paul. She didn't know quite what it was, but they just did not fit together like she'd hoped. She had sensed lately that when he asked her something, her opinion about the wine, or what she thought of a book, or whatever, her responses were being analysed and somehow found wanting. He kept asking her what music she liked, and when she'd said rock and jazz, he had seemed to withdraw. She knew that Celia had been a great music lover and a terrific pianist, but surely she wasn't supposed to change her tastes to approximate to everything Celia had been? She couldn't have done it even if she had wanted to.

Professionally, things were difficult between her and Paul as well. They'd been up against one another in court the other day, and she knew that he felt she'd tried to trip him up in a case about non-accidental injuries. But for goodness' sake, she was only doing her job! He said that she'd taken something he'd said during a personal conversation and had used it against him. She said that it was a matter of professionalism. Then she had got impatient and said they saw little enough of each other without spending their evenings bickering like an old married couple. Which of course was the worst thing she could have said.

It was just getting too complicated. Maybe she'd be better off out of it. She wanted to tell him personally, though, of her decision, even before she confirmed it with Bristol. She dialled the surgery, only to be told he was out. She tried his mobile (engaged) before finally leaving a brief message on his answering machine at home, simply asking him to ring her. Honestly. He was never there. It was like trying to have a relationship with the Scarlet Pimpernel.

*

Joanna was at the message trays when Paul arrived back at Wickton Road, just in the nick of time for afternoon surgery. She was shocked at how washed-out he looked. The good weather, which had been doing everyone else a power of good, didn't seem to have touched him at all. Though his face was lightly tanned, there were tight lines around his mouth and his eyes were tired.

'Sorry, sorry, it took longer than I thought...' he began, trying to pre-empt her tirade about outside work.

But Joanna had spent her time while sitting in the sun in the evenings doing a lot of thinking, mainly about why she gave Paul such a hard time. Thinking wasn't something she encouraged in herself. She had spent a lot of time thinking when she had first been on her own, and in the end she had found it counter-productive. So she had moved house and job and resolved to start again with no looking back. But the trouble was that everything you did in life related back in some way to what had gone before. It informed your choices, shaped your reactions. It was just not that easy to shake off the past. She had finally allowed herself to face the fact that Paul's pain in the face of Celia's death had been an uncomfortable reminder of her own recent loss and had forced her to relive emotions which she did not want to be aroused again, ever. So when he sought a means of escape in his police work, she was resentful. He seemed to be getting on with things. Good for him. So why did she feel so angry? Could it be because she was feeling left behind? But surely that wasn't really Paul's fault?

The next night she forced herself to be even more analytical, starting from where she had left off. She resented Paul's work because it took him away from the practice. It meant more work. But she wasn't afraid of hard work, never had been and it was true, as Nick and Shaaban were always pointing out, that she was recompensed for it. So – if she was being really honest with herself – what she minded, what she missed, was Paul himself, his actual presence. Which led to one inescapable conclusion: she had allowed herself to care for him.

She had to make a decision. She could either carry on trying to deny her feelings, which she now felt had been responsible for most of her griping, or she could give herself permission to care for Paul, and start treating him like a human being. The first course, the course she had taken, wasn't making anyone happy. All that remained was to try the second.

'Calm down, Paul, you've actually got thirty seconds to spare,' she grinned. She was rewarded by seeing a look of puzzled suspicion cross his face. He wasn't used to this sort of treatment from her. So she swiftly followed it up. 'I've been meaning to ask you. Have you had any news of Marty?'

Paul shook his head.

'No. He's spoken to Al, though. I feel a bit useless, really.'

Joanna impulsively stretched out a hand towards him. He had got a lot to cope with, and she knew that her frequent outbursts about outside work hadn't helped. But Julia bustled up importantly, as always enjoying being the bearer of bad news.

'The police are on again. They want you to do a bereavement visit . . . to a Mrs Burford.'

Paul sighed.

'Tell them I will, but it won't be until after evening surgery.'

'I'll go,' said Joanna quickly. She was amused to see in Paul's face a pantomime of surprise, and added sweetly: 'You've got enough on your plate as it is.'

Joanna got Paul to brief her on Mrs Burford and it transpired that the whole family had been registered at Wickton Road. When she got to Little Bagot, though, Lesley

Burford explained that her husband had been so healthy he never went to the doctor.

'He'd only been once or twice. He saw Dr Dangerfield, I think. Sore throat, that sort of thing. And now they're telling me he had a heart attack . . .' She tailed off, then started up again, reeling off the thoughts which had been wheeling round in her brain ever since she had heard the news. 'He left here at six o'clock last night. He rang me at seven-fifteen from Nottingham. What's that – fifty, sixty miles? So how come he died of a heart attack – at about the same time, they say – not five miles from here?'

'I'm sorry, I can't answer that.' Joanna felt out of her depth. It certainly did sound suspicious.

Lesley sat forward suddenly, her eyes bright. She was an ordinary-looking woman in her late thirties, slightly plump, inoffensively dressed in pastel chain-store clothes. Joanna had seen countless Lesleys loading the weekly shop into their Metros or waiting with other mothers at the school gates as she drove to and from her house calls. But what lifted Lesley out of her ordinariness was her conviction that something was not right.

'The police,' she said. 'They're not telling me everything. I know there's something wrong. I mean, what was he doing there? He was on his own, wasn't he? I mean if there was anybody else . . .' She stopped as the horrible possibility struck her for the first time. 'A woman? Was there?'

Al found him surprisingly easily, because the first place she headed for was the beach, and there he was, dragging a rowing boat up the sand. An old chap with tousled white hair came and spoke to him, and Marty grinned and carried on dragging the boat. But when Al approached, he shouted to the old guy that he was taking his break, and marched off up the beach with Al trailing behind, calling his name.

'Marty! Marty! Wait, will you!'

After a bit he rounded on her angrily.

'Why did you have to come?' he demanded. 'Can't you just go home? How did you know I was here, anyway?'

'I just guessed,' said Al. The wind whipped her hair into her mouth as she talked and she flicked it out. 'It's the last place we came with Mum. The last place we were all together. That's why you came here, isn't it?'

Marty scuffed the sand with his sneaker.

'We were a family when we came here, you know. It just felt so safe. We're not even a family any more.'

'Dad's trying,' urged Al. 'He's doing his best . . .'

Marty looked scornful.

'Yeah, well, he's not trying hard enough. He never talks to me. He never listens to me.' His voice rose in indignation. 'I mean, I might as well be invisible. What is the point of having a Dad if he's never around? I mean, he's always working!'

'But can't you see that's just his way of coping with it?' said Al gently. She had to make him see. 'If he keeps working all the time he doesn't have to face up to the fact that Mum's not here any more.'

He suddenly reached out for her. She stepped forwards and wrapped her arms round him, hugging him tight. She would never have believed she could have been so glad to see him.

'I just miss her, Al! I miss her so much!'

She could tell that he was close to tears.

'I know,' whispered Al. 'So do I.'

'Just got the PM on Burford.' Ken stuck his head round the door of Paul's room at the police station. 'You were right. Heart attack.'

'Ah ha,' said Paul. He had been called out at the end of evening surgery to examine a suspect when all he really wanted to do was get home and ring Kate. Al had said she was going to be out late and would probably stay over at a friend's tonight, so he was going to suggest that he might stay over at a friend's as well . . .

Ken beckoned to him.

'Want to show you something,' he said cryptically.

'What, dirty pictures?' asked Paul, fastening his bag.

'You jest,' said Ken.

He took Paul into one of the interview rooms where a TV monitor had been set up and showed him an amateur video. It was of a parked car, seen through the fronds of a hedgerow. As the camera zoomed unsteadily in on the car, a man got out, shouting angrily and approached the camera. The picture went crazily lopsided as whoever had been operating the video recorder turned and fled, with the tape still running. Now all you could see was ears of wheat. Suddenly the camera flew through the air, following an arc of blue, and landed on the ground, pointing at the cornstalks.

Paul shrugged.

'So?'

Ken seemed very pleased with himself.

'It's a tape we found in a video camera belonging to Burford. He dropped it in the field where he died.'

He moved over to a white wallboard where he had drawn the layout of the roads and field where Burford's car and body had been found.

'Look, Burford's here,' he said, pointing. 'He starts to video a couple canoodling in a car. The guy sees him. Burford starts running away. He throws the camera away – lands here.' Again he indicated the spot. 'He runs down this way towards his car. Gets as far as here. Has a massive heart attack, drops dead.'

Paul thought Ken might just be letting a plausible story get in the way of the facts.

'You can't tell he was a peeping Tom from the tape,'

he protested. 'He could have been doing anything! Bird-watching!'

Ken shook his head, pitying Paul's innocence, and changed the camera cassette for another.

'This one SOCO found in his car, hidden behind the rear seat. See the date – it's almost a year ago.'

Again, the tape showed a couple in a car. The girl couldn't have been more than about twenty, with long dark hair and a full, sexy mouth. As Paul watched, she peeled off her red-and-white spotted dress. The man took it off her and put it over the window sill of the car before reaching round to unhook her bra.

'OK,' said Paul, uncomfortably. He was cross with himself for not having recognized Burford as his patient when he'd examined him in the field – but then he'd only seen the man once or twice. Lesley Burford he'd seen rather more of, with her migraines and the children's coughs and colds. 'Look, Ken, what about the wife? How's she going to handle this?'

'She doesn't have to,' said Ken simply and Paul felt grateful relief. 'Saw a case like this once, in the Met. Wife topped herself. Why should the family have to go through hell? There's no need.'

'Yes, but what about the tapes?' asked Paul.

'Well, tapes,' said Ken, 'can be used over and over again.'

As Paul watched he pointed the camera at the white wall of the interview room.

'Just point it at something, press the record button, and it's wiped. Case closed.'

Lesley Burford seethed as she left the police station later that evening. How DI Jackson could sit there and tell her that there was nothing suspicious about Bill's death she didn't know. Ever since Dr Stevens had been round, and she had had her flash of insight about the possibility of there having been another woman, she had been searching the house. She had gone through his suit pockets, his dressing-table drawers, even the shed and the garage. Finally, stuffed at the back of the bureau, she had found a small black notebook containing a list of times and places.

'Selby Woods, six-thirty. Briar Lane, seven forty-five. Gipsy Common, nine o'clock.' Lesley couldn't make any sense of it. Finally she had asked her niece, Chris, who had come to help out with the children, if they meant anything to her. Chris's response had not been reassuring.

'Lovers' Lanes,' she had said.

Lesley could not find anything else. No hotel bills, or receipts from florists, or all the other evidence which she imagined would add up to an affair. But she had taken the notebook to the police station anyway, determined to get to the bottom of it. But Ken Jackson had resolutely denied either that Bill had been having an affair, or that he had been murdered. He said he had given her all the information that they had. So why didn't it feel right?

Paul was about to phone Kate with his suggestion for how they might spend the evening when he noticed the red light flashing on the answering machine and thought he ought to play back his messages first. He smiled as he listened to Kate's, which just asked him to call her, wondering what her response would be to his suggestion. She was so cool and collected that there was something very exciting about the thought of her being out of control just for once. Then he heard Al's voice, which pulled him up short.

'Hi, Dad, it's me. Guess what? I've seen Marty and he's fine. I'm getting the last train now, don't wait up. See you. Bye.'

He knew at once that he wouldn't be going out, still

less staying out all night. Don't wait up? He wanted to see her as soon as she got back. He rang Kate's number quickly, in case Marty was at this moment trying to phone him, though he knew it was unlikely. He was hardly surprised to find Kate's answering machine on, because she usually went to the gym straight from work. He left a message suggesting lunch the next day, unless she rang him back to say otherwise. That done, he had a shower, made himself an omelette and sat down to wait.

It was gone eleven when Al got back, dropped off by the taxi which she had managed to persuade to bring her all the way from Birmingham. She crept in to find Paul asleep on the sofa, his feet hanging off the end. She kissed his forehead.

'I told you not to wait up,' she scolded.

Paul sat up, rubbing his stiff neck.

'Where is he, Al? Is he all right?'

Al still couldn't tell him. She had promised Marty.

'I think he's going to come home,' she reassured him. 'He's just got to sort his head out.'

Paul sighed. It was all his fault.

'I just want him back, Al.'

'Don't worry, he knows that, Dad. I made sure he knows.'

Unusually, it was Nicky who phoned the next day to call him out on a police job and Nicky who briefed him when he arrived at the village church in Preston-sub-Edge. She explained that gravediggers had been asked to open up the grave of an elderly man who had been buried the previous summer, so that the coffin could be moved, at his sister's request, to a family plot in Yorkshire.

'The coroner didn't object. But when they lifted out the coffin, the gravedigger spotted something underneath: a second body, without a coffin. And before you ask, we've checked. There was only supposed to be one body in the grave, *and* it's against the regulations for a body to be buried without a coffin.'

Ken was standing at the graveside, his usual morose expression for once fitting the occasion.

'We need you to certify death,' he told Paul sardonically.

It was an interesting one.

'Long hair ... women's clothing ...' said Paul as he climbed out of the grave twenty minutes later. 'You're going to have to hope for some dental records. Thing is, there's some adipocere formation.'

'Oh, yeah?' said Ken, meaning, 'Translate, please.'

'When a body's been in wet ground for more than about six months the body fat starts turning into a sort of waxy substance,' explained Paul. 'Now, I think there are some grooves in it around the neck which could be strangulation marks. It's going to be interesting to see what the patho-logist says. Mind if I come along?'

'Feel free.'

Paul didn't often ask to be in on the post-mortem but today he wanted to have his time occupied. It was his day off, from the practice at least, and though he was meeting Kate for lunch – answering machine having spoken to answering machine – he didn't feel like hanging around at home all morning.

To his satisfaction, the pathologist confirmed his sus-picions. He was a prematurely balding man in his forties, who had grown a beard in compensation. His eyes, behind clear-rimmed glasses, were a pale aquamarine.

'Death was by strangulation,' he told Ken and Paul. 'The hyoid bone was fractured. I'd say tights were used, maybe stockings. She's about eighteen years old, dark hair, not pregnant and her teeth were well cared for, so hope-fully we'll get a match with the dental records.'

Ken was already heading for the door.

'We'll start on Missing Persons. Coming, Paul?'

Paul was watching one of the scientific officers placing

the dead girl's clothing in a bag. Streaked with mud, it had once been some lacy underwear and a red-and-white spotted dress. She had hardly been older than Al. All her life in front of her. Paul said softly, half to himself:

> 'Golden lads and girls all must
> As chimney sweepers, come to dust.'

'Eh?' Ken was waiting for him at the door. Paul grinned.

'Shakespeare, Ken. Nothing you need bother your head about.'

Kate was waiting for him on the riverbank, on a seat beneath a weeping willow. She stood up as he approached. It was warm. She wasn't wearing a jacket and she had unbuttoned the collar of her crisp white shirt which exposed the tawny skin of her throat and a hint of collarbone.

'Hi,' she said, a little muted, it seemed to Paul. 'I wasn't sure you'd make it.'

'Yes, sorry,' he replied. 'I got held up.'

He bent to kiss her. He annoyed himself sometimes. If he couldn't be on time on a day off, when could he be? But there was something bothering him about the post-mortem and the dead girl ... He tried to shake it off and give Kate his full attention. They saw so little of one another, she deserved that at least.

He took her arm and linked it in his and they began to stroll along the bank. The river was alive with pleasure boats which you could hire in the park and take as far as the weir by the castle. Paul was about to apologize for not having been able to see her last night: maybe her air of distance was because she felt he was trying to cool things down, which was far from his intention. But Kate spoke first, her words coming out in a rush.

'Paul, I wanted you to be the first to know. It looks like I will be going to Bristol.'

'Right,' said Paul automatically, stunned.

'I just wanted you to know that I'd made a decision, that's all.'

A decision she'd obviously felt able to make without him.

They walked on slowly, not speaking. Kate stared at her feet on the path, while Paul stared, unseeing, at the river while he tried to work out what she was really telling him and what she wanted him to say.

'Well, Bristol's not very far,' he said. 'We could meet at . . . it's not a problem.'

Kate stopped and turned to face him.

'Paul, let's be honest. Things aren't exactly working out between us, are they?'

'Well, it's not easy, is it?' Paul was instantly on the defensive. 'Mixing personal relationships with what we do.'

'It certainly doesn't help.' Kate was giving nothing away.

He ploughed on, feeling he had to say something, hoping he wasn't making things worse.

'It's just that – the problem never arose with Celia.'

'Oh, please!' She gave a bitter laugh. 'Don't compare me with your wife!'

'I don't mean to, Kate,' he said softly. 'I want you, really I do, you must know that.'

For a moment she looked tempted, and he thought that perhaps something could be rescued from the situation.

'There's got to be a fast train to Bristol, hasn't there?'

Kate looked up at him. Though he could see in her face that it was no good, he leaned forward to kiss her, as if compelled.

She looked down quickly, putting her mouth out of his reach.

'I'll see you, Paul,' she said and quickly walked away.

Feeling deflated, Paul wasn't sure what to do. He hung

about on the riverbank for a bit, trying to work out what he felt about Kate, and whether he had been lying when he said he didn't compare her with Celia. When he felt he was getting nowhere, and had seen the same woman walking her dog go past him and come back, he decided to move on. Feeling restless, he decided to look in at Wickton Road and collect some paperwork which he could do in the garden at home. He knew it wasn't healthy to work on his day off, but if it left you less stressed on working days, then surely it couldn't be that bad for you. Anyway, there was nothing else pressing, unless he wanted to go and camp out under Kate's office window and plead with her to change her mind, which he didn't think would be welcome.

As he loaded papers into a supermarket carrier which Julia had found for him, Joanna popped her head round the door.

'Can't keep away?'

'I've got a load of catching up to do,' he replied shortly. She should have been pleased; she was the one who was always droning on about his outside work taking up so much of his time. But she seemed in a mellower mood than usual. She came in and sat down.

'How's Mrs Burford?'

Paul stopped what he was doing and considered. Ken had told him about the visit Lesley Burford had paid him at the station.

'Not good, really, pretty much as you said.' Joanna had filled him in on her bereavement visit and the difficulties it had thrown up. He shovelled another few inches of in-tray into the bag. 'You know, I remember seeing her husband once.'

'What was the matter with him?' Joanna tilted her head on one side, curious. She was wearing dangly bronze earrings, one of which had become entangled with her hair. Paul had to resist a sudden urge to free it.

'Actually, he came in about her. She'd lost interest in him – sexually.'

'Ah.' There was a sudden constraint between them, as if he had touched a nerve. Their eyes met briefly. Paul tested how much more weight the bag would hold and Joanna changed the subject. 'What's the latest news about Marty?'

Paul resumed his packing operation.

'Al found him yesterday. He still doesn't want me to know where.'

Joanna pursed her mouth as she considered this.

'Is he all right?'

'I think so. Al doesn't want me to pressure him. It may pay off, he may come home.' He looked directly at her and gave a helpless shrug. 'We're a complicated lot, aren't we? What about you, why don't you ever have any problems?'

Joanna gave a soft laugh but did not give him an answer. Instead she leaned foward.

'Paul, when Marty comes back, find time for him. We can cover.' And with a smile instead of sarcasm, 'As you know, covering's not a problem.'

Paul could hardly believe what she was saying or, rather, who was saying it. It appeared that Joanna had had a change of heart. She looked so different when she smiled. He smiled back too, as if it was catching.

'Just spend some time with him,' Joanna went on. 'Tell him you love him. People tend to like that sort of thing.'

Then she leaped up, as if, again, she was embarrassed.

'God, is that the time! I've got a Family Planning clinic! See you!'

And she was gone.

Paul looked at the papers he had packed. Then he emptied them all back into the in-tray and went home to work on Marty's car.

*

The Missing Persons files came up with only one missing female in the age range of the body found in the grave. Her name was Susan Wainwright and, as her photo showed, she had certainly had dark hair.

'And . . .' Ken looked up at Nicky, who had handed him the file. She nodded. 'She was reported missing by her parents the day before the old man's funeral.'

'I tell you what, Boss,' said Nicky. 'When we get the dental records, if it is her, how's about *you* tell the parents?'

When Al got back from her day, she found Paul in the driver's seat of the Triumph, revving the engine.

'God, it's alive! Does it actually work?'

'Of course it works! Hop in and we'll give it a test drive!'

Paul had been secretly impressed by how much Marty had actually done to the car. He'd persuaded Alf, who came in to cut the lawn, to sit in it and steer while he towed it down to the local garage and got them to give it the once over. In the end, all it had needed was a new battery.

Paul and Al drove out towards Stratford in the brilliant late afternoon sunshine, getting stuck behind tractors carting straw bales in the narrow lanes, winding through villages where half-timbered cottages bulged out into the road. One village was in the middle of its week-long 'Summer Fayre', or so the fluorescent posters stuck on all the lampposts told them. Outside the church there was morris dancing. Paul halted the car for a better look, and as Al clapped along to the melodeon, his eye wandered over the crowd. He noticed a young girl talking to a couple of bikers.

He couldn't think what it was about her that was so familiar. She was half turned to him, her dark hair flicked back over her shoulder, and she was swaying in time to the music, making her red-and-white spotted dress swirl about her body. Where had he last seen a young girl with dark hair and a red-and-white spotted dress? Paul shook his head in irritation as he tried to remember. Then it flashed in front of him, along with another image he had not been trying to recall and had not been expecting. The dark-haired girl in Burford's video had been wearing a red-and-white dress . . . and so had the girl in the grave!

Paul fired the engine and threw the car into gear. Al, who had wound down the window and was leaning on the sill, was thrown forwards.

'Dad!'

'Sorry, Al. Just remembered something.'

He dropped Al at home, leaving her some garbled instructions about supper, swopped cars — Marty's car might be working, but he didn't quite trust it on police business — and, with a brief wave, was gone.

As he drove, he ran over all the possibilities. It could, of course, just be a coincidence. But they knew Burford had been videoing courting couples for the last two summers. Susan Wainwright had been put in the grave in July last year. Paul realized he could be making a complete fool of himself. Marty had always said scathingly that Paul liked his police work because he secretly hankered to be Sherlock Holmes. But Susan Wainwright hadn't died a natural death. Wasn't it worth even Ken's derision to catch someone's killer?

In fact, derision was the last emotion Ken seemed to be feeling. After Paul had explained his suspicions, Ken held up his hands.

'Right, let's start again. If it's the same red dress, was the girl in Burford's video Susan Wainwright, the girl in the grave and is the guy in the video the guy who killed her?' Nicky was ahead of him and proffered the two files: the file on Burford and Susan Wainwright's Missing Person's file. Ken grabbed them excitedly. 'Yeah, here we are.' He compared the information on each. 'Burford's video was dated 17th July and Susan Wainwright was reported missing eight days later. Yeah, yeah, Susan Wainwright could be the girl in the red dress!' Then the elation in his voice faded away as he realized. He covered his eyes. 'I've wiped the evidence. I've wiped Burford's tape.'

Paul glanced at Nicky who made a face.

'Maybe there's a copy?' she suggested. 'Perhaps he kept videoing the same couple, or her with different men. Course, we'd have to search the Burford house.'

Paul let out a breath.

'That would mean telling Mrs Burford.'

Ken was firm, mostly because he was furious with himself.

'What choice have I got? She's not the priority any more. This is a murder enquiry.'

Paul insisted that he went along to Little Bagot as well, and as they drove, he and Ken agreed that Paul should be the one to explain to Lesley Burford the reason for their visit. Of course, when they got there, Lesley thought that the police had uncovered something which would confirm her own suspicions and Paul had to explain it wasn't quite like that.

'The police just want to know if there are any video cassettes your husband made, that's all,' Paul explained. He took her arm and sat her down. 'The police think he may have accidentally videoed a murderer.'

Lesley looked at him blankly.

'Video? Why? What for?'

There was no easy way round this.

'Lesley, your husband liked to video people. Couples, Lovers. I'm afraid he was a bit of a peeping Tom.'

Understandably, Lesley didn't take it well. She screamed at Paul to get out of the house, refusing to believe it could be true. Paul wasn't surprised. She was still in shock and denial, convinced there was something suspicious about her husband's death, but unable to cope with the awful reality. He left Nicky calming her down, and Ken fretfully pacing the pavement outside, waiting for permission to search the place, refusing to rule out the possibility of a warrant if she wouldn't cooperate.

Paul went home and dutifully ate the supper Al had cooked. Half-way through, the phone rang. At the beginning of the week he'd arranged to meet Ken that evening for a drink at his local. They didn't see much of each other out of work, their shared rugby-playing days being more of a barrier than a bond in view of the very different paths their lives had taken. He expected the call to be from Ken, having to cancel because of what they had managed to turn up at the Burford house. But when he answered it, still chewing, it was Lesley.

She was awesomely in control.

'The police found what they were looking for,' she said. 'In the study, hidden. It was what you said. I – um – want to apologize.'

Paul was moved by her dignity, and was about to say so when she carried on.

'I just wondered if you knew . . . why he did it?' This must be so difficult for her, he could tell. Finally she managed to form the question she dreaded. 'Was it me?'

'You?' Paul repeated, playing for time.

'Well, he might not have had . . . er . . . he might have . . . not . . . been happy with me.'

Paul thought back to his one consultation with Burford and what he had said about Lesley. He thought about Ken and his attempt to protect her, and how dismally and messily it had failed, the additional suffering she had been put through because she had not been told the truth in the first place. But he didn't feel that now was the time for the truth, either.

'Oh, that's not true. That's simply not true,' he said decisively.

'How can you know?' wondered Lesley.

In the background, Al hovered, making signs that she was going to wash her hair. Paul waved her away.

'Oh, I do know,' he said into the phone, improvising as he went, trying to sound as certain as he could. 'He came to me last winter, for a flu jab I think it was, and I remember him saying what a good relationship he had with you. He told me how lucky he thought he was.' At the other end of the phone, he could sense Lesley start to relax. 'Look,' he went on. 'You have nothing to feel guilty about. Nothing whatsoever.'

'Thank you.' Paul could tell that Lesley was holding back tears. 'That means a lot. It means a great deal. Thank you. You can have no idea how much that means to me.'

Paul replaced the receiver gently and went back to his congealing supper. He no longer felt hungry. Boozie, whose mind-reading skills had developed over the years to clairvoyant proportions, scrambled out of his basket and glued himself to Paul's left leg. Paul bent and scraped bacon and pasta into Boozie's dish and was rewarded for his kindness by the thump of Boozie's tail on the side of his head. He put his plate and cutlery in the dishwasher and gulped down the rest of his wine, then shrugged on his jacket to go and meet Ken. Even if he didn't turn up, an evening's solitary drinking would give Paul the oblivion he required.

He walked into the village, hands thrust into his pockets, his shoulders sloped. It was a beautiful evening, the sky pink over the cut cornfields and the hedgerows alive, busy blackbirds swooping low over the road in search of sustenance for their young.

He'd made a mess of everything he'd touched that day. OK, he'd had the brilliant idea about the red dress, but it had meant another massive emotional upheaval for Lesley Burford. Was any of it worth it? Well, of course it was. What about Susan Wainwright's family and friends?

They'd lived for a year without knowing whether she was dead or alive. Now they knew for certain that they were not getting her back, didn't they at least deserve the truth, to know who killed her? That was what Kate would have said, cool, analytical Kate, with her lawyer's brain and, possibly, he now wondered, her lawyer's heart as well. He had thought Kate might be, if not *the* answer, then *an* answer for him, but it seemed that he had not even been asking the right questions.

He was glad when he reached the pub and was saved from his fruitless introspection. The garden was full of drinkers, groups of youngsters with bottles of lager, a few families trying to restrain their toddlers, but no Ken. Paul sought sanctuary indoors. He bought a pint for himself and an orange juice for Ken and perched at the bar. Ken joined him when he'd barely taken a couple of swigs.

'We found a stack of videos at Burford's,' he told Paul. 'None of them – none of them were of the girl in the red dress. I had a tape of the possible evidence in my hand, Paul. I wiped it and now I'm left with a case I'm no closer to solving than I was twelve months ago. Plus we had to tell Lesley Burford the truth and all we did was upset her.'

'She rang me tonight,' said Paul. 'I lied.'

Ken looked at Paul, wanting more, but Paul felt he'd compromised patient confidentiality, even dead patient confidentiality, even false patient confidentiality, quite enough for one evening.

Ken hunched over the bar, his leather jacket creaking.

'Well, it's the last favour I do for anybody. Wiping tapes! Just do the job, and keep it simple.'

'You're lucky,' said Paul, thinking of Lesley, and Susan, and Joanna, and Kate but especially of Marty. 'Wish I could do that.'

Ken looked at him, a sardonic gleam in his eye.

'You know something, Paul?' he offered. 'You're a miserable bastard.'

Paul grinned.

'It takes one to know one,' he said.

When he got home, he was surprised to see Joanna's car in the drive. As he approached the front door, it opened and she came out. She seemed very pleased about something.

'I just popped in to see Al,' she explained hastily.

'Well, stay and have a drink now you're here,' urged Paul, aware of the invitation extended before and never taken up. Joanna hesitated but when he took her arm, turned her round and shepherded her into the sitting room, she came without protest.

'God, what a day!' he exclaimed as he crossed to the drinks tray. 'Right, what'll you have?'

Joanna had moved to stand by the french window.

'Whatever you're having,' she shrugged, smiling.

Paul poured two whiskies, adding a splash of water to hers. As he walked up behind her with the drinks, he followed her glance through the window. Out in the dusk, under the old apple tree where the children had had their swing, he saw Al and Marty walking towards the house. He looked at Joanna and she beamed back at him.

'He turned up at the surgery,' she explained. 'I gave him a lift home.' Then she held out her hands for both glasses and stood aside. Paul thrust them at her and tore open the french doors. He crossed the terrace in two strides and came face to face with Marty on the lawn. Every emotion he could put a name to, and plenty more that he couldn't, churned in his chest: relief and anger and exasperation and remorse and love. He stepped forward and wrapped his arms round his son. Marty said nothing. But he didn't pull away. Al looked on, smiling.

Joanna stood on the terrace and watched. She felt enormously privileged to be present at the reunion, yet she was patently not part of it. Putting her glass down quietly

on the low patio wall, she tiptoed off round the side of
the house to her car. She had hardly got to the edge of
the terrace when Al spotted her.

'Joanna,' she called. 'Aren't you going to stay?'

Paul disengaged himself from Marty and caught her up.

'Joanna, come in,' he urged. 'Have a drink with us.
Celebrate.'

She shook her head.

'No, Paul. I think it's better if I don't. Really.'

'Come on,' he urged. 'Join us.'

'No.' She'd made up her mind. 'This is a family affair.'

Paul could see that she would not be persuaded, and
gave in.

'All right,' he smiled. And, aware of the irony, 'Another
time?'

'Yes,' she said. 'I'd like that.'

They all waved as she drove off but before she got to
the bottom of the drive, she saw in the rear-view mirror
that they had turned, Paul with his arms around both his
children, and gone back into the house.

She reached across and turned on the radio, wanting to
lose herself, not wanting to have the silence in which to
think.

8

'Can somebody give me a hand, please?'

Al stood at the top of the stairs with a sagging cardboard box balanced precariously against the banister. There was no response from the kitchen where she could hear her Dad and Marty talking over the background burble of the 'Today' programme.

'Dad! Marty!'

There was still no reply. None so deaf as those who don't want to hear, thought Al grimly and then, even more grimly, 'God, I'm turning into my grandmother'. Hoisting the box against her chest, she inched down the stairs. She had never realized a few paperbacks could be so heavy. Dumping the box on the hall table, she went into the kitchen, where Marty was having another go at wearing Paul down on the perennial theme of his loathing of school.

'What's the point?' he complained. 'You know what my mock results were like.'

'Yeah, but you did miss rather a lot of school last half term.' Paul slurped the dregs of his coffee. 'That's the point.'

'I wouldn't have minded a hand with my things for college, actually,' said Al. 'But don't let me interrupt.'

'Well, ask Marty,' replied Paul as he passed her, pulling on his jacket. Marty had already clumped upstairs. 'I understand manual labour's going to be his thing now he's given up on school.'

Al put out a hand and turned him to face her.

'Dad,' she said. 'I'm going away.'

As if Paul didn't know.

'Just down the road, Al, to university, not to Siberia,' he protested. 'Anyway, you're not going today, just moving your things into the halls of residence.'

'It would still be nice if I could talk to you before I go. But, of course,' she added sarcastically, 'you're pushed for time. As usual.'

Paul wondered if this was the moment. He had been putting off the talk Al wanted because, although he'd had months, well, years really, to get used to the idea that Al would be leaving home, it seemed to have crept up suddenly and ambushed him when he wasn't expecting it. There had been jubilation back in August, of course, when she'd got her A-level grades and they had more than met the entry requirements for Warwick. The phone had been tied up for two days solid as she swapped news with her friends, commiserating with some and congratulating others and Ken had complained that it was even more difficult than usual trying to get hold of Paul. But now, suddenly, it was October. The mornings had turned cold, the dew was heavy on the grass and the horse chestnut trees down the drive were beginning to bronze.

He half turned to go and then, as if it were an afterthought, reached into his inside jacket pocket and brought out a slim leather box.

'I nearly forgot.' He held it out to Al.

Surprised, she took it and when she opened it her face filled with colour. She lifted out a delicate Victorian necklace of garnets which had belonged to Celia's grandmother.

'It's Mum's,' she whispered.

'Yeah, well, it's yours now,' said Paul awkwardly. 'You know she promised it to you if you got to university. And she'd have been very, very proud of you.'

Al looked at him, her eyes starting to brim with tears. He hugged her to him. She was so young and so fragile, and yet she'd had to be so tough.

'Hey, come on . . .'

He didn't want her to go. That was why he'd been trying to ignore it, stepping over the black bin-liners stuffed with outgrown clothes and discarded pop posters which cluttered the landing outside her room, refusing to go in and see the outlines on the walls where she had taken down faded photographs or her old Pony Club rosettes. If Celia had been here . . . Al would still have gone, of course, but there would have been two of them to face this new phase in their life together. Instead he had to face the prospect of living in the house with Marty, who had still not really explained to Paul's satisfaction why he had run away during the summer. His insistence that he wanted to leave school was beginning to grind Paul down.

Al snuggled into his shoulder then looked up, in control again.

'D'you know, I'm really going to miss this place. And you, Dad.'

Marty jumped the last three stairs and landed thunderously beside them.

'And me?' he enquired.

Al grinned conspiratorially at Paul.

'Let's not get carried away,' she said.

Joanna wasn't very good at early mornings but she'd been determined to get to the hospital to talk some sense into her dad before going to surgery. Eight-fifteen certainly wasn't within the usual visiting hours, but if you couldn't pull strings occasionally, what was the point of being in medical practice? Now she sat by her father's bedside, his breakfast tray long cleared away, and tried to make him understand. She felt both exasperated by and sorry for him. Sure, it would be an upheaval. But he'd had a nasty fall, given his leg a bad break, and his flat was up two flights of stairs, for heaven's sake. How was he going to manage? But Harry Campbell was made of tougher stuff. He might have been seventy-six but his brain was as alert as when he'd fought with Montgomery at El Alamein, or when he'd been running a successful plastics business in Galashiels.

'I've been managing on me own since your mother died. I'm not going into an old fogies' home.'

'Sheltered accommodation, Dad . . .'

'Elephants' graveyard,' Harry cut in crustily. 'I'm not that far gone. I've broken me leg, that's all.' He squeezed her hand. 'I'll be all right, Jo.'

It may have been early but all over the hospital departments were humming, white coats were being donned for the day ahead. A white coat appeared now. It was Peter Evans, one of the radiographers, whom Joanna knew slightly. She'd always found him just a little bit too full of himself. He passed her an X-ray plate showing Harry's re-set leg. She took it gingerly, partly because of the plate, partly because she didn't want to jar his middle finger, which was covered by a finger-stall.

'Brought this down for Mr Callard's round,' he said. 'It's a lovely job. He'll be as good as new.'

'You're back early,' Harry observed to Peter while Joanna examined the X-ray.

Peter grimaced.

'Not much point in having a holiday in the rain . . .' he said lightly. 'Anyway, I'll leave you to it.'

'See,' said Harry triumphantly after he had gone. 'Good as new.'

Thanks, Peter, thought Joanna. I'll do you a favour some day.

'My father is driving me demented,' she confessed to Paul when she bumped into him at Wickton Road twenty minutes later. 'He's refusing to give up his independence.'

Paul smiled to himself. There was Al just striking out on her own, Marty desperate to do the same, and Harry Campbell refusing to be told what to do. Parents and children. They were as bad as each other.

'Well, I could have a word with him, if you like,' he offered.

'Oh, yes please, Paul,' said Joanna gratefully. Her mother had had a phrase, 'It sounds better coming from a man.' It wasn't that, exactly, but Harry might just take advice from someone with less of a subjective interest in the matter. And he had always liked Paul.

Before she could say any more, Paul's mobile rang.

'Got to go,' he said when he'd finished the call. 'That was Ken. They've found a body in the canal, by the Bracewell bridge, near the pub . . .'

'Paul . . . we've got a practice meeting,' Joanna reminded him gently.

'Oh, my God . . . look, I'll be back soon,' Paul promised. 'And about your dad . . . Come for supper tonight. About seven. Take pot luck.'

Joanna smiled resignedly.

'OK, you get off,' she said. 'And, yes, we'll cover.'

It was freezing by the canal. It was the sort of cold that creeps up your sleeves and into the very heart of you. Finding a body was never pleasant but this had to be one of the dankest places anyone could have died in. Paul tugged on his boots and followed Ken along the towpath. To the right of the path was a steep bank which dipped down to the water through a belt of trees. Part of the bank had been taped off to form a sterile area and a couple of SOCOs were trying to search it, aware that every step they took could be trampling something underfoot. Paul followed Ken down, slipping on the walking plates which were already treacherous with mud.

Half in and half out of the water, her torso in the canal and her face on the bank, a blonde-haired woman lay face downwards, dressed only in an anorak.

'There's blood on the lips and chin from a possible head wound,' said Ken. 'She was found about an hour ago by a jogger. Cudworth and Spenser were down here straight away.'

Paul nodded and, bracing himself, splashed down into the water. Even through his boots and thick socks he could feel his toes start to curl up in protest.

'Subject mid-thirties,' he said, feeling the woman's skull. 'No obvious sign of skull fracture. She has a cut above the right ear, superficial from the look of it, as is the bruising to the right cheek.'

'Drowned?' asked Ken.

'No obvious evidence,' Paul replied. 'No rigor.'

No rigor . . . he suddenly whipped his stethoscope from his pocket and, as he fixed it in place, felt frantically for a pulse in the woman's neck.

'What are you doing?'

He felt a flutter. He was sure.

'Get an ambulance!' Paul yelled. 'She's still alive.'

As Ken did so, Paul gave orders.

'I want her out of the water and into the field . . . come on!'

Nigel Spenser and a couple of other constables scrambled down to help. Paul chucked his car keys at Ken, telling him to get someone to get his other bag from the car.

'Why didn't somebody check?' he asked angrily.

In a small voice, Georgie Cudworth said: 'I did check.'

Paul had the woman laid on the ground on a pile of coats, and covered her with his own Barbour and Ken's overcoat. He began mouth-to-mouth resuscitation. Then he gave her a shot of adrenalin. Anything, till the paramedics got there.

Ken took Georgie Cudworth on one side. This was a real mess.

'Sure there was no pulse?' he asked her gently.

Georgie was only young, but precisely because of that she was conscientious. She would have checked.

'She was freezing ... there was nothing...' Poor
Georgie looked agonized.

'I believe you.'

When Ken turned back, the paramedics had arrived.
They were preparing to shock the woman's heart, greasing
the body where the paddles would go in. Cudworth looked
as if she was going to throw up.

'Make your report very specific; I'll do the same,' muttered Ken. 'Let me have a look at it before you hand it
in, OK? But the doc says there was a pulse ... got a
problem.'

He glanced over at Paul who shook his head. The
woman had failed to respond.

'All right, Ken. We're going to call it a day.'

Everyone looked bleak. You saw it every night on the
telly in some medical programme or other, especially the
American ones, but seeing them trying to revive some poor
woman on a bloody freezing canal bank in England wasn't
quite the same as seeing it done in a New York ITU from
the comfort of your armchair.

'OK, thanks, everyone, as you were,' called Ken. 'First
off, get your coats back on, for God's sake.'

'There was a pulse.' Paul's mouth was determined as
he came over to Ken.

'If you say in your report that there was a pulse,
Paul, you land Cudworth in the cart, you know that,
don't you?'

'Ken ...' said Paul reproachfully.

'I'm just asking you to think very carefully before sub-
mitting your report, that's all, if it's going to be critical
of the team.'

'It isn't like that, Ken,' Paul protested. 'Come on.'

What had Ken himself said, only that summer, over the
business with Lesley Burford, about not doing anyone any
favours any more? By asking Paul to falsify what he'd
found on examining the body, Ken was asking him to

compromise his professional judgement and training. And in a way it was no criticism of Cudworth. A pulse was notoriously difficult to find if the subject was very cold.

Ken turned and surveyed the canal bank which, what with four pairs of feet all over it, and dragging the body out, was a quagmire.

'Look, I'm going to need all the forensic help we can get with this mess,' he said, jerking his head towards the taped-off area. 'Can you drop in on the lab from time to time, keep a check on it?'

'I'll do whatever I can. You know I will, Ken.'

Paul was grateful that Ken hadn't pushed the question of his report any further. He knew that what Ken was saying was shorthand for the fact that, since there was an element of doubt about whether the woman had been dead or alive, he wanted – no, needed – a result on this case, so that Paul's report, and Cudworth's, could be sub-sumed in the weight of other evidence.

Nigel Spenser approached.

'Your coats, gents,' he said.

Ken took his long overcoat gingerly. It was caked with mud all down the back where the paramedics had thrown it aside. Paul reached for his Barbour, which was rather more resilient, and pulled it on gratefully. It wasn't getting any warmer.

'I'll be in touch,' he said to Ken, and left him there, looking at the best part of £200-worth of wool and cash-mere, ruined.

Paul drove quickly – not dangerously fast, but faster than he should have done – back to the practice, where he caught the end of morning surgery and a look of gratitude from Julia, who was, after all, the one who had to field the patients who were kept waiting. It was about time he bought her another box of chocolates, or bottle of sherry, which he did from time to time as a token 'thank you'.

The practice meeting was fairly routine and by twelve he was on his way to the forensics lab. The forensic support officers hadn't had much time, but with all the gismos they had these days, they could get a long way pretty quickly. He had decided that there was only one way he could phrase his report which would both be fair to the fact and which might let Cudworth off the hook. It would have to be: 'I thought I detected a heart beat.' Even then, Cudworth could still get it in the neck from Ken's superiors, or what Ken termed 'the suits'.

The scientific support officer on the case was new to Paul. She was young, Scottish, and very, very keen. Her name was Terri Morgan.

As Paul had expected, she said that she hadn't had a lot of time, but he was impressed by the facts she could marshal for him.

She told him that the woman had had a lot to drink, and had recently had intercourse, but that there were no indications that it had been rape. The PM had not revealed any definite cause of death, though hypothermia was indicated. The slap to the cheek and the head wound had certainly not caused her death and she had bitten her tongue. Terri pointed to the blown-up photographs from the post-mortem.

'She was a well-groomed woman,' she observed in her sing-song Scottish accent. 'Manicured hands, quality make-up.' She stared up at Paul, who must have been nearly a foot taller than she was, her head on one side. She reminded Paul of a little bantam hen which Celia had kept for a while. Her dark curly hair was screwed up on top of her head in the same slightly chaotic way as a hen's ruffled feathers. 'Who was she?'

'Well, you're not going to tell me that, are you?' grinned Paul.

Even forensics had its limitations.

'No, but you'll like this,' Terri went on, 'or the DI will.

Skin and blood under the nails of the right hand. She'd attacked someone recently. Bruising to the upper arms and shoulders; somebody holding her off, or perhaps she was defending herself. We also recovered body hair – not hers, so whoever she scratched wasn't dressed. And her blood's interesting.'

She showed him a printout from a machine which could analyse blood for everything going: percentage of alcohol, blood type, drugs . . .

'She was taking sodium valproate.'

'An epileptic!' said Paul. 'A grand mal attack . . . that would be consistent with the bitten tongue.'

'There's only a small amount in her blood,' said Terri. 'Not a therapeutic level.'

'Yes,' said Paul. 'But if she hadn't taken her regular dose and had an attack . . .'

Terri shrugged. Conjecture wasn't her business. Just facts.

'Oh, and it was a man's anorak. It would have gone round her twice.'

Paul found Ken in the ops room, in his element. As he punched numbers into the phone, he was issuing orders to check any vehicle which had been seen parked along the lane by the canal, get the dead woman's photo faxed to Intelligence liaison and comb through Missing Persons. Paul had just managed to relay the salient points of his chat with Terri Morgan when Cudworth appeared.

'If that's your report, put it on my desk,' said Ken shortly.

'No, sir,' faltered Cudworth. 'I was called to a car abandoned in a pub car park. Someone had nicked the stereo and the alarm was going off. The pub was the Bracewell Arms. It's on the canal, sir.'

Ken was attending now.

'I've checked it with the owner, sir, a Mr Callard. He's

a surgeon at Warwick County. It's his wife's car. He says she left it at New Street station car park, going to Dumfries to visit her sick mother. That's in Scotland, sir.'

Paul stifled a grin, but Ken said kindly, leading her over to a map on the wall, 'Show me. And I don't mean Dumfries.'

Georgie showed him where the car had been found. Ken wheeled round.

'Nicky . . .' he called. 'Get scientific support to pick up this car and check it over, right?'

Nicky nodded.

'Well done, Cudworth,' said Ken.

Joanna covered her glass with her hand as Al raised the bottle questioningly. It was nearly eight-thirty and there was no sign of Paul. Al, used to his timekeeping, had made supper for herself and Joanna, and stuck Paul's in the oven, saying there was no point in waiting. Joanna emphasized that Paul had asked her round specially but though Al didn't say anything, she knew that if he was caught up on a police job, that wouldn't make the slightest bit of difference. If Joanna was thinking of sticking around – and she had 'just dropped in' once or twice lately – she'd better learn fast where she would come in the pecking order. Al poured herself another glass anyway.

'Getting some practice in?' laughed Joanna. 'For when you're a student?'

'I'm going to university to study, not for a piss-up,' said Al, half indignant.

'Well, you'll be a rarity then,' smiled Joanna. 'Most of my student days were spent in a complete blur.'

They both laughed. She was OK, Joanna.

'You looking forward to going?'

'Yeah. Yeah. I'm just worried how Dad and Marty are going to cope.'

'They'll manage,' Joanna reassured her. 'If they can't, tough luck. They're not your responsibility.'

Al took a sip of her wine.

'I know I'm stupid, worrying about Dad, but I just can't help it. I just wish he'd talk. I mean, actually sit down and talk. It's not as if we can't cope with it.'

'Your Mum, you mean?' probed Joanna.

Al seemed not to have heard.

'I mean, we are coping . . . daily routine and all that,' she carried on. 'But you don't have to be so strong all the time. You can own up to your feelings, can't you?'

Joanna nodded her agreement but she couldn't help feeling slightly hypocritical. It had taken her ages to own up to herself about her feelings for Paul and now that she had, she had to face the fact that what Al was saying was not exactly encouraging. She knew that Paul was still very wrapped up in Celia's death. Al was right. He would have to work through those feelings first before he could feel anything for anyone else. The front door banged across her thoughts.

'Aha,' said Al, getting to her feet. 'The wanderer returns.'

As Al and Joanna moved through to the hall, Paul hung up his Barbour. The worst of the mud had brushed off against the car seat, but there was a strange damp smell emanating from his jacket which was an unpleasant reminder of how the day had begun. He turned to find Al and Joanna, arms folded, staring at him, smiling.

'You're just in time to say goodbye to Joanna,' Al informed him.

Paul groaned.

'I'm really sorry, Joanna. Can you stay a bit longer?'

'No, I can't,' said Joanna firmly. 'I want an early night, Paul. See you, Al. Good luck!'

She kissed Al goodbye and gave Paul a cheeky little wave. Then she left them: Al to finish her packing, Paul to pick at the somewhat congealed remains of supper. As he was putting the casserole dish in to soak, Al came down to the kitchen to make herself a coffee.

'You ought to talk to Marty some time,' she said casually.

From the insistent bass rhythm pounding upstairs, Paul gathered that Marty was in his room, occupied in what he called 'doing his homework', in other words, gazing idly at the walls. Al spooned coffee into two mugs.

'He's confused. He doesn't know what to do.'

'Thought that was a normal condition at his age?' asked Paul flippantly.

But he knew he was doing it again. Before Marty had come back from Aberdovey, it was Joanna who had urged him to find time for his son. Now here was Al doing the same. What was it that came between him and Marty? Celia had always had a magic way with him, coaxing him out of his sulks, getting him to confide in her. Whenever Paul tried, it always ended in a row.

'Think about it, Dad,' said Al. 'Night, night.'

'Night, night.'

Her last night at home. She'd be home for the holidays, of course, but it wouldn't be the same. Well, he wouldn't be able to say he didn't have the opportunity to talk to Marty once it was just the two of them.

Scientific support had had a field-day with the car from the pub car park, as Terri explained to Ken and Nicky in Ken's office early the next morning.

'The prints are on the steering wheel, the bonnet, the boot lid, the gear stick and the handbrake,' she told Ken. 'Your body has been in that car. And . . .' She produced another set of enlarged prints. 'This set was on the boot, and part of the set on the passenger door handle. It's funny, though . . . only three fingers, see?'

Ken motioned to Nicky who was already in her coat

and clutching the file on the dead woman, into which Cudworth had clipped the report on her chat with the car's owner, in case there was a connection. Georgie had already told Ken that Callard had seemed strangely unconcerned by the discovery of the car, and had shown no anxiety about his wife's whereabouts. The husband's theory was that the car had been stolen from New Street station and dumped at the pub.

'Home or work?' asked Nicky as they walked towards Ken's metallic blue Sierra. Ken looked at his watch. Callard would be at the hospital by now. They started early, those consultants, so that they could see their private patients at home in the afternoons.

'Work,' he replied.

As Ken drove, Nicky read him the background they had established on Callard.

'He's fifty-eight, senior orthopaedic surgeon, educated St Thomas's, Oxford. Married twice. Divorced the first . . . oh, years ago. Current wife thirty-four. According to him she's in Scotland visiting her sick mother. Dumfries.'

'Yeah, I remember. Hmm. Old man,' reflected Ken, pulling out rather riskily at a roundabout. 'Is it the old story? Was somebody tromboning his old lady?'

Nicky winced at the crudity.

'Boss . . .' she protested. But Ken was busy hooting at a cyclist as they turned into the hospital car park.

Paul had lain awake for what seemed like all night rehearsing possible ways to approach Marty, and in the end he used none of them because he had come up with, he thought, a rather subtle plan. He'd decided to let Marty take the day off, tell him he'd heard all he'd said, tell him to get down to the Job Centre and get a job, and when Marty saw the pathetic range of opportunities for unskilled work, he'd be back at school like a shot. That was the theory. Paul knew it was a long shot. His bluff might be called. Marty might pick up something worthwhile, but it was unlikely. Even if he did accept a menial job, Paul doubted that he'd stick it for more than a week. It would be well worth missing a week of school at this stage to get him to carry on with the rest of the academic year.

'Look, Marty,' he began, 'I've been thinking.'

'God, that's a bit drastic,' muttered Marty into his Shreddies.

'I'll have a word with your headmaster, you can take a trip down to the Job Centre, and if they've got one *and* you stick at it, then I'm prepared to listen seriously to anything you've got to say, even if it means leaving school.'

Marty's spoon clattered into his dish.

'Really? I mean, do you really mean that?'

'Is that a deal?'

'Yes. *Yes.*' Marty got up, already pulling off his hated school tie. 'Thank you, Dad. Thank you. That's brilliant. Cheers.'

Paul was pleased with his tactics all through morning surgery and was still smiling to himself when he bounded up the police station steps in response to Ken's call. Ken told him he needed a suspect declared fit for questioning.

'Victor Callard. You might know him, he's a surgeon,' Ken told Paul. 'We got on to him through his wife's car, which had been abandoned at the Bracewell Arms. Had him identify the body from the canal – and yes, it's his wife. Much younger wife. Get him outside and he comes over all funny with an asthma attack.'

'And he's a suspect?' hazarded Paul.

'Well, he told Cudworth his wife was in Scotland seeing her sick mother, didn't he? We rang the mother just now. She's as healthy as we are. So, yeah. Somebody's telling fibs.'

Paul felt almost sorry for Callard. He knew him by

reputation; in fact, he'd been the man who'd operated on Harry Campbell, Joanna's dad, and made a very good job of it, so Joanna had said. He was a typical consultant of the old school, deeply chauvinistic, treated his housemen like dirt, expected the nurses to treat him like God. Perhaps not the easiest of men to live with. Perhaps not the easiest of men to deceive, and get away with it . . .

He opened up to Paul, though, as Paul took his blood pressure, perhaps as one medical man to another.

'Moira was young, attractive,' he mused. 'I was surprised she didn't leave me years ago. Because I was under no illusions. I knew there were other men. She didn't try to hide it. Used to taunt me, as if to say, "You don't own me, I can do as I please". Oh, she'd go away — as I presumed she had this last time — but she'd always return and I'd always take her back. Love? Or an old fool's vanity? I don't know.'

'I can . . . er . . . postpone your interview with Inspector Jackson,' offered Paul, slightly embarrassed by Callard's revelations.

Callard shook his head.

'No, I've got nothing to hide. I was in the operating theatre that night. There's plenty of people who can vouch for that.'

Much as he wanted a result, Ken gloomily had to conclude, having interviewed Callard, that they were really very little further forward. Thanks to Callard's identification of the body, they might know who the dead woman was, but with her husband's alibi holding up (he had been in theatre with six other staff), they still had no clue as to how she died or even if she was killed.

'We're more or less back to square one,' he said to Terri, having called at forensics to see if there was any more news. Paul, mindful of his promise to keep an eye on things, happened to be there too. Terri had indeed been busy, working with infra-red on a scrap of sodden paper which she'd found in the pocket of the anorak the woman had been wearing. It turned out to be an invoice for industrial diesel, presumably for a boat or barge, which seemed to be made out to someone called Martin Frobisher. Ken was so busy jumping to conclusions that Paul could not get a word in until he'd already despatched Nicky to ring Intelligence liaison to see if they knew anyone of that name, convinced that if they found Martin Frobisher they had found the only person who knew the truth about Moira Callard's death.

'Ken . . .' said Paul finally, when Ken paused for breath, 'Martin Frobisher is the name of a sixteenth-century British Admiral.'

'It's the name of the boat, Ken,' put in Terri gently.

Ken was silent for a moment, nursing his embarrassment.

'I know people who pay for this kind of humiliation,' he said at last.

Then he yelled for Nicky, who reappeared looking quizzical.

'Forget ILO, we're going for a drive. Down to the canal.'

It didn't take them long to find the *Martin Frobisher* – far less time than if they had been looking for a living, breathing person. At the canal basin the bargekeeper showed them the boat, but that was about all the help he could give them. He said that the *Martin Frobisher* had been hired by someone on his own, calling himself Smith ('What else?' muttered Ken) who was apparently middle-aged, middle height, middling build, browny sort of hair . . . Ken looked at Nicky. This guy really was Mr Observant. It got better, though.

'If he was away for a few days' passion he'll have picked up his lady friend at the Bracewell Arms,' the bargekeeper told them. 'They all do. Anyway, he paid his deposit. I showed him the ropes and off he went. He come back early. The narrow boat was in its mooring when I came down yesterday first thing.'

'Nicky,' ordered Ken. 'Get Terri Morgan from forensics.'

Nicky began dialling on her mobile. Ken turned to the bargekeeper.

'Nobody goes on that boat unless I say so, OK? Nobody.'

The local paper had got hold of it pretty quickly, Paul reflected, as he sat by Harry Campbell's bed that afternoon looking at the X-rays of Harry's leg as the old man read the lunchtime edition. The headline was 'SURGEON'S WIFE CANAL DEATH'.

'Mr Callard's my surgeon, you know.' Harry lowered the paper. 'Here's his wife dead of a fit . . . It's shocking.'

Paul nodded, putting the plates to one side.

'Well, your leg's certainly on the mend. You'll be out of here soon.'

'Yes, and I'll be glad to be back in my own home, I can tell you,' grumbled Harry. 'I'm bored witless in here.'

'Yes . . .' said Paul, as if considering. 'I've said I'll give Joanna a hand with the arrangements. You'll need looking after, won't you?'

'I don't need looking after,' said Harry stubbornly. 'I shan't be a burden on anyone. I value my independence.'

'Sure,' replied Paul. 'She's just worried you're going to end up marooned in your flat, dependent on everybody. Anything but independent.'

It took time but, over the next twenty minutes or so, Paul managed to wring from the old man a grudging acceptance that he would find it hard to cope on his own, and that somewhere on the ground floor, with a warden on call, was a sensible option, and one that was at least worth a look. Paul breathed a sigh of relief. He knew that Joanna had been getting to the end of her tether.

Something else had been preying on his mind the whole time he had been talking Harry Campbell round. As Paul got up to go, he asked casually: 'By the way, who told you that Mrs Callard had had a fit?'

'Mrs Callard?' Harry struggled to remember. 'Oh, who was it?' He drummed his gnarled old fingers on the bedcover then suddenly pointed. 'Oh, it was him.'

Paul followed his gaze and saw Peter Evans in the corridor outside, talking to a nurse. Then the ward doors swung open and Evans entered. Seeing Paul with Harry, and the X-rays spread on the bed, he came across.

'Good, aren't they?' he said. 'Mr Callard has performed his usual miracles.'

Paul handed the plates to Peter who, still inhibited by his finger-stall, had trouble in getting them back in the envelope.

'Actually . . .' Paul began, 'I wonder if I could take that latest one to show Joanna. Just to put her mind at rest.'

Peter handed it back.

'I don't see why not. Just ask her to bring it back when she next visits.'

It was a long shot, a really long shot. He might be way off target. But Evans would have had the opportunity to meet Moira Callard at medical functions and thus the opportunity to start an affair. He had a finger-stall on his middle finger which could account for the strange three-finger prints on the car. And most of all, he knew that Moira had had a fit. There had been not one word about it in the paper. So how could he know, unless he had been there? Unless he was the mystery man who had hired the *Martin Frobisher* for a relaxing few days with his mistress and had brought it back early . . .

Paul went to Ken first and then they both went to Terri. She kept them waiting only long enough to drink a powdery and over-sweetened hot chocolate from the machine, then she beckoned them back in.

'The three-fingered prints on the car were also on the lock key I recovered from the barge,' she said, slapping down enlarged prints in front of them one after the other. 'Now these are off the X-ray plate you brought in. Your man was on the barge and in the car. That's game, set and match, really.'

Ken picked up Evans at the hospital. He had already sent Paul on to the station, because he wanted him to check Evans over for injuries consistent with the skin and hair found under Moira Callard's fingernails. Sure enough, when Evans took off his shirt in Paul's examination room at the station, he had three parallel scratch marks down his shoulder on to his chest.

'I didn't attack her,' he kept saying.

'The police will be asking you about that,' said Paul, concentrating on what he was doing.

'They think I killed her,' Evans babbled on. 'I wanted to end the affair but I didn't kill her.'

Then it all came out.

'She said she was going to tell my wife. It wasn't so much that ... Elaine's suing me for divorce anyway – irreconcilable differences. It was just a game to Moira but if it had got out that I'd been having an affair with Mr Callard's wife, I wouldn't have a chance of getting custody of my son, Davy.'

'Someone hit her,' said Paul, not liking Evans's tendency to whine. 'And her shoulders were bruised.'

'OK,' said Evans. 'We made love. Then we had a row. She got hysterical, started screaming and scratching ...'

'So you slapped her?'

'To stop her screaming. She was going crazy. Then she went up on deck. I waited a while, tried to calm down. I wanted to reason with her, make her understand how much I have to lose. Then I went up top, and found her lying there.'

'You thought she was dead.'

'There was no pulse. Blood. Of course she was dead.'

'So you dumped her in the water?'

'Well, she was dead,' said Evans. And, realizing, 'Wasn't she?'

'No, I don't think she was,' said Paul. 'Not then.'

It all came back to the discrepancy between what Cudworth's report said and the pulse which Paul believed he had felt. At the end of the afternoon, with Evans still held for questioning, Paul and Ken went over to see Terri again. It was six-thirty but she was still there. An enthusiast and a worker. They'd struck lucky with Terri.

They all stood and brooded over the PM photos of Moira Callard.

'Well,' speculated Paul. 'She could have had a fit and received a head injury in the resulting fall.'

Terri nodded. 'It's possible, yeah.'

'So if she was alive when he dumped her, and then she died, he can be done for murder, right?' asked Paul.

Ken made an impatient noise.

'Evans is adamant that she was already dead when he left her. Now, if I'd agreed with you that she was alive when we found her . . .'

'Then she must have been dumped alive,' realized Paul.

'But my report agreed with Cudworth. It insisted that Moira Callard was dead when found, so she could have been dead when he dumped her.'

'What about my report?' asked Paul, remembering how carefully he'd couched the wording.

'Beyond reasonable doubt'? I don't think so,' snorted Ken. 'A defence lawyer would have a field-day.'

'So what can you do him for?' insisted Paul. Moira Callard may have had her faults, but no one deserved the death she'd had in all its indignity.

Ken laced his hands behind his neck and stretched to relieve the tension.

'Failing to notify a death,' he said bitterly. 'The best part of sweet FA.'

When Paul got home, Joanna's car was on the drive. So was the little Mini he had bought Al for passing her exams. Marty was stowing another huge sack of something in the back.

Al and Joanna came out of the house. Marty gave Al a big bear hug, then disappeared indoors, as fearful as his father of showing any emotion.

'Hey,' Al greeted her father. 'Guess what? Marty's got a job. Well, an interview,' she added hastily. 'On Monday.'

'That's great,' said Paul quickly. 'What for?'

'I'm not sure.' Al was absorbed, checking in her usual careful way that the boot was properly closed. 'Well, this is it, Dad.' She came round the car towards him and stood very close. She was wearing jeans and a skimpy grey top with a navy sweatshirt knotted round her neck. Her hair was loose round her shoulders and she was glowing with excitement, which was presumably what stopped her feeling the cold. Joanna was wearing a pale camel coat and black boots.

'You can't go,' said Paul, only half joking.

'I can, it's only down the road,' grinned Al. They had had this discussion before. Paul had wanted to take her to college and settle her in. She had said no.

'You can't go till you've given me a hug,' said Paul, reaching out for her. He pulled her close to him, smelling her clean hair and smooth skin. She hugged him back. It was a reassuring hug. Through it she told Paul clearly that she'd be all right, that she was up to this. He wished he felt the same and he wished, not for the first time, that he felt more like Al's parent, and less like her child. He hugged her tighter but she laughed and loosed his hands from behind her back.

'Bye, Dad,' she said softly. Then, emphatically: 'And don't worry.'

Then she pulled away and swung into the car, slamming the door.

'Give me a ring when you get there, let me know you've arrived safely,' he called.

Al nodded, humouring him.

'Bye'.

Paul forced a smile as she started the car and skittered off down the gravel drive. Joanna, who had been hanging back in the porch, stepped forward and stood at his elbow. He could smell her perfume, musky and exotic on the cold, clear air, so different from the girlish smell of Al.

'Well, I came to say thanks,' she said. 'I don't know what you said to my dad, but it worked.' And seeing Paul staring down the drive into the darkness, she added softly, 'She'll be fine, Paul. Just fine.'

I wish I could say the same for me, he thought to himself. But he looked down at Joanna and smiled.

'Can you stay for a drink?' he asked. He remembered another evening when he had badly wanted her company but she had refused to stay. They had been having one of their silly rows. They didn't seem to fall out so much these days. So perhaps this time she'd say yes.

'Yes,' she said.

And they both laughed at the abruptness of it, that single syllable, crisp in the October air.

9

Terri Morgan wasn't just an enthusiast about her job in forensics though, for Paul, with the results she was able to achieve, that would have been good enough. As they were poring over photographs one Friday afternoon in the lab, she said something about looking forward to Sunday, and when Paul asked her what it was she'd be doing, she replied enigmatically: 'Flying the hawk.'

'I'm sorry, did you say hawk?'

'That's right,' said Terri casually and turned away to study a photograph of blood splashes.

Though he had lived in the country for the past ten years, Paul had had very little to do with the country way of life. He loved watching the countryside changing through the seasons, enjoying its colours, smells and textures, but he was not involved in it. Thanks to his walks with Boozie, he now knew the difference between wheat and barley, and could distinguish a field of potatoes from a field of kale, but that was about the extent of his knowledge. Similarly, he had never taken up any country pursuits. He'd been clay pigeon shooting once, courtesy of a drug company, and had found the earplugs they'd given him very useful for blocking out the sound of Marty's electric guitar, but beyond that he'd had nothing to do with country sports. Hawking might not be up there with hunting and shooting, but it involved a living creature, you did it in the fresh air – perhaps this would be one way to start.

'D'you think I could tag along?' he asked Terri.

'Sure,' she replied. 'There's lot of raw meat involved, but at least I know you're not squeamish.'

On Sunday, after he'd watched her fly her hawk, who rejoiced in the name of Joey, Terri mentioned that she knew of a bird which was looking for a home.

'Oh, come on, I only came out of interest. I didn't say I was thinking of taking it up as a hobby . . .' Paul began.

'I think you'd enjoy it, Paul,' Terri smiled. 'It's a great release. I get out as much as I can. I spend most of my days in a darkened room, looking down a microscope, remember. It's good to see some sky.'

'Well, yes, I know that feeling,' agreed Paul ruefully. But he could also imagine what Joanna would say. Hadn't he got enough commitments already?

But Terri was very persuasive. Every time she saw him she enthused about hawking and before long Paul found himself enquiring after Joey's progress. There had been something so primitive and powerful about the bird, with its mean beak and talons, its cruel eyes and yet its impossibly elegant soaring flight. Terri smiled at his interest.

'That bird I mentioned's still available,' she said. 'What d'you say, Paul?'

He said yes.

The next thing he knew, Terri was over at Church House, sizing up the outbuildings, and declaring them, once adapted, just perfect for keeping a hawk.

'Congratulations, Paul,' she smiled. 'I think you've just found a way of occupying all the free time you have — and more.'

Marty was incredulous.

'What is this, the male menopause?' he asked cruelly. 'Why not just get a sports car like everyone else's dad?'

But once Paul had decided on something, he was determined. Terri, the hawk and the hawk's handler came over the following week to settle him in.

'And what's its name?' Paul enquired, when the bird

was established on the perch he had acquired, looking around balefully. 'Polly, I suppose.'

'Mr Harris,' Terri informed him. 'Named after a friend of the family. Don't ask.'

Paul knew it would be a while before he could fly Mr Harris, because he had to get the bird to trust him first. But Terri quite often brought Joey over at the weekends and they would fly him, early on a Saturday or Sunday morning, watching him dip and soar in the pale autumn sky, then retreat inside out of the finger-nipping cold for mugs of tea and toast.

Paul was surprised but pleased with his new hobby. Al's departure for university had left a gap, there was no doubt about it. Having Marty around just wasn't the same. At least he seemed less belligerent since he had been permitted to leave school. The 'job interview' had turned out to be for what amounted to dishwashing at the hospital, of all places. Though Marty tried to dress it up for his friends' and grandparents' benefit as a 'Kitchen Hygiene Supervisor', what he really did all day was wash piles of enormous cooking pans and utensils.

Nevertheless, it wasn't such a bad place for him to be. Maybe it was having seen his father learning to cook from scratch, but Marty had himself turned into a very good cook, and was often to be found in the kitchen at home chopping vegetables or grinding spices for stir-fry. So Paul reconciled himself to the situation, reasoning that if, by a miracle, Marty stuck at the job, he was at least in an environment where he might learn something about catering, which was one career option for him. And if he didn't last the course and went back to school, which was what Paul still hoped for and expected, he would have had a useful insight into the hard world of work which would not do him any harm. Mr Smith, the head chef, was ex-army and he ran his kitchen like a parade-ground. It might also make Marty see what an easy life he had at home and how Paul, whom he always castigated for being the 'heavy' father, was in reality anything but.

In general, though, life was much easier with Marty than it had been for some time, and Paul was relieved. Al also seemed to have settled in at university. She'd been back home a couple of times, once for books, once for supper, but Paul got the impression she wanted to make a break, which he understood. If she'd gone further away, to Bristol or to York, say, he wouldn't have seen her for weeks on end, so he didn't complain and made the most of her visits and phone calls. About three weeks into term there began to be a lot of references to someone called Ben: 'Ben says this,' or 'Ben and I did that'.

'This Ben . . . is he your boyfriend?' Paul had asked, tentatively.

'Oh, Dad, you're so old-fashioned!' Al smiled down the phone. 'You'll be wanting to meet him next!'

'Well . . .'

'OK, I'll bring him home some time. Now I've got to go, there's a band playing at the Union tonight and anyway my money's run out. Love you!'

Marty spent a lot of his off-duty hours at the hospital. There were some good sports facilities which Paul had vaguely been aware of, and he was getting involved in a lot of things, including a wheelchair basketball team. Paul didn't enquire too closely. Marty was going to work without complaint, which was an improvement on his attitude towards school, he was healthily occupied in the evenings, he was earning money for CDs and computer games. Life seemed more settled than it had for a long time.

Another thing that pleased Paul was the fact that he had at last become friends with Joanna. After her father, Harry, had agreed to go into sheltered accommodation, it was Paul who'd gone with Joanna to show him round the place she'd found for him, Sheerwater Flats. Harry had put up a token protest about the menu ('Never did like treacle tart. Sticks your teeth together!') and the regular Bingo evening ('I don't think it's compulsory, Dad'), but in the end he had accepted the ground-floor flat which was vacant and, after only a month or so, seemed to be thriving. Joanna had told Paul that Alan Stewart, the warden, said he was the focus of attention for at least half a dozen elderly ladies but he seemed to be paying most attention to a Mrs Doris Attwood, who was in fact one of Paul's patients.

It was Mrs Attwood, who was, in truth, a bit of a hypochondriac, who summoned Paul to Sheerwater Flats one crisp blue morning at the beginning of November. He found Harry tidying up a flowerbed near the main entrance.

'I see they've got you earning your keep,' Paul called in greeting as he got out of the Discovery.

'Got to make myself useful somehow,' Harry replied.

Paul explained that he'd come to see Mrs Attwood.

'Nothing serious, I hope?' Harry asked. 'We're going out to the races tonight.'

'Oh, you're *dating* Mrs Attwood, are you?' asked Paul with a mischievous smile.

'Good heavens, no,' said Harry rather too quickly. 'It's just that Alan's keen on the horses and Mrs Attwood's a member at the race course. It's really for Jo's benefit. I talked her into coming along.'

'Oh, good for you,' said Paul, slightly surprised. Joanna hadn't mentioned it.

'In favour of it, are you?' said Harry quickly. 'Well, you'd better look sharp.'

'How do you mean?' asked Paul, mystified.

'A good-looking girl, my Jo,' stated Harry, not brooking any disagreement. 'And that Alan's a bit of a charmer, you know . . .'

With an obscure sense that he was being tested, Paul

said his goodbyes to Harry and, amused, went to find Alan Stewart in his office. Paul wasn't sure about 'charming' but he had always found him a genial enough chap, probably mid-forties, well turned-out and well educated. In fact, it was a bit of a mystery to Paul what he was doing running a place like Sheerwater Flats. He would have thought that Alan Stewart would have been cut out for something a bit more stimulating than the day-to-day concerns of twenty or so septuagenarians.

Paul gave Doris Attwood a thorough examination. He didn't think he'd find anything seriously wrong, but he had a superstitious belief that the one time he was less than conscientious with a patient like Doris would be the one time that she was not crying wolf. But her heart and lungs were fine: her breathlessness was probably down to the fact that she was carrying too much weight.

'Tell her to lay off the steamed puddings,' he said to Alan Stewart as they walked across the courtyard. 'Oh – and have a good evening. Harry told me about your little jaunt.'

'Thanks.'

Alan Stewart raised his hand in farewell as Paul reversed and drove off. Watching him in the rear-view mirror, Paul saw him turn and go back inside. He drove thoughtfully back towards Warwick.

Earlier that morning, Paul had had a call from Ken asking him to get over to the hospital when he had a moment. When he arrived he found a small boy of about nine, Richie Collins, whose back was a mess of weals and grazes. Ken's suspicion was that they were 'non-accidental' injuries. Nicky Green was there with the boy and after Paul had done his examination, which confirmed Ken's conclusion, she filled him in on the boy's background. As she told him about the family, Paul realized that they were patients at Wickton Road, though not patients of his, and would have been referred to the hospital from there in the first place.

'Says he fell off his bike,' said Nicky disbelievingly. 'He's obviously terrified.'

'Well, they'll keep him in, anyway,' said Paul, trying to be reassuring. Even Nicky, who had seen far worse injuries on adults, seemed moved by the little boy. 'He's out of harm's way here.'

Nicky nodded, thanked Paul for coming, and went back to Richie's room, muttering something that sounded like 'animals'.

Paul was just unlocking the car, and fantasizing about getting a lunch hour for once, when Joanna's car pulled up next to his.

'Hi,' he said as she got out.

She was wearing a trouser suit in a dull blue with a big silver brooch on the lapel.

'Are you here about the Collins boy?' she asked, putting her car keys in her handbag.

'Yeah. You dealing with that?' asked Paul.

'I referred him,' she replied. 'The mother, Beth, brought him to see me first thing. He'd been sick before school. That was all she came about. When I got his shirt off to examine his stomach, I saw all these weals on his back.' She looked straight at Paul. It seemed she was seeking his approval. 'I had to call in Social Services,' she went on. 'They called the police. Beth was pretty upset, you can imagine. She says she has no idea how he got them.' She shook her head, as if shaking off the memory of what had obviously been a pretty heated disagreement. 'So, what's happening?'

'Well, non-accidental injuries, I'm afraid,' Paul confirmed.

'Yeah, that's what I thought . . .' Joanna's voice tailed off. 'The parents,' she whispered to Paul and he followed her gaze in the direction of the hospital entrance where a couple were coming down the steps. Beth Collins was slight and fair and only in her mid-twenties. You could see the resemblance to Richie: she looked like his big sister. Mr Collins was older, early thirties perhaps, with greasy dark curls and a day or so's growth of beard. Both were wearing jeans and leather jackets.

'Is this the one?' he said aggressively to Beth, indicating Joanna. 'What's going on, eh? Why won't they let us see our boy?'

Paul stepped in quickly, glad for Joanna's sake that he was there.

'They're just doing some tests at the moment.'

'And who are you?' spat Collins.

'Dr Dangerfield.'

'Another doctor?' sneered Collins. 'That's all we need.'

Beth nudged her husband. 'Shut it,' she hissed. Then to Paul: 'Can't you help, Doctor?'

Paul explained that the tests were to establish if Richie had any internal injuries and that she would be able to see her son as soon as they were completed.

'And me?' demanded Collins. 'They reckon I might not be able to see him because I'm not his real dad, just his step-dad. Who brought him up, eh? I did – and I'm taking him out of here!'

'Please, Mr Collins, you have to understand . . .' Joanna intervened.

'Oh, yeah?'

'. . . that if you try and discharge Richie then they are going to obtain an emergency protection order to stop you.'

Collins thrust his head forward.

'Are you threatening me?' He spat at the ground. 'People like you, oh, you always know what's best for the likes of us, don't you?'

Beth tugged at his arm.

'Come on, Gerry . . .'

Gerry Collins shrugged her off and pointed at Joanna, his finger with its ragged nail just an inch from her face.

'Don't think you can treat me like dirt and get away with it.'

Paul stepped protectively towards Joanna but Collins turned abruptly and marched off, Beth trailing behind him.

'You OK?' he asked.

Joanna, who had been staring straight ahead, shocked by what Collins had said, turned to look at Paul.

'Mm. Threats already and it's not even lunchtime.' She was trying to make light of it but her voice sounded shaky. 'Just my day, isn't it?'

Back at Wickton Road, Joanna tried to forget about Gerry Collins and his unpleasantness, but Paul must have mentioned it to Shaaban. During afternoon surgery Shaaban took her on one side in a gap between patients and asked if there was anything he could do. Joanna shook her head.

'I just hope I'm not being too hasty . . .' she mused. 'As Beth herself said, would she have brought him here if she'd known anything about it?'

'Maybe, maybe not,' soothed Shaaban. 'Sometimes it's all part of the covering up. Maybe Beth Collins genuinely didn't know what was going on.'

'So you think it was the boy's step-father?'

Shaaban shrugged minutely.

'I don't know, Joanna, and neither do you. Our job is to diagnose the injuries and take the appropriate action, and that's what you did. As far as I'm concerned, you did absolutely the right thing in calling in Social Services.'

'Thanks, Shaaban,' said Joanna warmly, putting her hand on his arm. 'I wish Mr Collins could see it like that.'

Shaaban smiled.

'Try to forget about it. It's your night at the races, isn't it?'

'God, yes, I've got to go straight to pick my father up when I've finished here. I'd better get on. Mrs Ellis, please,' she called.

'Enjoy yourself,' Shaaban said.

She didn't think she would. Frankly, standing about on the rails on a freezing evening hardly sounded like fun, but she felt her dad ought to be encouraged to get out and about and make new friends at Sheerwater Flats and if this was one way of doing it, then it was a small price to pay. In fact, it turned out to be rather fun. There was a covered grandstand, for a start, which cheered her, and a bar where she could have a warming whisky mac before the first race. She was lucky with her bets, too. Alan Stewart seemed to know quite a bit about horseflesh and he translated the programme for her and she understood for the first time exactly what 'form' meant.

Harry and Doris pottered off somewhere together and she took the opportunity laughingly to accuse Alan of matchmaking.

'It never works, you know,' she scolded.

'You should tell that to your dad,' he replied. 'He's hoping you'll marry again – preferably Dr Dangerfield.'

Joanna managed a social sort of laugh, but inside she was mortified. She would have to have stern words with her father. Just because Paul had managed – where she had failed – to talk her father into moving into sheltered accommodation, he was suddenly husband material. Not for the first time she cursed Paul's charm. Even her dad had fallen for it. If Harry Campbell had known how Joanna had struggled to contain her feelings for Paul, and how tight a rein she had to keep on them in order to enjoy the friendship she now seemed to have achieved with him, he would not have spoken so lightly about the two of them getting married. And to Alan Stewart, of all people! That meant Harry had probably confided in Doris as well. She'd tell all the other old biddies and before Joanna knew it, every time she came to visit she'd be surrounded by a knot of semi-senile well-wishers asking to see the ring.

'Yeah, well, that's Dad's fevered imagination, I'm afraid,' she said dismissively to Alan in reply. And, desperate to swivel the spotlight away from herself, asked: 'What about you? Have you ever married?'

'Came close once. I don't think I'm cut out for it,' he said with a shrug, then, to her dismay returned to the subject of Joanna and Paul. 'I mean, you can understand Harry pairing you off with a doctor. A fellow professional, got the charm, got the looks, tireless servant in the common cause of humanity, sort of person people look up to . . .'

'Excuse me,' smiled Joanna. 'Are you being sarcastic?'

'Of course not,' said Alan. 'It's true, isn't it?'

'I think he'd be rather embarrassed to hear himself described like that.'

Alan grinned.

'Of course he would; he's modest too!'

'My dad's having a very bad influence on you, Alan,' laughed Joanna, but she was relieved when Harry and Doris came back, full of a tip they had been given for the next race but one.

They left at about ten. Alan insisted on taking Doris and Harry back in his car, saying that the drive to Sheerwater Flats would take Joanna out of her way, which was true.

'And you've got to be fresh for the morning. I daresay you'll be in surgery bright and early,' he added.

Jo smiled.

'No, I've got the morning off, actually. Thought I might go shopping, treat myself.'

'I'm sure you deserve it,' replied Alan.

'She does, she works too hard,' said Harry.

Joanna finally managed to extricate herself and drove

home, which was a renovated artisan's cottage on the outskirts of Warwick. It was small, just two up and two down, but it was all she needed and she had painted it white inside to make it look bigger and filled it with the bits and pieces she picked up on Sundays, browsing at antique fairs. It had felt strange, living on her own at first, after Charles's death, but she was used to her own space now. Why had she suddenly started thinking about Charles? she wondered as she parked the car. It was odd. She thought she had buried the pain, but it still bobbed up like a cork, from time to time, as if to make sure that she wasn't enjoying life too much.

She had thought she would never get over it. Coming home and finding him there, in the garage, hanging . . . She had had no idea why he had done it. She still had no idea. At first she had thought it was her fault. That he must have been unhappy with her. Everyone told her that was nonsense, he had been so proud of her, enjoyed showing her off, his attractive young wife. So why? There had been no problems at work. It wasn't as if one of his patients was suing him for negligence, he wasn't about to be made redundant, or to move hospital in a 'rationalization'; in fact, he was one of the most respected ENT surgeons in the area – the top man, many said. When the will came to be sorted out, she had dreaded money worries, a mistress, a child, or even, in her worst fantasies, another wife. But there was nothing. No note, no clue as to why, at the age of fifty-five and at the top of his profession, with a new young wife who adored him, he should take a length of blue plastic washing line and string it from the beam in the garage, clamber up on a ladder and place a noose round his neck – and jump.

She hadn't told anyone about it when she first moved to Warwick, just said that her husband had died and she wanted a fresh start. She had told Paul, finally, only recently, soon after her father had moved into Sheerwater

Flats. Harry had engineered the two of them into going out to dinner together and it had just come out, somehow, after her third glass of wine. Paul, in fact, had been the last person she wanted to tell in case he thought she was using it in some way, to find common ground with him, as if to say, 'We've both lost a spouse in tragic circumstances – let's pool our misery, we must be made for each other!'

Joanna let herself in and went through to her tiny kitchen, which was a quarter of the size of Paul's. She filled the kettle. A nice hot drink and straight to bed, she thought. No more memories.

She had just made herself a cup of tea when she heard it: the sound of running water. She cocked her head on one side but it wasn't coming from the bathroom upstairs and it wasn't coming from the sink, where she'd turned the tap off firmly because it had a tendency to drip. Then she realized it was coming from outside. There was a tap under the kitchen window, fed from the same pipe, where she attached the hose in summer to water the garden. She unlocked the back door and peered out. Water was gushing from the tap. She racked her brains for any reason why it should have happened. Something burst? Something to do with a valve? She stepped outside and turned it off, trying not to get too wet in the process, and, in the silence which followed, her relief at finding the source of the noise turned to disquiet. How had it happened? Taps didn't turn themselves on. She straightened and looked around the blank, black garden. She couldn't even detect the shape of the lawn or the outlines of the trees, let alone if there was anyone out there. With a shiver which had nothing to do with the cold, she scurried back inside and locked the door. Thank God she'd got tomorrow morning off. She'd have a good look round in the daylight. There must be some explanation.

*

Next day, on his way to a house call at a farm about ten miles away, Paul noticed the fair on Midsummer Common. Gerry Collins was something to do with the fair, wasn't he? He knew that the Collinses were travellers. They weren't fair folk because they didn't move on as frequently as the fair, but he had a feeling Gerry took on casual mechanical or maintenance work with the rides. He took a left turn down the next lane and soon found the field where all the caravans were camped. He asked a small girl about Richie's age, who should have been at school, if she knew them, and she pointed him in the direction of a caravan standing by itself in a far corner of the field. Even the Discovery's wheels slipped in the mud at the gateway, but Paul persevered and once he got on to the grass, which had been flattened into a rough track, the going was better.

As he pulled up, he was aware that Beth was standing in the doorway, wiping her hands on a tea-towel.

'I was passing,' said Paul, unconvincingly. 'I thought I'd pop in.' As Beth didn't reply, he carried on. 'Look, Beth, I wanted to explain . . .'

'What is there to explain?' asked Beth bitterly. 'They've got my kid, thanks to that friend of yours.'

'You can't blame Joanna, Beth,' said Paul quickly. 'It's my responsibility.'

As police surgeon, he was the one who had determined for certain that Richie's injuries were non-accidental.

'You think it was Gerry, don't you?' she demanded.

'The police will want to question him,' Paul admitted. Out of the corner of his eye he saw a battered red pick-up approach and park under a shrivelled oak tree.

'If I thought Gerry had done it,' Beth was saying, 'he'd be the one needing a doctor. It's true he's got a temper, specially when he's had a drink. But he loves Rich like the kid was his own.'

Paul heard Gerry before he saw him – or rather, he

heard the dogs which, released from the cab of the pick-up, rushed over to Paul, barking furiously.

'What's he doing here?' demanded Collins, not attempting to call off the dogs which were growling at Paul. 'We don't need your help, not you or that blonde bitch. We sort things out own way, all right?'

It was not the sort of question that invited a negative answer, not if you wanted to keep all your teeth. Paul beat a retreat and drove off, hoping he hadn't actually made things worse for Joanna.

Later that day, Ken came to see him at the surgery.

'Collins has got previous,' he informed him, playing with a paperweight. 'Two counts of ABH and three of drunk and disorderly.'

'But the boy isn't even on the At Risk register,' protested Paul.

'Doesn't mean he hasn't been thumped,' replied Ken.

'I can't believe Beth would allow it to happen.' Paul considered what he'd seen of her maternal instincts and judged them sound. 'And anyway, why would she bring him to surgery?'

'Maybe she didn't know about it, or perhaps she was being clever.' Ken had an answer for everything. 'You bring the kid in here, look surprised when the shirt comes off. It's usually one or both of the parents.'

Paul nodded, sickened, knowing that what Ken said was true. Terri, who'd seen the pictures of Richie's back, believed the injuries had been caused by a chain. That was a pretty vicious weapon to use on anyone, let alone a child.

'Anyway,' Ken went on. 'Me and Nicky paid Collins a visit and guess what, he's got these two bloody great Alsatians. Which of course have chains. Terri's looking at them. That should tell us something one way or the other.'

*

Joanna had had a lovely morning – spending money always cheered her up – but she was, in a way, glad to get in to work in the afternoon and have something else to think about, because when she had got back to her car in the multi-storey, two of her tyres had been let down. Not gone down, punctured, but let down, with a matchstick in the valve. She had called the attendant, called the recovery service, and got it sorted out, but it was unsettling, especially after that silly incident with the tap last night. The car park attendant said that there were gangs of kids roaming the town's car parks all the time up to no good and she allowed herself to believe him. She didn't want to become paranoid. She was on call that evening and if she got in a state about going anywhere, or about staying in the house alone for that matter, she was going to be no good to anyone.

She was unlucky in that her first call was to the Bluebell estate. It was the worst part of town which they covered from Wickton Road. Never had a housing estate been more hopefully yet wrongly named. There was scarcely a blade of grass to be seen there, still less a bluebell, even in spring, and on a November night it looked more like the set for a depressing investigation into the evils of the welfare state than the woodland idyll the name tried to evoke. Joanna parked under a streetlight which pierced the murk, craning her head up at the twenty-seven floors of Primrose Tower above her. Luckily, she had been called to Crocus Flats which were a three-storey low-rise. She put on the car alarm and the steering lock and picked her way across the cracked slabs to the badly lit stairwell. Number 5 was no better or worse than any of the others: a regulation maroon-painted door with a bit of torn net curtain across the frosted glass. She rang the bell. The door was opened by a skinny man in his fifties who brought with him a reek of tobacco. When she said she had come to see his wife and explained who she was he asked none too pleasantly: 'Is this some kind of wind-up?'

'No . . .' said Joanna, bemused. 'I'm . . .'

'I don't have a wife,' he said, and closed the door.

Joanna checked her notebook for the address. This was certainly the place. Uneasy, she looked around, peering into every shadow as she walked back to the smelly concrete stairs. Relieved when she was in her car, she locked herself in and drove off as fast as she dared.

Back at home, everything seemed fine. She had left the radio on to suggest that someone was in, as the police told you to do, but when she got in she snapped it off, and stood and listened. The little grandmother clock which had been in her father's family for years ticked and whirred. It was only ten but she thought she'd feel safest tucked up in bed, with the burglar alarm on, so she set it and went upstairs with a magazine. She looked in every room, though, before going into her own bedroom, feeling angry with herself for being so silly. Honestly, she was turning into a nervous wreck. Crossly, she realized she hadn't made herself a hot water bottle, and was just debating whether she could manage without one when she heard a noise downstairs. She froze, her hands still behind her neck where she had been undoing her zip. Then she crept gingerly along the landing and looked down into the hall. Someone had pushed something through the door. It looked like a video tape.

Paul was in the kitchen when the doorbell rang.

'Who's that at this time of night?' he asked Marty, who shrugged.

When he opened it, it was Joanna, of all people.

'Paul . . . I'm sorry . . .' she began. 'I know it's very late . . .'

She looked dreadful. Half frozen and somehow distracted.

'Come in,' he said, standing back to let her pass.

She allowed him to take her coat, swapping a package from one hand to the other to get her arms out of the sleeves. It looked like a video tape.

It *was* a video tape. It was an amateur tape, filmed in black and white, which somehow made it more sinister, because you saw so little in black and white these days. And it was all of Joanna.

It showed her going into her cottage, leaving her cottage. It even showed her inside her cottage, talking on the phone, making a cup of coffee, drawing the curtains in her bedroom last thing at night. It also showed her looking mystified in the garden beside the running tap, peering at her car tyres in the car park and knocking on the door of 5, Crocus Flats. Joanna stared fixedly ahead while it played, her mouth compressed, her hand at her neck.

'And you never noticed anything?' asked Paul. One possibility had sprung into his mind straight away. 'When did it start? Was it before or after you referred the Collins boy?'

'After, I think.' Joanna tried to remember. She felt so shaken she couldn't think straight.

'You came straight here tonight? You didn't call the police?'

'No ... I ... just needed to be with someone. I just want to feel safe.'

Paul took her up to Al's room which, though denuded of most of its decoration, was still recognizably a teenager's bedroom. There was even a teddy bear on the bed. Joanna smiled as she remembered her own much loved 'Huggy', a ghastly yellow cloth dog which she had loved until it literally fell to pieces. Feeling a little better, and relieved to be in someone else's house, where her safety was someone else's responsibility, she crossed to the window and drew the curtains. She might not have felt so safe if she had known that in the garden, from various vantage points, the camera had been trained on the house since she arrived and was recording her even now.

Next day, Paul took her to see Ken. Paul was convinced that it was all the work of Collins, getting his own back for what he saw as his unfair treatment over Richie's injuries, but he had to admit he had no proof. Marty had already given him an ear-bending, saying he was picking on Collins because he was a traveller, and even Joanna said that there was no proof against him.

'Look, maybe it's a complete stranger and he's picked my name out of the telephone book?' she suggested.

Nicky Green shook her head.

'No, they're usually known to their victims.'

'Are you going to bring Collins in?' Paul asked Ken impatiently.

Ken rubbed his face thoughtfully.

'He's not the sort to fall apart under questioning, but whoever it is, he's taking some risks, getting a bit close. Tell you what.' He turned to Joanna. 'Have you got anything planned for tonight?'

Ken outlined a plan which, Joanna said, sounded like something from a film. He wanted her to come home at the usual time, and let herself into the house. Then she was to leave by the back door, letting in Cudworth, who would already be in place under cover of darkness in the back garden. Cudworth, with a radio link, would sit in the house as a decoy in case the stalker – whoever it was – tried to get closer still. Meanwhile, Joanna was to make her way through the garden gate to where Paul would be waiting to drive her to his place.

Joanna agreed, but inside she felt numb. Everything was out of control. What had started as a couple of odd incidents which, though unsettling, she could dismiss, had turned into something she felt she couldn't handle. She was Joanna Stevens, for heaven's sake, a forty-one-year-old GP in a county town, not Sharon Stone in a newly-released thriller. She couldn't believe that she was going to be the centre of a police surveillance operation. It was – and she regretted ever having used the term flippantly before, about a bad train journey or a visit to the hair-dresser – a nightmare.

Paul was very attentive. He drove her back to Wickton Road and even while she was seeing patients, kept popping his head round the door or bringing her cups of coffee. At lunchtime he wouldn't let her be on her own. He said he didn't want her to brood. It was a nice day for November: cold, but with a wan sun in a bare blue sky. He took her for lunch at the pub – not that she could eat anything – and then, as they still had time, they wandered across the bridge and down to the river. He was trying to help, but in a way, by stopping her working, by giving her time to think, he made it worse. Joanna couldn't get it out of her head. Paul felt that the police could have done more, but Joanna knew his indignation was futile.

'He has to attack me.' She was having to concentrate really hard to stop her voice from trembling, and it was giving her a headache. 'I've had women patients who've been through this with men stalking them. The police don't do a thing until he makes a move.'

'At least we've got this surveillance thing tonight.' Paul didn't sound convinced.

Joanna didn't know what Paul had expected Ken to do: give her a twenty-four-hour armed guard? She'd been thinking a lot about all the other cases she'd heard about in her professional capacity, sitting on the other side of the desk, secure and safe, with her window-locked cottage to go home to and a new, reliable car to take her there. She had listened as these pathetic women asked for 'something for their nerves' because their ex-husband or ex-boyfriend or ex-something had come up to them in the pub and called them a slag, and told them that he'd get them, and the children, if there were any, because they were rubbish, and good for nothing and deserved to be treated like dirt. And the scary thing was, some of the women had believed it.

She stopped walking and turned to Paul.

'Those women who came to me, you know, I could never really picture myself in their position. Not because I was unsympathetic but because, somehow, I had the idea that if it ever happened to me, then I'd know what to do about it, because I'm capable. Now suddenly I feel just as vulnerable, powerless.' Her voice started to crack and Paul guided her to a bench. She sank down, feeling its wooden slats strike damp through her skirt, taking no notice. He sat down close beside her. 'I mean, I'm single, I live alone. Why should it happen to others and not to me?'

'Have you ever thought about living with someone?' Paul asked. His tone was one of pure curiosity.

'You mean get married again?'

'Well, not necessarily. I mean just sharing your life with somebody.'

'No. I've got used to the idea of living alone now.' She paused, thinking, wondering whether to say it to him, then went on anyway. 'You know, when I was in Al's room last night, it reminded me of my old room at my parents' house. How I could always go back there when I was a student, when the world got too heavy. And then you grow older, you get used to the idea of being a grown-up with grown-up responsibilities . . . but somehow there's . . . there's always a part of you that yearns for that childhood room, where you felt snug and protected, and loved.'

Her voice had been getting higher and thinner as she was talking, and now she looked down and saw tears tumbling on to her lap. Paul put his arm round her and pulled her against him. He felt warm and strong and just so . . . solid.

It was a good job that Joanna didn't know just how much work the police had been doing on her behalf because she would not have been reassured by their findings. After she and Paul had left, Ken had done two things: he sent the video to Terri to see if she could come up with something, and instructed Nicky to send a copy to the Intelligence Liaison officer, to coordinate reports of any other similar incidents in the area or beyond and to get profiles on any known suspects of this type of thing or any unsolved related crimes. By the late afternoon, things were coming together. The video hadn't revealed much: all Terri could tell from the camera position was that the operator was about five feet ten, and definitely male, because he cleared his throat at one point. But the ILO came good on the known suspects. Five of the six possibilities he suggested were already banged up, leaving just one mystery man.

At seven, Ken and Nicky briefed the team who were going to be in on the surveillance operation on Joanna's cottage.

'All we've got,' said Nicky, consulting one of a sheaf of faxes, 'is an offender profile based on two murders for which they think the same person may be responsible, one in Worcestershire, one in Cornwall.'

'Women victims?' asked Georgie Cudworth.

'Yeah, but the psychologist doesn't think the motive's primarily sexual. Power is what this guy's into. He thinks he's something special. He's got a secret. It gives him an edge.'

'He's a psychotic,' put in Ken, helpfully.

Nicky shot him a look.

'He's not going to kill someone every day,' Nicky

explained. 'He wants the murders to be special. Perhaps it marks some particular point in his life.'

'Now Mr Collins,' Ken reminded them, 'is a traveller.'

There was a murmur among the assembled constables. If Collins could beat up his step-son . . . Nicky held up her hand. Terri had told Ken that the dog chains from Collins's caravan were not the ones, in fact, which had been used on the boy. The welts on his back had been caused by a chain with a wider link. Nothing had been proved against Collins, yet.

'Well, whoever it is,' said Nicky, 'he's getting closer to his target, and before he goes too far, we've got to be ready.'

'So how do we know when he'll strike again?' piped up Cudworth.

Ken smiled thinly.

'We don't.'

Joanna thought it was the most scary thing she had ever done. She hung on at work until as late as possible, then drove towards home still feeling that disembodied 'this isn't happening to me' sensation which had been with her since the previous night. The fact that she knew that Ken would be in an unmarked police car outside her cottage when she got there, and that Georgie Cudworth was waiting in the back garden, did nothing to reassure her as she put her key in the lock and, trying frantically to stop her fingers from shaking, switched off the burglar alarm. Only pausing to drop her medical bag in the hall, she moved through to the conservatory, still in the dark, which itself was terrifying, and fumbled open the door. She blundered out into the black garden, startled by Georgie's whispered 'Well done' from the shadows. Clutching herself, as if trying to hold herself together, she stumbled down the lawn to the gate which led into a lane at the back. The catch clattered as her frozen fingers scrabbled at it, terrified that she would be jumped on from behind. Why ever had she agreed to this? She had felt more scared in the last five minutes than she had even last night. Finally, the stiff latch jerked open and she flung the gate wide, half falling, half running towards the silver shape of Paul's Discovery which was parked right outside. Wrenching the door open, she scrambled in and sat for a moment, panting, her eyes closed. Paul reached over and squeezed her hand.

She opened her eyes.

'Let's go,' she said.

Paul fired the engine and the Discovery moved off.

'I must phone my dad,' she said worriedly. 'If he rings me at home and gets no answer . . .'

'Don't worry,' said Paul. 'It's no problem.'

Joanna smiled at herself. It was true that that was the least of her worries. She wondered how Ken was getting on. She had seen enough police dramas on television to know that there would be another unmarked police car parked in the lane near the Collins's caravan, which would follow Gerry Collins should he leave the site that evening. She shivered, and tried to stop thinking about it.

Paul's house had never seemed so welcoming. A log fire was burning in the sitting room, and Marty was messing about in the kitchen, half the table taken up with the ingredients of his pasta sauce, the other half with a muddle of bits of string, dog biscuits, junk mail and old newspapers.

'The cleaner's gone to Tenerife for a bit of winter sun,' Paul explained. 'You just can't get the staff.'

Joanna laughed, feeling her shoulders lower themselves inch by inch. Paul gave her a glass of Chardonnay and she sipped it gratefully.

'Thanks for this, Paul,' she said. 'And I don't just mean the wine.'

'Any time,' he smiled.

Marty cooked, and Joanna had another glass of wine, and she started to believe that everything would be all right; that Ken would pick up Collins, or whoever it was, and that by tomorrow her life could begin to get back to normal. She would never have to go through this evening again, and she would never have to go through anything worse than this evening, of that she was sure. In a way, she ought to take an obscure comfort from it: the worst had happened. Then the phone rang.

'Right, well, that was Alan Stewart. It's Mrs Attwood,' said Paul when he'd finished the call. 'He wants me to go over there and have a look at her. Joanna, I think you'd better come with me, for safety's sake.'

'Oh, no . . .' Joanna had just got comfy on the sofa with an old Sunday supplement.

'Come on, you can go and see Harry,' insisted Paul. His voice made it clear that he would not take no for an answer. 'Marty, thanks very much, excellent meal.'

'Sorry about this, Marty,' said Joanna, getting to her feet reluctantly.

'S'OK,' said Marty. 'Oh, Dad. Al rang. She's coming over later.'

As usual, Doris Attwood was in a panic about nothing. Paul felt even more exasperated than usual and, to make things worse, as he was packing his bag and making the expected soothing noises, his mobile rang.

'Who? Mr Pearson? You'll have to speak up? Where did you say?'

He met up with Joanna as arranged back at Alan Stewart's office. She was not exactly thrilled to hear that he'd had another call.

'Parkfield? That's the other side of Warwick!'

'Problem?' Alan Stewart emerged from inside.

Paul explained what had happened.

'Not your night, is it?' said Alan wryly.

'Not mine either,' added Jo. 'I've got to tag along with him.'

'Well, I can always give you a lift back,' offered Alan. 'I'm going your way.'

'I might as well, Paul,' said Joanna. She was heartily fed up with the way the evening had turned out.

Paul wasn't sure, and said so.

'Don't let me be the cause of a tiff,' said Alan, rather pointedly, Jo thought. She suddenly remembered their conversation at the race course, his insistence that Joanna was marked out for Paul. 'Yes or no?' he persisted.

Some perverse streak in Joanna, which minded that other people thought she and Paul were ideally suited when it was up to her to decide, made her say: 'If you don't mind. Thanks.'

Paul still seemed reluctant, but he accepted it.

'All right,' he said, shifting his bag to the other hand. 'Thanks, Alan. Bye.'

'Bye,' said Alan. And then to Joanna: 'I'll just lock up and then I'm all yours.'

The least she could do when they got back to Paul's was to offer him a nightcap, she thought. She let them in with the key Paul had given her and called: 'Marty! I'm back!'

Alan picked up a note from the hall table and held it out to her.

'Gone to pub,' read Joanna. 'Typical!'

She grinned at Alan, then led him through into the sitting room. No amount of Marty's clutter could detract from the beautiful proportions of the room, the soft light thrown by the table lamps and the dozing fire, the beautiful muted colours which Celia had chosen. Alan paused in the doorway, taking it all in.

'So this is where he lives,' he said. 'Very grand.'

'It's a lovely house, isn't it?' said Joanna warmly, moving to the drinks tray.

'Yes, people like him usually get what they want.' There was an edge in his voice which made Joanna look at him sharply but he went on, smiling. 'I mean, some blokes have all the luck. It's sickening.' He moved to the piano and picked up a photograph of Celia as Joanna poured them each a whisky.

'Nothing worse than the pain of loss,' he said thoughtfully.

'Are you speaking from experience?' Joanna sat on the sofa and placed their drinks on the table. Alan came across to sit beside her.

'I told you, I nearly got married once. We were engaged, but she called it off.' He picked up his glass and drank. 'It was years ago, when I was young and trusting. She fell for someone else. I was angry with myself more than anything. There was I, thinking she was the perfect being, but she was flawed, just like the others.'

Joanna wasn't sure that she knew him well enough to be on the receiving end of all these revelations. Still, some people felt that, just because you were a doctor, you were the right person for their confidences, however intimate.

'We're all flawed, Alan,' she said lightly.

'But I demand perfection,' he insisted. 'Everything in its place, just so.'

'Yeah, well, the world isn't like that.'

'Then it should be.'

'Oh, come on . . .' He sounded so serious, Joanna almost wanted to laugh. 'You're sounding like some irate child who's stamping his feet because he can't get his own way!'

'Well, I'm sorry you think that,' he said, sounding hurt. 'Still, forget it. It was a long time ago. Hardly worth talking about. Mind you, at the time I felt like killing the bloke.' He laughed. 'Don't worry – I didn't.'

Joanna smiled uncertainly. He wasn't quite the unassuming, even-tempered individual she had thought him to be.

'Excuse me,' she said, standing up. 'I need to go to the loo. Help yourself to another drink.'

Alan smiled up at her.

'No, thanks. This is fine.'

Keith Lardner unlocked the door to let Paul through to the custody area, his face signalling surprise.

'No, you're right, you didn't call me out,' said Paul in explanation. His evening was going from bad to worse. When he'd got to the address he thought he'd heard for the Parkfield patient, it had turned out to be a row of boarded-up shops. 'Look, I'm sorry to be a pain but I was called to a house round the corner. There must have been a mix-up over the address and the mobile's gone dead on me.'

Keith indicated the back office.

'There's a phone through there. Be my guest.'

As Paul edged round the front desk, Nicky came out of her room.

'What are you doing here?' she asked. 'Where's Dr Stevens?'

'She's at my place,' Paul explained. 'Alan Stewart drove her back from Sheerwater Flats.'

'Who?'

'The warden. Look, she's all right, Marty's there and Al . . .'

Nicky looked worried.

'Yeah, but the only people who should know about this are those who *need* to know.'

'Well, we didn't say anything to Alan.'

'But you told him she was staying with you.'

Then it hit him. He hadn't told Alan. And he didn't think Joanna had mentioned it either. So how had Alan come to make the assumption? From the fact that they had arrived together? They might just have been out to dinner. Or did he know more about Joanna's movements than anyone had suspected? What had Harry Campbell said? 'A charmer?' Just the sort of man who . . .

'Oh, my God,' he said under his breath.

Nicky picked up the front desk phone and held the receiver out to him.

'Call her,' she said.

The phone rang just as Joanna was coming out of the bathroom. She could hear a phone trilling upstairs as well as down so she followed the sound into what she assumed must be Paul's bedroom to answer it. It felt very intimate, standing there by his bed, with the book he was reading splayed open on the bedside table and a kicked-off pair of shoes by the chair. It was Paul, sounding tense.

'Alan dropped you off OK, yeah? No problems?'

'No,' said Joanna, puzzled. 'Why should there be?'

'Good,' he said. 'Can you put Al or Marty on?'

'They're not back from the pub yet.'

'What? So you're there alone?'

'No.' What had got into Paul? She was safe here, for heaven's sake. It wasn't like she was at home. 'Alan's here.'

At that point the line went dead. Joanna shook the phone.

'Paul? Paul?'

There was nothing. Gradually it broke over her, like a wave in slow motion. All that stuff about people being flawed, and Paul always getting what he wanted. It wasn't Gerry Collins who had been following her, videoing her, spooking her. It was Alan!

She put the receiver down carefully, quietly. She was in the house with him. He was in the house with her. Joanna swallowed hard. She had to get out. And to do that, she had to keep calm, and think logically. She knew the layout of the house. Alan knew she was upstairs, so she had to get downstairs and out of the front door. Now that wasn't very far, just along the landing, down the stairs and out. But he wouldn't just be sitting there. He'd obviously heard the phone, because he'd cut her off. So he'd be waiting somewhere to grab her. At this thought, her legs almost gave way. She felt herself sway, but she grabbed hold of the headboard and steadied herself. She'd got to get out. She'd got to. Feeling every step, dreading a creaking board, she edged carefully out on to the landing. The house was quiet and there was no sign of Alan. She crept along and began to inch down the stairs, keeping close to the wall, keeping her eyes fixed on the front door, willing herself to stay strong, trying to still her thudding heart. Then the lights went out.

At the police station, Ken, Nicky, Spenser and Cudworth ran for the cars, coats flying. Nicky had told Paul they'd given up on the surveillance operation after Collins had left the caravan site but headed off east, in the wrong direction, to spend an innocent night drinking and playing pool with his mates. Ken was obviously cursing himself for having pinned all his hopes on the wrong bloke. Paul was just cursing himself. Why had he let Joanna out of his sight? With anyone? If anything happened to her . . .

'We'll follow you,' shouted Ken to Paul. 'Stick your emergency light on. Just drive!'

At first Joanna froze against the wall, a sick panic swelling in her chest. She swallowed hard. She knew without a doubt that she was fighting for her life. She fumbled her way back up the stairs, her only thought now of hiding. The first door she came to was Al's room, where she had spent last night. Craving light, even moonlight, she made for the window, then pressed herself back against the wall, as she thought she heard footsteps coming up the stairs. Then she knew she heard them on the landing.

Then she heard Alan's voice. He knew she was there. He knew she would be listening. Joanna felt sick as she heard him say: 'I did tell you I don't like people who let me down.'

The door to Al's bedroom was pushed slowly open and he entered the room. He crossed the carpet silently towards her where she stood at the window. How could he see her? It was pitch dark. Maybe he could scent her fear.

She could hear him smiling as he came closer.

'But that's not much use to you now, is it?'

He was close to her now, looking into her face, not that he could have seen more than an outline. Rigid with fear, Joanna pressed herself hard against the wall as his hands reached out towards her. Unsure she could make herself do it, she raised her right arm, holding a can of hairspray which she had found on the windowsill. Would her fingers work? Would she be able to press the button? Desperately, she pointed it at his face and he staggered back, howling in pain as the stuff stung his eyes. Joanna pushed past him, running for the door, running for her life. She almost fell down the stairs and even as she reached the bottom she heard Al's door bang back as he came after her. She flung herself at the front door. To her horror she realized that he must have locked and chained it. She scrabbled back the chain, tugged at the bolts, but the deadlock defeated her. She fled into the sitting room, but the french windows were locked and security bolted and she had no idea where the key might be. She wondered about trying to smash a pane with an ornament or something, but then she heard him coming down the stairs and changed tack. If she could get to the kitchen . . . the key was always in the back door.

As she crossed the hall, he was half-way down the stairs. She saw him and he saw her. But her fear, which had made her clumsy, had reached a new pitch now. This was self-preservation. Slipping on the tiled kitchen floor, she raced for the back door and managed to turn the key in the lock. Flinging it open, she found herself in the yard outside. But now what? There were no neighbours, no one she could run to for help. Paul's house was completely isolated. Had she just made herself more vulnerable? She didn't have time to think. She heard the sound of his feet on the kitchen floor, and ran.

Paul had never driven so fast. Ken had had the sirens on as they left the town, but there was no traffic on the quiet country lanes and no more need for them. The Discovery's headlights picked out Alan Stewart's car as Paul drove up to Church House. As he got out, he heard the hawk's cry and noticed the door to the old stable block standing open. Instinctively he ran towards it, followed by Ken, who had already sent Spenser and Cudworth round the back of the house while Nicky tried the front.

The aviary door was open. The first thing Paul saw was Joanna huddled in the corner, not moving, just a heap of clothes.

'Joanna?'

The relief when she raised her head was indescribable. Her face was contorted with terror and her eyes were fixed on a dark shape beneath the hawk's perch. Mr Harris appeared to be standing guard. Paul nodded at Ken who handed Paul his torch as he stooped and hauled Alan Stewart to his feet. Mr Harris shuffled proprietorially on his perch and gave a piercing cry. Alan Stewart leaped back, gibbering.

'Keep it away from me!'

He had a livid gash, trickling blood, on his right cheek and the backs of his hands had deep parallel scratches where he had put them up to shield his face.

Paul stepped forward and spoke softly to the bird,

knowing that the hawk needed to be calmed as much as Joanna did – more so, if he was not to attack anyone else.

Ken hustled Alan Stewart away and Paul went over to Joanna. She must have been beside herself to try and hide in here. He had told her repeatedly just how dangerous these birds were. You might be able to train them but you could never tame them – ever.

He crouched down beside her and held her hands in his.

'It's all right,' he said. 'It's all right now.'

A couple of nights later, Ken took Paul and Joanna out for a meal, along with Nicky. He called it a celebration. It was a feather in his cap, putting away a man like Alan Stewart, responsible for two deaths and who knew how many more if he hadn't been apprehended?

'His employers had started asking some awkward questions, checking the references he'd given when he got the job.' Ken poured them each a glass of wine. 'Turns out he'd written them himself.'

'So he knew it was time to move on again?' asked Joanna, looking up from the menu. She still had a fragile, haunted look about her, and whenever she thought, not so much about what *had* happened, terrifying as it had been, but about what *might* have happened, the shaking started again.

'Everywhere he goes, it's the same,' added Nicky, remembering something Alan Stewart had said during his interview. 'Small people conspiring to bring him down.'

Paul wanted to steer the conversation on to something a bit more cheerful, or at least give Joanna the chance to think about something else.

'What's happened about the Collins boy?' he enquired. 'I haven't had a minute to check up on him.'

'It was one of the nurses who got it out of him in the end,' Nicky explained. 'Turns out he'd been picked on by a gang of bigger boys at school. Didn't want to say anything because they said they'd torch the caravan. Had it in for him because he was a traveller.'

'Didn't we all?' said Joanna softly. 'I mean, we were as guilty as anyone of thinking the worst about Gerry Collins just because of the way he chooses to live his life.'

'He had got past form, Joanna,' said Ken defensively.

'So had Alan Stewart, as it turned out,' replied Joanna, her level gaze holding his. 'But because he seemed like a nice middle-class chap in a caring profession we all thought he was above board. You can see why blokes like Collins get abusive.'

They were all silent for a moment, unable to deny the truth of what she had said. Then Paul spoke.

'Well, I'm having the mussels followed by the poulet à l'estragon,' he said, snapping shut his leather-bound menu. 'This is the first time Ken's ever bought me dinner.'

'At these prices, it'll be the last,' grumbled Ken. 'Whose idea was this place, anyway?'

Nicky glared at him. The suggestion had been Joanna's. But Joanna laughed her infectious laugh and, relieved, they all joined in.

'Expensive tastes, you see,' she said, raising her glass to the others. 'Alan Stewart could never have afforded me, anyway.'

11

Things settled down a bit after that. Chastened by what had happened with Alan Stewart, Harry Campbell pulled back on his matchmaking efforts with Joanna and Paul and they were left to their own devices. The trouble was that neither of them seemed able to take the step which would have eased them from a close friendship born of shared professional interests and remarkably similar personal sorrows into something deeper and closer still.

Paul thought about it often as he flew the hawk. He and Mr Harris had reached an understanding now. Paul could encourage the bird to leave his gloved fist, to swoop and dive in the air, to reach the top of the tallest tree, without the fear that he would never return. If only he could overcome his fear of another relationship as easily. He didn't quite know what was holding him back. Now that Joanna had dropped the protective spikiness which had done its job in warding him off for most of the time they had worked together, he had come to know her as a warm and intelligent woman with a soft beauty which she had also, it seemed, held in check before. She knew him and understood his predicament from a personal and professional point of view as much as anyone could; she understood about his police work and his home life and the way that Al and Marty would always come first, and she didn't seem to mind. If she resented anyone for taking up his time, it was probably Mr Harris, despite the fact that the bird had saved her from her attacker. Joanna had come with him on one occasion to fly the hawk; in fact, it had been the first time Paul had flown him alone, without Terri's support.

'Right,' Paul had said, staring into Mr Harris's un-winking eyes, 'I'm going to stay here with the chicken giblets and you're going to go to the top of that tree. And when I call you in, you're going to come. All right? All right?'

It hadn't worked the first time. Paul raised his fist into the air but Mr Harris hesitated, squawking feebly, and refused to move. Joanna glanced at Paul and pulled a face. Then she gave an encouraging smile.

'Try again.'

'Now let me run this past you one more time.' Paul addressed the bird seriously. 'I'm here with the giblets. You're going to the top of the tree, we're going to take a little walk and then we're going to call you in. Right. Here goes.'

He raised his fist boldly into the air. Mr Harris stretched his impressive wings and launched himself, soaring up into the cold December morning.

'Yes!' Joanna clenched her fists in triumph. 'I knew he'd do it. He trusts you!'

He did. He trusted Paul to be there with the chicken giblets, like Boozie trusted him to take him for walks. Nothing seemed to destroy that trust in an animal, once it was established. But as for Paul ... it wasn't that he didn't trust Joanna. She had been hurt herself by the loss of her husband. He felt as sure as he possibly could that she would not willingly hurt him. But he couldn't trust himself not to hurt her. He didn't know if he could sustain another relationship, even now. After all, his attempt with Kate had come to a pretty uninspiring end and, as she herself had pointed out, things hadn't been exactly brilliant between them even before her move to Bristol. If he embarked on a relationship with Joanna and it didn't work out, they would be back to all that awkwardness at Wickton Road, maybe even the sparring which he had found so exhausting, and he would have lost her friendship for good. Was it worth it? The current state of affairs was so much more restful. So much safer.

Joanna thought she'd been patient. Very patient. After all, it would hardly have been a whirlwind romance. She had known Paul as a colleague for over five years and they had become friends over the last twelve months. Of course he would be cautious, she understood that; who wouldn't be, having lost Celia in the way that he had? But she had lost Charles, too. She had wept, and raged, and blamed herself. If she was willing to try again, surely he could find it in himself to take the risk? She even hankered for the simple days, before that awful business with Alan Stewart, when her dad had tried his clumsy efforts at matchmaking, like the time he had suggested that they all had dinner together as a thank you for Paul's involvement in securing him a place at Sheerwater Flats, only to cry off at the last moment because he felt tired.

'You two go and enjoy yourselves,' he had said, transparently.

Joanna had wanted to die of embarrassment at the time, but, she had come to conclude, Paul was so backward in coming forward, that it was exactly the sort of push he needed. A more modern woman would have had no qualms about asking Paul out herself, seducing him, even, but Joanna was traditional enough to want Paul to do the asking. She knew he liked her; no, more than that, was fond of her. But what if that was all it was? Paul had an abundance of natural charm which made you feel special. That was why there were patients – all of them women, let it be said – who would wait for days to see him, suffering the pain of their sore throats or strained ligaments, in preference to one of the other doctors at Wickton Road. He used that charm on everyone. It wasn't a conscious thing, it was just part of him. But it would be terrible, Joanna thought, and her self-confidence might never recover, if she were to make a move, only to discover that she'd been on the receiving end of no more and no less than the sort of attention Paul gave to Nicky Green, say, or Doreen, his cleaner. He just couldn't help being charming and attentive, and he didn't know how charming he was, which of course was what made him so attractive. But what if he didn't find her attractive? Maybe he saw her as a colleague and a friend, nothing more.

There had been one occasion when she had pushed it. It had been quite soon after Alan Stewart. Paul had invited the partners and their wives round to dinner, for no other reason, Nick said, than that he wanted to show off his cooking. It had been a lovely evening. All the men had dressed for the occasion: Shaaban was in one of his beautiful hand-made suits from the Turkish tailor he knew in Birmingham; Paul in a dark jacket, collarless shirt and waistcoat, which, he said, had been a present from Al; and even Nick had on a bottle-green velvet jacket instead of his usual baggy corduroy. Amina wore an almost iridescent lime-green sari, Jean was elegant in a black and ivory print and Joanna wore a midnight-blue evening suit tailored like a man's but with a plum-coloured silk camisole. She let her hair down but pushed it back from her face with two pearl combs. Paul had laid the table in the dining room with a white damask cloth and there were candles and long-stemmed glasses and a wonderful meal of soup, and pheasant, and a pudding steeped in Grand Marnier. Knowing that she would want to drink, Joanna had ordered a taxi to collect her just before twelve, and, five minutes before it was due, when she had said her goodbyes to the others and excused herself to get her coat, Paul came with her into the hall. He held her coat for her and when she had shrugged it on, she turned to face him. They were standing very close and he didn't move away.

'Thank you for a lovely, lovely evening, Paul,' she smiled.

'It's a great pleasure,' he said seriously. 'I'm sorry you have to go.'

He was looking at her intently, his eyes not moving from her face. She leaned towards him. She had intended it to be nothing more than a social kiss, but something happened; either she moved or he did, and the kiss landed not on his cheek but on his mouth, and became not a social kiss but something more significant. Then the taxi hooted and, startled, Joanna pulled away, feeling uncertain. He squeezed her shoulders.

'Goodnight, Joanna.'

Nothing more had been said and the moment was never repeated. She went round to Paul's for supper occasionally with him and Marty, or they went out for a drink, but though he kissed her goodbye at the end of the evening, on the mouth, it was a gentlemanly rather than a passionate kiss and he never seemed to want or expect anything more.

And now the winter had passed, and they were into summer again, Paul reflected as he drove to work one Monday morning in early June. The municipal hanging baskets were vibrant with colour and the wisteria on the front of Wickton Road was out in all its glory.

Amazingly, Marty had stuck his job at the hospital. Mr Smith, his boss, was a bully, but Marty had found a good mate in Angie, another of the kitchen workers. He also, Paul suspected from the odd telephone call he'd overheard, had a bit of a thing going with a girl called Carol, who was wheelchair-bound following an accident, and was at the hospital for intensive physiotherapy. His interest in sport and cars continued unabated and, luckily for Paul, the fact that he spent all day in a kitchen had not dimmed his enthusiasm for cooking at home. Paul was often grateful for the note from Marty which said, 'In the fridge is something I prepared earlier', when he got in late from a police job. These days, except for special occasions, such as having the partners round to dinner, he didn't do much cooking himself.

In fact, despite, or maybe because of, the glorious weather – 'record-breaking', was the phrase most frequently used to describe the temperatures they were experiencing – Paul felt sluggish and lethargic. Everyone seemed to be enjoying themselves – except him. Marty had his interests, which was as it should be; Paul didn't in any way begrudge him. Al seemed totally wrapped up in university and in Ben. Paul had met him now. Al had brought him home before Christmas, and Paul had been surprised by the serious-looking, bearded boy with his bright shirt, not what he thought of as 'Al's type' at all. But then she'd never had the opportunity to meet anyone except the clean-cut boys from Warwick School who had been the mainstay of her social life before she'd left home. University presented all sorts of other options – that was the point of going. Ben was in his second year, studying Oriental History, but he had a wide-ranging general knowledge as well and a wacky sense of humour. He teased Al the whole time but he obviously thought the world of her, and by the time the Easter vacation came and Al opted to spend half of it at Ben's home in Staffordshire, Paul suspected that Al was in love. Not long after Easter, Al had told him that she and Ben were planning a camping trip to Snowdonia after their exams. They were going with two other friends from university, Kathy and Simon. Only relieved that it wasn't to Manchuria, of which Ben was making a special study, Paul gave the trip his blessing. He wasn't quite sure when they were going – one of the things he'd had to get used to with Al being at college was not knowing what she was doing every minute of every day – but he had a feeling it was this week. At least the weather would be good for them.

That night he got home feeling more drained than usual

from a perfectly normal day; that is, two police call-outs, two surgeries and a clutch of house calls. As he flopped on the sofa, too weary even to pour himself a drink, Marty thumped downstairs and into the room, wielding a sports bag.

'Bad day?' he enquired sympathetically.

'Busy,' sighed Paul. 'Busy, busy, busy. Can't be bothered to do supper tonight, Marty. I'll make it up to you to-morrow.'

'No, it's OK, I'm going to a basketball match,' explained Marty. 'Do you want to come?'

Paul could think of nothing he'd like less, and made his excuses.

Marty shrugged.

'OK. But you know, Dad, you should get out more.'

Paul smothered a grin.

'You think so? That's the voice of experience, is it?'

'Yes,' said Marty firmly. 'When was the last time you were on holiday?'

Paul shook his head.

'Er . . . nineteen sixty-seven?'

Marty clicked his tongue impatiently.

'Oh, come on, Dad, be serious.'

'I don't have the time,' said Paul tetchily. And added, 'Anyway, there's no one to go with, is there?'

'That's pathetic!' Marty wouldn't even allow him to wallow in self-pity. He paused, then added cheekily: 'I know someone who would love to go with you.'

And leaving Paul to think about it, he shouldered his kitbag and left, whistling.

Paul was still thinking about it next morning, sifting through his mail after morning surgery. Suddenly aware that he was being watched, he looked up to see Joanna leaning against the doorframe. She was smiling. She had obviously been sunning herself at the weekend because she had a light golden tan which was striking against her cream raw silk jacket. She had on a fine gold chain and she was running it through her fingers as she watched him.

'Anything interesting?' she asked, indicating the mail.

'There never is. Once, just once, you'd think they'd write to you and say thank you for making me feel better or improving the quality of my life or something . . . instead of which we get complaints about how long somebody's mother had to sit in the waiting room.'

Joanna's face dimpled as she controlled a laugh at his grumpiness.

'I see. One of those mornings, is it?'

He looked up and smiled ruefully. He must sound a real old misery.

'I'll leave you to it.' She turned to go, then turned back. 'Are you doing anything tonight?'

Paul bit his lip.

'Joanna, I'm sorry, I can't tonight. I promised Marty I'd be in . . .'

'S'OK.' She smiled first at Paul, then at Nick, who had appeared in the corridor behind her. 'No problem.'

As her high heels tapped away down the corridor, Nick came into Paul's consulting room shaking his head in despair.

'Nick. Hi, how are you?'

'Paul, you're a fool. I'm sorry, but it has to be said.'

Paul knew what he was talking about, and was kicking himself already. For one thing, Marty was the one encouraging him to go out more; he wouldn't have held his father to a half-promise to cook him supper tonight. And secondly, he could have invited Joanna over to join them. But he wasn't about to let Nick see that he knew he had handled it badly.

'I'm sorry?' he hazarded.

'Turning down an invitation to go out with a beautiful

young woman . . . Lovely personality . . . similar interests. You must be mad.'

'I'm doing something tonight,' said Paul, adding quickly, 'Not that it's any of your business.'

'I wouldn't call staying in with Marty "doing something".'

'Oh, you heard all that, did you?' said Paul, annoyed. 'Look, what are you all of a sudden, my mother?'

'Paul.' Nick spread his hands on Paul's desk and leaned forward. 'Live a little. Before it's too late. Go out with Joanna. Marty can fend for himself.'

'Thanks for the advice, Nick. Now, was there anything medical you wanted me for?'

Nick straightened, defeated.

'No. No, just sticking my nose in where it isn't wanted. Good morning.'

Mock-wounded, he left.

Paul called after him, as the phone began to ring: 'If it's any consolation, my son thinks I'm quite boring, too.'

It wasn't long before Nick was back. He apologized for having interfered where he wasn't wanted, and then proceeded to tell Paul that he'd been scrutinizing the leave rota. Paul, he said, was owed a lot of holiday.

'Oh, look,' said Paul wearily. 'I've had this out with Marty. I don't have the time.'

Nick pointed a knowing finger at him.

'That's what I used to say. It's absolute nonsense. Nobody is that indispensable. It's ego, pride, your sense of self-importance making you say that . . . or fear,' he added, tellingly. Paul looked up sharply. 'You're not the only one who's owed a lot of holiday either. As I said, I've been checking.'

'Have you,' said Paul, beginning to feel outmanoeuvred.

'Yes. We could manage without you, you know,' Nick went on relentlessly. 'It would be difficult, but we'd cope. You need a break. You both do. I'm out of order, I know, but somebody's got to give you a good kick up the behind. It might as well be me.'

After Nick had gone, Paul pushed his chair back and put his feet up on the desk. Outside his window, a white lilac was in full bloom, brushing against the pane. As he watched, a blue tit rested on one of its branches, briefly, before flitting off back to its young. Nick was right. Al had gone. Marty didn't need him. What was he waiting for? And clever old Nick had put his finger on it. Fear. He was afraid of spoiling things with Joanna, and he was afraid of everyone else knowing about it if things didn't work out. But Nick had presented him with the perfect opportunity. He would ask Joanna to go away with him. Then they could see how they got on, just the two of them. And if it didn't work out, at least they would have kept their dignity. It would be their secret and no one need ever know.

He sneaked into the office when no one was about and deftly pencilled in two days' leave around the following weekend, Friday and Monday. That was the easy bit. Now all he had to do was to find the right moment, and the courage, to ask Joanna.

The opportunity came sooner than he'd expected, when she came out into the back car park that evening as he was putting his bag into the Discovery. Paul smiled shyly.

'Doing anything interesting this weekend?' he asked.

Joanna frowned.

'Nothing in particular. Why?'

If he asks me to go and fly that blasted hawk, she thought, I'll scream.

'Um, I just wondered . . . I'm taking a long weekend, fancied getting away from it all.'

'How spontaneous,' said Joanna, wondering what all this was about. 'Well, good for you. What are you going to do?'

There was a pause you could have washed your socks in.

'Well, that actually rather depends on you.'

'On me? Why?'

Now she understood. But she was damned if she was going to help him. Beyond saying yes, of course.

'Look, I'd really like it, um, I mean I was wondering if . . .' Paul stuttered, 'if you'd like to . . . go away too. W-with me,' he added, unnecessarily.

Joanna felt a great smile well up within her. At last.

It was tough going in Snowdonia and not just because of the terrain. Simon was turning out to be a total wimp. When Kathy had first invited herself and Simon along, Al hadn't felt able to refuse. And Ben had been very good about it, seeing as the trip had been planned, in the beginning, as a romantic interlude for the two of them. But for the entire first day, Simon had done nothing but moan, about the weight of the tent, the meagreness of the rations, the lack of a decent pub, to name but three. On the second day, he seemed a little better. Though he did drone on and on about his blisters, he was bearable. But by the third day, he had reverted to full-blown moaner mode.

'We're thinking of going back,' Kathy announced after breakfast.

'We've only just started,' said Ben. They were aiming for Pinnacle Crag and they'd only got as far as Devil's Kitchen.

'We thought we'd go to that pub in Betws-y-Glyn you know. The Betws-y-Glyn Arms. We could meet you there on Friday.'

'I'm sorry, mate,' put in Simon sheepishly. 'I'm just holding you back and I'd rather spend a couple of days back in civilization.'

Ben looked at Al and shrugged. In his opinion the other two were no loss.

'OK, then. Have it your own way.'

'Are you sure you don't mind?' Kathy asked Al.

'No, of course not.'

Al and Ben watched the others begin their descent, Simon leaning heavily on Kathy's shoulder for the steep bits, and dissolved in giggles.

'He's just not hard, like me,' said Ben in a mock Liverpool accent.

'Don't push it, you,' said Al, digging him in the back.

'I'm glad I've got you all to myself, though,' said Ben, seriously, nuzzling her hair.

'Me too,' said Al.

Joanna had a nasty moment when, having accepted Paul's invitation, she tried to book the Friday and the Monday off.

'Ah. Paul, that's when you're off, isn't it?' said Shaaban, sounding concerned.

'Er, is that a problem?' asked Paul ingenuously.

'Not at all!' said Nick breezily. 'We can cope, can't we, Shaaban?'

'Can we?'

'Yes, of course we can,' said Nick, taking a pen from Julia and filling in Joanna's name below Paul's against the days in question. 'If we get stuck we can get a locum.'

Paul and Joanna escaped to the corridor with a sigh of relief.

'So, where are we going?' she whispered.

'I don't really care – as long as it's quiet and peaceful,' replied Paul. She smiled up at him, her eyes sparkling with mischief, at the promise of forbidden treats. 'I'm very glad you said yes,' he added, meaning it.

'I'm very glad you asked me.'

'Excuse me.' Shaaban squeezed past them with an apologetic smile.

'You don't think they know, do you? They don't, do they?' hissed Joanna.

'Does it matter?'

Suddenly it didn't matter to him, not one bit. He was sure that when they got to wherever they were going, everything was going to be fine. And so, soon, everyone could know.

'No. No, it doesn't.'

'Right. Well, there's no need to whisper then, is there?'

And they both burst out laughing.

Ben had pitched the tent on a grassy slope below the crag. The views down the mountain were breathtaking. Every way you looked there was just green on green. Above them, the grass got scrubbier and the grey of the rock poked through, but that, too, was stunning in its way against the vivid blue sky with its dazzlingly white clouds. It was jolly cold, though. Al could feel the damp grass right through all her layers of clothing, and her sleeping bag. She snuggled up to Ben.

'You didn't like me when we first met, did you?' he asked, as she lay with her head in the crook of his neck. 'Go on, be honest.'

'I wouldn't go that far,' said Al. 'I just wasn't sure about you, that's all.'

'And what about now?' said Ben, serious for once.

'I'm pretty sure what I think about you now.' Al propped herself up on her elbow so that she could see his face.

'I knew how I felt about you the first moment I saw you.'

Al leaned down and kissed him.

'Your nose is cold,' he said.

'I'm cold,' said Al.

'Well, we can't have that, can we?' Ben wriggled into a sitting position and began to unzip first his sleeping bag, then Al's. 'We can zip them together,' he explained. 'Make one big bag.'

Al held up her arms to him. He was so lovely. She was so lucky.

'Forget zipping them,' she said, pulling him down to kiss him.

After much agonizing and consulting of brochures, Paul booked himself and Joanna in at the Woodside Hotel, which promised them a relaxed stay in five acres of grounds in the beautiful Oxfordshire countryside, their every need taken care of by attentive and courteous staff, their palates tempted by dishes from their four-star kitchen.

'That'll do,' thought Paul, lifting the receiver to make the reservation. He noted that they had a honeymoon suite, but thought that a de-luxe double would probably be more fitting.

Next day, after lunch, Marty waved them off.

'Have fun!' he called.

'Thank you,' said Joanna, without a trace of embarrassment. 'We'll try.'

She got in and slammed the door. Paul waited for her to fasten her seatbelt, then he fired the engine and put the Discovery in gear.

'There's something wrong with this scenario, you know,' he said as they moved off.

'What?'

Joanna waved back at Marty who had picked Boozie up and was making him wave his paw.

'Well, the teenage son stands at the door waving his father goodbye, telling him to have fun . . . he accused me of not being able to have any fun, you know.'

Joanna raised an eyebrow.

'Well, we'll just have to prove him wrong, won't we?'

It didn't seem as if they were going to have much trouble, in fact. The drive only took about forty minutes, which meant that they were at the Woodside in time for afternoon tea, which they then worked off with a stroll round the grounds. On the way back, Paul caught Joanna's hand. He looked at her questioningly, but she nodded, so he twined his fingers with hers. They walked for a while without speaking, then he stopped her beneath a horse-chestnut tree and turned to face her. Bending his head, he kissed her softly on the lips.

'I like it here,' she said, putting her arms round his neck. 'I'm really glad we came.'

'Yes,' he said simply. He kissed her again. 'I think we've managed to escape. You know – I've wanted this for a long time, Joanna. It just, it didn't seem right, you know, back there.'

Even now he was putting off the moment of making love to her, but only because he was enjoying the feeling of wanting her. He wanted to savour the heightened feelings between them so that when, at the end of the evening, the moment came, they could both enjoy the release. When they came back upstairs, giggling after a delicious dinner and too much wine, he knew the moment had come. He unlocked the door of their room and ushered her in, then guided her towards the bed, drawing her down beside him. Joanna was luminous in her beauty, her skin glowing, her blonde hair tousled. With his forefinger he traced the line of her jaw and then her neck, noticing her shiver and her eyes darken with desire. He leaned to kiss her, only to be startled by the jangle of the bedside phone. He closed his eyes with a sigh. Reluctantly she let him go and he rolled away from her and snatched up the receiver.

'Hello?'

'Hi, Dad, it's Marty.'

'Marty!'

Behind him Paul felt the bed move as Joanna sat up, concerned. She knew he wouldn't have disturbed them without good reason.

Marty sounded upset.

'Dad, Al and Ben have been reported missing near Betws-y-Glyn and they need you to go over there.'

'Look, slow down . . .'

Joanna crawled across the bed to Paul and put her arm round his shoulders.

'OK.' Marty took a deep breath. 'The mountain rescue people have been called out and they want you to go over there. What shall I do?'

Paul rubbed his eyes. This couldn't be happening.

'OK. Ring them back and tell them I'm on my way.'

Joanna was superb. She changed, and made him change, she packed for both of them, she called Reception and got them to prepare the bill, which she paid on her credit card. Then she made Paul give her the keys to the Discovery and she drove them, at speed, to Wales.

The Betsw-y-Glyn Arms was the only building in the village showing a light. Joanna parked round the back and they found a side door open, which led straight into a small bar. By the fire were two scared-looking youngsters of about Al's age, poring over a map. They introduced themselves and Simon explained that the rescue team were resting while it was dark but that they were going to start up again at first light.

'They'll be fine, Dr Dangerfield,' said Kathy urgently. 'They've got a tent, a stove, and food. They're just lost.'

She was trying to be helpful but it wasn't reassuring. 'Just lost' on a Welsh mountain was not a good thing to be.

Simon indicated the bar.

'Told us to help ourselves,' he said.

Joanna took Paul's arm and drew him to one side, behind the bar.

'Ben's done it before,' she said. 'He'll know what to do.'

Paul was suddenly aware of what she had given up to be here.

'Well, it's certainly not the weekend I had planned,' he said, accepting the brandy she had poured him. 'I'm sorry.'

Joanna slid an arm round his waist.

'Don't apologize,' she said. 'I'm glad I was with you. Look, Paul, I'm not in this for cosy meals in restaurants. I think we're beyond all that, don't you?'

He clinked his glass against hers and kissed her hair. He was glad she'd been with him, too.

Ben and Al huddled together and shivered. It had been raining earlier and the wetness wouldn't leave them. Al looked at Ben, worried. It was all her fault. They had been coming back along a shale-covered plateau, towards Betws-y-Glyn, so nearly there, but she had begun to feel really, really tired, as if her legs wouldn't go any further. Ben had said it would be more tiring coming down than going up, and he had been right. She was worried that they were losing time, and would be late for their meeting with Kathy and Simon, but Ben, ever considerate, had pointed out that Kathy and Simon were in the warm, they could wait an hour or so if needs be. He suggested that they stop for a rest. Al agreed gratefully. She looked back to where they had begun, tracing their route back down.

'I can't believe we've come all that way,' she said.

'I know.' Ben stretched his back, easing his rucksack to the ground. Al, less patient, let hers slip off. It struck Ben's and before either of them could do anything about it, both rucksacks had tumbled over the edge, down the sheer drop. They peered cautiously over. The contents were scattered over the boulders below.

'Ben, I'm really sorry,' said Al in a small voice. 'They've got everything in them.'

Ben squeezed her shoulder. 'It's not your fault. But I've

got to get them back. If we get stuck, we're going to need the tent.'

'Don't,' said Al, panicky at the thought of being left alone. 'We'll manage. We're nearly there.'

But Ben was already lowering himself off the ledge. Inch by inch he disappeared from view. Al could hear his boots scrabbling for a foothold. In the end he found one and began to climb gingerly down, Al's frightened face peering over the edge of the precipice. He looked up at her once, and grinned. She smiled back weakly and then, in front of her eyes, he fell. Not far, but hard. She heard him cry out as a sharp rock jabbed into his side, but he seemed to recover himself.

'Ben?' shouted Al. 'Ben!'

'I'm OK,' he called weakly, but Al saw him crawl to lean against a rock for support, clutching his side. That was when she had known she had to get down there and join him. The descent had been the worst few minutes of her life. That was probably all it took, but she had thought she would never get there. Ben kept looking up and encouraging her and she knew she had to do it for his sake. It was all her own silly fault anyway, for dropping her rucksack like that. Finally, she felt him catch hold of her ankle and guide her foot to a safe place, and then she was crouched beside him. He was dreadfully pale and his hands were torn and bleeding.

'Your poor hands!' Al took them tenderly in hers.

'Oh, I'm all right!' He attempted a smile. 'You know me, tough guy.'

'I'm still going to give you a cuddle.' She snuggled up next to him. He moved slightly to accommodate her, and she heard him gasp in pain.

'What is it?' she asked, worried.

'Nothing,' he insisted. 'I'm fine.'

It got dark. She must have dozed. They must both have dozed off and on all night. She was suddenly aware of a noise coming closer, the rough, sawing noise of a helicopter. She struggled to her feet in the grey dawn, her legs stiff with cold.

'Ben! Ben! It's a helicopter!' she cried.

Ben made no reply. His head had fallen sideways on to the rock. He must be exhausted, poor love. Al took off her scarf, her yellow scarf and waited for the helicopter to come in view. Then she waved and waved. At first she thought it hadn't seen them, but then it came closer and circled above them in the grey mist of early morning.

'Ben! It's all right! They've seen us!'

But Ben was still asleep.

Joanna was determined to go with Paul to the mountainside next morning. Planning a weekend in a plush hotel, she hadn't really packed anything suitable for 5 a.m. on a Welsh mountain, but she put on every layer of clothing she had with her, including two pairs of trousers, and clambered into the mountain rescue landrover with him. The landrover deposited them at the foot of the mountain and, as they arrived, the radio spluttered the good news that a couple, a boy and a girl, had been spotted by the helicopter and the team had gone in. They reckoned they'd be down in about forty minutes. It was Al and Ben.

As the time got nearer, Paul got out of the landrover, where they'd stayed for warmth, and scanned the mountainside with binoculars. As soon as some tiny figures appeared, he thrust the binoculars back on to the passenger seat and ran to meet them. Joanna followed.

He saw Al first, wrapped in a silver space blanket, being led down and supported by two of the team. Paul ran over to her, stumbling on the rough ground. The rescuers guided her to him and tactfully melted away. Al just stood there. Shocked and exhausted, she seemed in another world. Paul reached out for her and held her tight, wanting to wipe away everything she must have gone through in the past twenty-four hours. His throat was too tight with relief and anxiety to speak and he knew that it wasn't the wind which had stung the tears out of his eyes.

As he tried to blink them away, he froze as the rest of the team approached and he saw the burden they were carrying. He'd seen them enough times. It was a body-bag.

Joanna, standing at a discreet distance, watching Paul and Al, saw it too. Ben was dead. What would it do to Al? And, though she cursed herself for her selfishness, what would it do to Paul – and to her?

12

Ben's funeral took place at the uncompromisingly modern crematorium on the outskirts of his home town. It was high summer again and Paul couldn't help comparing it with Celia's funeral at the old stone church in the village. He was so glad that Celia had a permanent resting place there. Ben's parents were going to take his ashes and scatter them in their garden, so that they could feel him near them, he presumed. He hadn't realized until after Ben's death that he had been their only child and he could understand that they felt doubly robbed because he had died in a place and in a way which was nothing to do with them and completely alien from their experience. Then they had had to wait nearly three weeks for the formalities of the post-mortem and the inquest to be concluded. Now, they were literally 'taking him home'.

It was strange, and rather unsettling, to see so many young people at a funeral. Ben's best friend, Tim, read a lesson, and broke down. Afterwards everyone milled about uncertainly outside. Most of these kids had probably never been to a funeral before, Paul reflected, except maybe to a grandparent's, which would have been considerably less disturbing than the loss of a contemporary.

Ben's mother, Margaret, was sweet to Al.

'He was so happy he'd met you, you know.'

Paul saw Al bite her lip, hard, as Ben's father joined them. He looked so like Ben.

'Perhaps if he hadn't . . .'

'Don't be silly.' Margaret Wright put a hand out to her. 'What happened . . . you weren't to blame . . . nobody was.'

'I'd like to come and visit if that would be OK?'

Yes, good, thought Paul. The two other people in the world who are grieving as much as she is, with whom she can talk about Ben to her heart's content.

'I don't think that'd be a good idea,' said John Wright curtly, turning away to shake someone's hand.

'He's . . . he's upset,' said his wife quickly. And to Paul: 'I'm sorry.'

Paul nodded his understanding. He knew what it felt like. God, he knew what it felt like, and he knew how you took your grief out on anyone who was there. But he had also seen Al recoil as if she had been slapped, and he hurt for her too. Gently he led her away to where Joanna and Marty were waiting.

Spinney Woods were looking really beautiful. The sun, filtered by the canopy of trees, fell to the ground in shards of light which glowed on the forest floor. The trees were still that vibrant, early summer green, and birds were everywhere. So, too, were the SOCOs and the police photographer. Nigel Spenser moved forward as Ken's car crunched into the car park. He raised his hand in greeting as Ken and Nicky got out. Ken, whose one concession to summer was to discard his black leather jacket in favour of a tan one, was feeling the heat. Nicky looked cooler in natural linen trousers and a rust and navy striped sleeveless top.

'OK, let's see the body,' said Ken in his businesslike way. No 'lovely morning' or 'nice to see you' for Ken.

Nigel led the way across the car park, pointing out a taped-off car on the way.

'Sunderland's car?' asked Ken.

Nigel nodded.

'Park warden says it could have been here for weeks.'

Nigel led them off the wood-chip path, up a bracken-covered slope and into the woods. They could hear the police activity before they came to the clearing and when they got there they could see the body of a man, in jeans and a denim jacket. It wasn't nice. He was lying face down in the soil and his hands were tied behind his back with a serrated cable clip. The smell was appalling. Nicky retched and covered her nose with a handkerchief. Terri, wearing a paper face-mask, was photographing the body from all angles.

'Looks like animals have got to it. Badgers, that type of thing,' said Nigel helpfully, causing Nicky to heave again.

'I don't think that was the cause of death, Nigel. "Eaten by badgers"!' said Ken sarcastically.

Released from their tension, Nicky and Terri laughed.

'You managed to contact Paul yet?' Ken asked Nicky.

'I tried him at the surgery,' she replied, removing the handkerchief from her mouth. 'He's at a funeral.'

Ken looked back at the body dispassionately.

'There's no great rush,' he said.

Al was alone, sitting on the wall which bounded the terrace, staring unseeing over the garden.

'Al, I'm making coffee.' Paul approached her from the house.

'Not for me, thanks.;'

Paul knew that she was thinking about Ben's father and his dismissal of her.

'Al, don't take it to heart,' he said. 'It's obvious he was distressed . . .'

'No, I can understand that he blames me,' said Al flatly. 'It was me that dropped the rucksacks. It was because of me Ben fell, trying to get them back . . .'

Paul sat down beside her and took her hand. The wall was warm. He turned her fingers over and over in his. She was so young and she'd been through so much.

'Al, accidents happen – especially on mountains.'

'I just didn't know he was so badly hurt.'

Her voice was a whisper. Al had told her father how they had cuddled together, all night, waiting for the morning, waiting to be rescued, and how she had thought Ben had fallen asleep. She wasn't to know that the fall had ruptured his spleen and that he was slowly bleeding to death inside. He would have slipped gently into unconsciousness, but when? How long had she spent huddled up against Ben's dead body? It haunted Paul. But not as much as the realization that he might have lost her, too.

With his usual sense of occasion, Marty yelled unceremoniously from an upstairs window.

'Dad. Police on the phone.'

'Well, tell them I'm . . .' flared Paul.

Al gave him a little push.

'Dad, go on, I'm OK.'

Paul tried to make his excuses to Ken; if there was one time when his family needed him more than the police, it was now. But it was the holiday season. Andy Rawnsley was away. Eventually, under pressure, Paul agreed and scribbled down the directions Ken gave him on the back of a Tesco's receipt he found by the phone. Spinney Woods wasn't far away; a local beauty spot where he sometimes took Boozie for a walk on Sunday mornings. He told Ken he'd be there in half an hour.

Ken told him what they knew about the victim as they walked through the woods towards the body.

'His name's Tommy Sunderland,' he puffed, as they climbed a slight incline. 'Former soldier. Wife reported him missing about three weeks ago. That's his car you saw down there. There was no soil on top of the body, just this layering of branches and stuff.'

'Right,' said Paul, stooping to begin his examination. He felt as if he was operating on automatic pilot. 'Well, he's been here some time. Looks like the foxes have been at him.' He turned aside to get a lungful of slightly fresher air. 'OK. He's gagged. The thumbs are held by some sort of clip. Looks like somebody didn't want him found. I certify death at 14.32.'

Nicky, meanwhile, had been detailed to tell the wife. They had first met three weeks before, when Lucy Sunderland had reported her husband missing. She was a physiotherapist at the county cricket ground. Now that's the job I should have gone for, thought Nicky, as she climbed the stairs to Lucy's treatment room, manipulating cricketers' groin strains, instead of crawling about in the undergrowth and investigating thefts from cigarette-machines. Gareth, her married man, was away in Minorca with his wife and kids and she was going through her annual, though short-lived, 'what's in this for me?' phase. Thank God he'd be back on Sunday.

Lucy was between patients when Nicky knocked on the door. Her room was clean and white with a treatment couch and various posters showing muscle and sinew in lurid colour. Through the open window came the sound of cricketers practising in the nets. Lucy herself was dark-haired and attractive in an obvious sort of way, thought Nicky bitchily, with a well-defined Cupid's-bow mouth and big brown eyes. She kept herself in good shape and liked to show it off: she was wearing tight leggings and a T-shirt instead of the usual physio's shapeless white overall. Her face showed that she knew at once why Nicky had come and Nicky's face told her that the news was not good.

'We've found a body,' Nicky began, 'along with your husband's wallet. His car was parked nearby.'

'You think it's Tommy?' asked Lucy in a low voice.

'Well, we still have to make a formal identification.' Through dental records, probably, she thought, unless Lucy had a strong stomach.

'How did he die?' asked Lucy. Her hand had gone to the neck of her T-shirt which she was pulling at nervously.

'We're not certain yet,' said Nicky carefully.

The next bit would be delicate. At the beginning of June, a week before Lucy had reported him missing, Tommy Sunderland had been to his local police station at Delwoodley and made an accusation against his wife and a man called Sean Brook, a sergeant from his old company, saying that they wanted him dead.

'Mrs Sunderland,' she said. 'How did Tommy seem to you just before his disappearance?'

'How do you mean?'

'Well,' continued Nicky, 'the last time we spoke you told me his career had been ended by an injury. That he'd been shot during an army training exercise.'

'Yeah, right through the head. They were amazed he survived.'

'And according to you,' persisted Nicky, 'this had brought about a change in his personality.'

'Not just "according to me",' said Lucy firmly. 'The army doctors told me it damaged his brain. Before, he really was the kindest of men. After, he was for ever turning on me.' Her voice dropped. 'The day before he disappeared we had an almighty row and he stormed off. I figured he'd come back when he'd calmed down a bit.'

'And the next morning you reported him missing.'

'Yeah.'

Lucy's dark brown eyes met Nicky's, and didn't waver.

Meanwhile, Ken was having pretty much the same conversation with Sean Brook. He was still a regular soldier, so Ken had had to come to the army base to find him. It gave him the creeps, reminded him a bit too much of his own training at Hendon.

Sean was not a big bloke, but he was wiry and muscular, the sort of bloke who would surprise you in a fight. His brown hair was cut army-regulation short and he had a tidy, clipped moustache. Ken asked him to sit down.

'You know Thomas Sunderland, I believe?' he began.

'What's happened?' asked Sean at once.

'I've got some bad news, I'm afraid,' said Ken silkily. 'We found his body in Spinney Woods this morning and we believe the circumstances to be suspicious.' He watched Sean's reaction closely. 'You knew that he was missing, I take it?'

Sean nodded.

'Did you also know about the allegations that he made?' Sean Brook gave a puzzled frown, so Ken continued. 'He reckoned that you and his wife were having an affair and that you were planning to kill him.'

'Kill him?' Sean seemed genuinely surprised.

'He was reported missing about three weeks ago, June the 9th,' said Ken, changing tack. 'Where were you then?'

'Um, Cyprus,' said Sean, thinking back. 'Training exercise. Flew out on the 4th, returned on the 11th.'

Out of the country. That shook Ken a bit but he recovered himself.

'So you were out of the country at that time? I'd need corroboration of that.'

Sean Brook flashed Ken a contemptuous look.

'There's about two hundred squaddies can tell you I was in Cyprus. Will that be enough for you?' he asked defiantly.

Al sat alone at the big pine kitchen table. The house was quiet, except for Boozie's panting as he sought some relief from the heat of the day by stretching out on the cool tiled floor.

After her dad had been called out, Joanna had offered to stay with her, as Marty had to get to work, but she had sent her to Wickton Road. It was really easier to be on her own, instead of people tiptoeing round her and making her cups of tea and trying to be kind. If other people were there she had to put on a performance for them, either a cheerful performance or something which was a mockery of the real sadness she was feeling, just so that they could feel better. Dad understood. With him, she could just be sad, but the others . . . Slowly she took the photographs out of the envelope; she hadn't felt she could look at them till the funeral was over. Now they brought it all back. Ben in Snowdonia. Ben, Simon, herself and Kathy that last morning at Devil's Kitchen. Ben clowning around, waving the map in the air, the wind tugging at it. Ben in his silly hat. And the two of them, the camera held at arm's length, on their last night together, after they had made love. No. She still couldn't look at them. It was too soon. Quickly she slid the photographs back in the envelope, and, getting to her feet, stuffed them in the dresser drawer. She pushed her hair back fiercely from her face and, as she did so, caught sight of her Mum's old cookbooks. That was what she would do. Mum had always said how soothing it was. She would cook.

Ken's felt-tipped pen squeaked on the shiny paper of the flip-chart. Both he and Nicky were back from their respective interviews with Lucy Sunderland and Sean Brook, neither of them wholly convinced by what they had heard.

'The army's confirmed that Brook's company was in Cyprus at the time that Tommy was reported missing. It doesn't mean he didn't do it, though.' Ken began writing dates on the chart as he spoke. 'Look . . . it starts here, June the 2nd. Tommy makes a statement at Delwoodley alleging that his wife and Brook are conspiring to kill him. Delwoodley police contact his GP, who's Dr Stevens incidentally, and she confirms that he's unstable, so they shelve it. Two days later, June the 4th, Brook flies out to Cyprus.'

'And June the 9th Mrs Sunderland reports her husband missing.'

Ken wrote June 9th on his chart, followed by June 11th, the date Brook returned from Cyprus.

'But if Brook's involved,' said Nicky, 'it would have to be before June 4th or after the 11th.'

'And more likely to have been before,' said Ken, recapping the marker pen. 'Otherwise, where was Tommy when Brook was in Cyprus? He was seen alive – at Delwoodley – on June the 2nd. Forty-eight hours before Brook left. So if it turns out that Tommy died some time within that forty-eight hours, Brook's back in the frame.' He rubbed his forehead. 'Let's hope the PM can help us with the time of death.'

After he had finished at Spinney Woods, Paul sat in the Discovery with the window down, listening to the pigeons calling, and debated what to do. He didn't want to crowd Al. He knew from his own experience that sometimes, all you wanted was to be on your own, so in the end he rang her to try to gauge how she was. When she answered the phone she informed him cheerily that she was cooking supper and asked what time he'd be back. This rather scotched Paul's unformed question about whether he should come home or not, so he told her seven o'clockish and rang Wickton Road to say he'd be in for afternoon surgery. Julia was ecstatic. Shaaban had been called out to a woman with chest pains, and she promptly passed Paul a couple of his home visits, which he felt he had no choice but to accept. When he finally made it back to Wickton Road, Joanna stopped him in the corridor and motioned him into her office.

They had had no time together to speak of since their abortive weekend away. He had spent all his free time with Al, just sitting with her, saying nothing. Joanna hadn't complained, hadn't pushed it. But they hadn't quite reverted to being 'just good friends'. There was something between them, something unfinished, something barely started. And when the time was right again . . . She was coming to supper tonight. Maybe then . . .

Joanna closed the door behind them and went to sit at her desk. Paul sat uneasily on the chair facing her. This seemed very formal.

'Are you involved with the Tommy Sunderland death?' she asked abruptly.

'Well, yes,' said Paul. So it was to be business, not pleasure. 'Why, what's your connection with him?'

'WPC Cudworth came to see me this morning to see what I could tell her about him,' Joanna explained. 'He became a patient of mine about a year ago when he left the army,' she went on. Paul hadn't realized that Sunderland had been registered at Wickton Road. 'I put him in a box clearly marked paranoid. Told the police as much when they asked me earlier this month because he'd made a complaint about people being out to get him. They didn't believe him and neither did I and, well, now it's too late to listen.'

'Look,' replied Paul reasonably. 'You told the police what you knew of his condition and that's all you could do.'

'Yeah, but what happens if I was wrong? If there *was* someone out to get him?'

'That's not your concern.' He knew what Joanna was like when she got these crises of confidence. She was a good doctor and she should have had more faith in herself.

'Maybe not,' said Joanna, but her tone was defiant. 'But I'm not going to let it rest. I'm going to try and see his old Army MO.'

'What?' This seemed to be taking it too far.

'We were at the Middlesex together,' she said quickly, in explanation. 'Perhaps he can shed some light.'

Paul gave a half-laugh.

'Are you quite sure this isn't all about looking up some old flame?' he enquired.

'Oh, well, now you come to mention it . . .' Joanna flashed him a sly smile. 'Oh, Paul! Your face!'

Marty didn't exactly get the warmest of receptions when he turned up at work over an hour later than he'd said he'd be.

'It was a funeral, Mr Smith,' he protested. 'I couldn't just walk out in the middle.'

Smith said something scathing back and stomped off, leaving Angie to tell Marty about the exciting list of chores which awaited him. But when, after he'd washed a pile of pans, mopped the floor and sterilized the cutlery, Smith couldn't resist coming over and finding fault, Marty snapped.

'This is what you call a clean saucepan, is it?' his boss had demanded.

'No, that's my idea of a saucepan that should have been chucked out years ago,' retorted Marty.

'I don't know what irritates me more, Dangerfield,' said Smith, in that cod-headmasterly way of his, 'your incompetence or your attitude.'

Fury boiled inside Marty but he didn't sweep all the pans off the draining board on to the floor or smash the chipped, thick glass tumblers. Instead he calmly undid the strings of his apron.

'Well, I don't know what irritates me more about you, Mr Smith: your lack of humour or your complete absence of humanity,' he said with dignity. 'But that's not something I'm going to have to dwell on. Thank you very much for teaching me how to wash up saucepans – and goodbye.'

It was the longest conversation he'd ever had with Mr Smith. And he was determined it would be the last. Flinging his apron on to the draining board, he walked out.

Afterwards of course, as he mooched around the hospital corridors, killing time for the rest of the day, he began to have regrets. Not about leaving that stinky job, because Smith had had it coming to him, but how was he going to tell his Dad. He had to be realistic. As a failed dishwasher, his employment prospects were zero. He could imagine the conversation: 'Oh, Dad. D'you remember when you said that I should have stayed on at school a bit longer and not thrown myself on the scrapheap? Well, you were right.' He was going to look such a prat.

He didn't have the bottle to tell his dad that evening, and of course Joanna was round to supper, which Al had cooked, and there were all these solicitous remarks about had Smith given him a hard time, and hang on in there, Marty, give as good as you get. He excused himself early and went up for a bath, but not before he had found himself accepting a lift to work next day from his dad. Terrific. So now he'd have to be dropped off at the hospital, then find somewhere to hang around all day.

What with Marty skulking about, and Al excusing herself to write a letter, the evening was rather muted and Joanna said she'd welcome an early night. All this grief was exhausting. Tomorrow was her morning off but she'd arranged to go and see Sunderland's MO, Colonel Colclough, or Lee as she called him, at ten and she wanted to read up on Sunderland's notes before she went to bed. Paul walked out with her to the car.

'Al's thinking of going back to university straight away,' he said.

'Is that wise? It must be nearly the end of term now.'

'Yeah, well, I've told her I think she should rest for a few days.' Paul shrugged. 'But ultimately it's her decision.'

Joanna reached up and put the back of her hand to his cheek.

'Maybe while Al's like this, we should keep us on hold, yeah?' she said softly.

Paul thought about it, then nodded regretfully. He bent his head and kissed her lingeringly, but not for as long as he would have liked.

'I'll see you in the morning,' he said.

'Come on,' said Ken to Nicky as soon as she got into work the next day. 'We're going visiting.' He handed her a lidded polystyrene cup of coffee. 'You can drink it in the car.'

'You spoil me,' said Nicky, taking the cup. 'Anyone I know?'

Ken held the door open for her.

'The name Lucy Sunderland ring a bell?'

Lucy Sunderland's flat was a surprise. In a modern block in a quiet part of town, it was feminine in the extreme, all pastel colours and flowered wallpaper, every surface cluttered with cut glass and the tiny crystal animals which she obviously collected. Nicky tried to imagine Tommy Sunderland, all six foot of him, clumping round in this tiny space, and failed.

Ken, looking equally out of place, asked Lucy to sit down. She sat bolt upright on the edge of the pink Dralon settee, fiddling with the fringe on a cushion.

'You told DC Green yesterday that your relationship with Sean Brook was strictly platonic. Are you still saying that that was the case?' One thing you could say about Ken: he didn't bother about the niceties.

Lucy paused, and fiddled a bit more. Then she looked straight at him.

'I'm sorry, I didn't mean to lie.'

'So why did you?' asked Nicky, thinking how unconvincing she'd been anyway.

'Panicked,' said Lucy with a nervous giggle. 'Thought you'd jump to conclusions.'

'You mean that perhaps your husband wasn't so paranoid after all?' asked Ken. 'And that maybe you and Brook really were planning to kill him?'

'No!' Lucy was vehement. 'We'd never hurt Tommy!'

'But you're saying that you are having an affair with his best friend?'

Lucy leaned forward, her big brown eyes doe-like, imploring.

'That was the other reason I didn't tell you about Sean and me. I was ashamed. I mean, I know how other people'll see it. They'll think I deserted him when he needed me. But he changed when he left the army. Believe me, I tried to help him! So did Sean. We both loved Tommy. But the Tommy we knew was gone. In some ways it would have been kinder if . . .'

'If the bullet on that training exercise had killed him?'

Lucy looked down at her feet in their sparkling white trainers.

'Yes.'

When Ken and Nicky had gone, she phoned Sean.

'Sean? The police have just been here!'

There was no doubt about it, thought Joanna, Lee Colclough was gorgeous. Tall, dark and handsome, he had that pink-cheeked, clear-eyed, well-fed look that can attach only to someone who does not have to live life as lesser mortals do; that is, to the very rich and to commissioned officers in the armed forces. Lee had been through public school, medical school and now the army. He had never cooked a meal in his life – even on exercises there were squaddies to do that for him – never ironed a shirt, never had to unblock a drain. He had never had to fish around in the dirty washing basket for a pair of socks because he'd run out. He had never had to navigate round Doncaster with a child wailing in the back seat and a dog being sick in the front. No wonder he looked so well, and didn't seem to have aged at all.

'It's lovely to see you again, Joanna,' he said, as he held open a swing door for her to pass. 'Couldn't believe it when I got your call.'

'It's been a few years, hasn't it?' smiled Joanna.

'You're as pretty as ever, though,' said Lee. Joanna fixed him with a sceptical look and he brought himself up short. 'I know we're not supposed to say that sort of thing these days . . . but the army's one of the last bastions of male chauvinism.'

'Isn't that why you joined?' teased Joanna.

He shot her a look, the same look which had caused many a sleepless night in the nurses' home.

'You always did see right through me.'

He took her through into the officers' mess. If you wanted the bachelor life, this was the place to have it, thought Joanna, as she took in the regimental portraits on the walls, the sagging armchairs and tidy racks of newspapers which were probably taken away and ironed between readers. A white-jacketed steward brought them tea.

'Did you see much of Tommy Sunderland when he was in the army?' she asked, declining sugar and taking her cup.

Lee put two lumps in his tea – where else did you see lump sugar, these days? – and stirred it, the spoon tinkling against the crested bone china. He sat back in his chair.

'Too much,' he said, 'after his accident. His injury left him prone to severe depression and mood swings. It was clear he couldn't continue in the army.'

'So you agree that he was paranoid?' Joanna asked, seeking reassurance.

'Oh, yes,' agreed Lee. 'Mind you, considering what's happened . . . you remember the old joke: just because you're paranoid, it doesn't mean people aren't out to get you.'

'Well, someone got Sunderland, all right,' said Joanna uneasily.

'Buried him in a shallow grave, you said?'

'Yeah, it was odd – hidden with branches and things.'

'Hmm.' Lee pursed his mouth, considering. 'Perhaps not so odd.'

The steward returned with a plate of warm scones, jam and cream.

'Tuck in,' ordered Lee. 'Before the defence cuts do.'

Maybe it was the fact that Joanna was involved in Tommy Sunderland's case, maybe it was because Paul had nothing better to do, but he found himself spending most of the time between surgeries that day at the police station, closeted with Ken and Nicky, awaiting the latest titbit from Terri or from the pathologist. It was a long, hot afternoon and, at first, they seemed to be going round in circles. The pathologist's report, when it arrived, concluded that, contrary to their expectations, Sunderland had not actually been dead when he had been put in the grave. He had been buried alive and had suffocated.

Nicky was adamant.

'I'd say this puts Lucy in the clear,' she asserted.

'How d'you reckon that?' enquired Ken, looking up from the detail of the report.

'Burying a man while he's still half alive, leaving him to suffocate, I don't see a woman doing that.'

'Got to be some brute of a male, right?' Ken challenged her.

'Well, I agree with Nicky,' cut in Paul. 'I mean, if Sunderland was still alive when he was dragged from the car to the woods, then Lucy couldn't have done it on her own.'

'Who said she did do it on her own?' Ken persisted.

'Well if Brook was in Cyprus when Sunderland went missing . . .'

229

'No, Paul. Brook was in Cyprus when Sunderland was *reported* missing. And it was Lucy who reported it. Brook could have killed Sunderland and flown off to Cyprus thinking he had a hell of an alibi lined up. Maybe they hired someone. Whatever. They're still in the frame. The pair of them.'

Paul and Nicky exchanged glances. When Ken got an idea in his head . . . But later that afternoon, when Ken had just sent Nicky to the van outside to get them a cornet each, Terri came up with something else.

'Sunderland's blood contains Temazepam,' she announced proudly.

'So what does this tell us?' asked Ken eagerly. 'Could it have killed him?'

'No, there's not enough,' replied Terri. 'But he'd sleep well.'

'So they drugged him.' Ken turned to Paul with his 'told you so' look in his eyes.

Nicky came in, minus the ice-creams.

'Boss, I've just had word Brook's with Mrs Sunderland,' she explained. 'Are we going to pick them up?'

As Ken and Nicky climbed the stairs they could hear raised voices from Lucy's flat.

'Lover's tiff?' whispered Nicky.

Ken turned his mouth down at the corners.

'I wouldn't fall out with Brook, not if I was her.'

At that moment, just as they reached the landing, there was the sound of smashing glass from inside the flat and a shriek from Lucy Sunderland. Ken was about to hammer on the door when it opened and he stopped with his fist raised in the air, to be confronted by Sean Brook. He lowered his fist to his side.

'Sergeant Brook . . . need to ask you a few more questions,' he said charmingly.

Brook just stared at him. He was cradling his right hand

to his chest. Beyond him, in the doorway to the sitting room, Lucy was sobbing. At her feet were the remains of several crystal vases and some of her glass menagerie.

'Nasty cut you've got there, Mr Brook,' said Nicky, looking at Sean's hand which was oozing blood on to his shirt. 'We'll get a doctor to have a look at that down at the station.'

Everything always happened at once, thought Joanna. She ushered Marty who had, according to Julia, been hanging round the waiting room with a face like a wet weekend, through to her room and, as she closed the door, the phone rang.

'Colonel Colclough for you.' Julia sounded impressed.

'Thanks, put him through,' said Joanna warmly. It did no harm to keep Julia guessing about her private life. With her hand over the mouthpiece she gestured to Marty to sit down.

'I was just wondering if I could have a word,' Marty said stumblingly. 'If it's convenient.'

Joanna nodded encouragingly at him as Lee's voice came down the line.

'Joanna, I wonder . . . could you bear to come and see me again?' he asked. 'I've located some more information about the Tommy Sunderland case.'

This was unexpected.

'Well, yes.' Joanna recovered herself. 'I'll come round straight after surgery, say half six?'

'Fine. I'll see you then.'

Joanna debated within herself the relative merits of winding Paul up a bit more about her past association with Lee, and having him with her. She knew which she'd prefer.

'Oh, and Lee, would you mind if I bring a colleague with me?'

Having finished her call, Joanna turned to Marty with a smile.

'Sorry about that. What can I do for you?'

It all came tumbling out. How he had packed in his job and he didn't know how he was going to tell his dad and how he was a hopeless failure and how his dad would go on at him ... Joanna couldn't help smiling. Marty invariably made things much worse for himself by imagining the worst possible scenario instead of just getting it over with.

'Well, you can't keep up this charade indefinitely,' she said, hearing how he'd had to accept a lift to work from Paul that morning.

'I know. That's why I came to see you. Um ... what do you think about me working in disabled sports?'

Joanna's first thought was that it was a bizarre departure. Then she remembered something Paul had said about how Marty had got involved in wheelchair basketball matches, and with a girl called Carol who was in a wheelchair.

'I think that could be a great idea,' she said cautiously.

'I get such a buzz from it,' he enthused. 'D'you know how I could get into it or do you have any contacts or anything?'

'I don't think it works like that, Marty,' said Joanna, as gently as she could. 'My guess is that you'd have to become a physio. Which means going back to school. A-levels.'

Marty looked miserable.

'Which is what Dad said in the first place.'

Joanna glanced at her watch. Her first patient was due any minute.

'Uh-huh,' she smiled. 'Look, do you want me to tell him?'

'N-no,' said Marty reluctantly. 'I think I've got to do it.'

'I think you have too,' she smiled. 'He'll probably be fine about it.'

'Yeah?' Marty looked disbelieving. 'And I have it on

good authority that Luton are going straight to the top of the Premier League.'

Sean Brook was a professional soldier. He had dodged sniper bullets in Northern Ireland and policed the so-called 'safe havens' in Bosnia: he was hardly going to be rattled by the odd few hours in police custody. And after years of army discipline – and canteen food – he was hardly going to get cabin fever banged up in a detention cell. Even so, Ken found him a tough customer to interview. He sat across the table from Ken, his bandaged hand held loosely in his lap. He answered Ken's opening questions calmly and even when Ken turned up the heat a bit, he didn't show a flicker of emotion. He must have absorbed every word of his training about how to stay cool under interrogation because, half an hour in, Brook was still batting back every question Ken asked him. Ken didn't like it; Nicky could tell.

'You weren't in England when Tommy was reported missing. Maybe he was already dead by then?'

'I had no reason to kill him.'

Ken registered surprise.

'You were involved with his missus. She told us.'

'Their marriage was dead, all right?'

Brook sounded slightly on the defensive. Ken seized the nearest thing he'd had to an opening since the interview had begun.

'The marriage might have been,' he said, forcing Sean Brook to look at him, 'but Tommy was very much alive. And in the way. Brain-damaged, unpredictable. Could have caused a lot of trouble if he'd felt like it . . . and he probably did feel like it.'

Sean Brook stared Ken out.

'If I'd wanted him to disappear, I'd have made a proper job of it,' he said mulishly. 'You'd never have found him.'

Ken sat back and folded his arms.

'There is that. You are a professional.'

'I've learned a few things in the army, that's all I'm saying.'

Ken leaned forward again.

'But the circumstances were tricky. You didn't have time to get the details right. You were supposed to be flying off on this training exercise . . .'

'I did fly off,' said Sean, patiently. This was the point at which most other prisoners would have begun losing their rag. 'The army have confirmed the dates, haven't they? I never killed Tommy.'

'Then who did, do you think?' enquired Ken, leaning back again and stretching his legs out in front of him. 'Lucy?'

Sean looked incredulous.

'Sure, he was drugged,' continued Ken, 'and she would have found it hard to drag him through the woods and bury him, but not impossible.'

Nicky suddenly remembered the dumb-bells in Lucy's treatment room, the exercise bike at the flat.

'You don't believe that?' Sean demanded.

Ken shook his head.

'' Cos I think you're old-fashioned about these things. You wouldn't let a woman do your dirty work for you. Well, would you?'

Sean Brook looked at Ken as if the question were not worthy of a reply.

'Do I get a cup of tea?' he asked.

'Why not?' said Ken, tired of making no progress. He leaned over to click off the tape recorder. 'Interview suspended eighteen thirty-five.'

'This is a bit odd, isn't it?' asked Paul. 'Is dragging me off to meet Lee your idea of a cosy threesome? Or am I just the chaperon?'

Joanna smiled broadly but she didn't take her eyes off the road.

'Colonel Colclough to you,' she replied.

She had to stifle another smile when she introduced Paul to Lee and noticed the polite restraint with which they shook hands. Lee had obviously expected some old fuddy-duddy instead of Paul, and she knew that other men always found Lee irritatingly good-looking. They were in Lee's cream-painted office this time. Lee motioned them to sit down and installed himself behind his desk. Any awkwardness between him and Paul evaporated as he started to explain why he had asked Joanna to come back.

'This morning,' he began, 'I didn't give you the full picture. I've now discussed matters with the station commander, and he agrees that I should pass on to you additional information.' He looked up, and glanced at both Paul and Joanna. Joanna smiled encouragingly. Lee looked down at the file on his desk, then spoke. 'I've always believed that Sunderland's brain injury was self-inflicted. Despite what his records might say.'

'You mean he shot himself in the head?' asked Paul.

Lee held up his hand to dismiss this idea.

'Oh, no. The injury happened on the rifle range, as recorded. But it appears that Sunderland just wandered on to a rifle range during practice. Now an army rifle range is a clearly designated area. Live ammunition is always used. Every soldier knows that.'

Joanna looked over at Paul as Lee continued: 'His records say it was an accident . . . I've got no proof. But it looked very much to me like an attempted suicide.'

'So you think he tried to take his own life even before his brain injury?' Paul asked.

'Yes.' Lee sounded grave.

Paul sat forward in his chair, his hands clasped between his knees.

'I'm sorry, I'm not quite with you. What bearing does this have on the case?'

'I think it perfectly possible that a soldier could make his own grave and get himself into it. Digging shallow hides is a common military exercise.'

Paul looked sceptical.

'His hands were tied together behind his back with a plastic clip.'

'Applied to the thumbs? Yes.' Colclough was matter-of-fact. He opened the middle drawer of his desk and pulled out a pair of cable clips. He demonstrated as he talked. 'Standard army issue. With practice, easy to do to yourself, even behind the back. Now, the gag would be no problem; he could have put it on before he tied his thumbs together.'

'Yes, but how would he lift the canopy of branches and get into the grave?' asked Paul incredulously.

Lee Colclough picked up an exercise book and a pencil. Raising the book at an angle of about sixty degrees to the desk, he propped it up with the pencil.

'Rolls himself into the grave, having bound and gagged himself,' he said dispassionately, demonstrating with a finger and then knocking away the pencil with one movement. The exercise book, its prop removed, flopped flat on to the surface of the desk. 'Kicks away the stick that's propping up the branches, bracken or whatever – he's now concealed. However, the next bit is more tricky,' Lee continued. 'It's no easy thing just to lie down and asphyxiate, no matter how determined you are to die. It's sheer human impulse to seek oxygen.'

Paul glanced at Joanna. He couldn't see any harm in sharing with Lee what Terri had discovered.

'He was drugged,' he said. 'We assumed by his attacker.'

'It fits, Paul,' said Joanna, wonderingly. 'He must have taken Temazepam himself so he was already losing consciousness by the time he got into the grave.

So he didn't give himself a chance to have any second thoughts.'

'But what about the car?' Paul asked, as she drove them both back to his place for a drink.

'Well, I think he left the car there as a marker because he needed to be sure his body was found.' Joanna changed down a gear to overtake a tractor. 'I've been trying to imagine the thoughts going through his head. His whole world had disintegrated. His three loves – the army, his best friend, Lucy – well, they all betrayed him. So what was there to live for? Except that he wasn't going to let Sean and Lucy get off scot-free because they'd done the dirty on him and now he's repaying the favour by getting them framed for murder.'

'You genuinely believe Sunderland killed himself and make it look like murder?'

'You heard what Lee said,' replied Joanna, craning this way and that at a junction. 'Sunderland had a death wish even before the accident. Combine that with paranoia and delusions . . .' She pulled out on to the main Warwick road. 'Paul, you have to speak to Ken.'

Paul looked out of the window. Two men were carting hay in the twilight in a field beside the road. Why couldn't his life be as simple? Sow the seed, cut the crop. He knew a farmer's life was far from simple, of course, and fraught with just as many decisions and choices as his own, but did Joanna seriously expect him to tell Ken that he'd been taken for a ride by Sunderland, that charging Sean Brook was just what the corpse wanted him to do, that it was all a sick man's fantasy, a macabre joke? He could hear Ken laughing already.

To give Ken his due, he didn't laugh when Paul told him Joanna's theory next day, but he did look as if he were thinking of sending Paul for a psychiatric report himself.

'You really believe it was malicious suicide?' he said. 'I'd have thought people about to top themselves were beyond playing daft games.'

'Sunderland was a sick man,' said Paul. Joanna had done a good job of convincing him. 'Look, he did what a suicide bomber does. He had a cause – to destroy Lucy and Sean Brook – and he was prepared to die for it.'

'Sorry, Paul, I'm keeping Brook here till I've firmed up my enquiries. I'm still waiting for the entomological report from the path lab.'

'No, you're not. Got it here.' Nicky entered with a slim green file. 'Can you translate this for us, Paul?' she asked. 'Terri's in court.'

Paul took the report from her and scanned it.

'Does it give us anything?' asked Ken impatiently.

'Hang on a minute . . .' Paul read on. 'Yes, it certainly does.'

'Well, don't keep it to yourself!' Ken was literally breathing down his neck.

'Ken, according to this report there's no way that Brook could have killed Tommy Sunderland. They've established the time Tommy died. Oh yes, this is very clever stuff.'

'What?'

'Well,' explained Paul, 'what they've discovered is that there's a particular species of bluebottle that landed on Tommy Sunderland's body and laid some eggs, right? And there were empty pupae cases on the body when it was found. In other words, some of the pupae had started to hatch. Now then, in this species, the length of time between the flies laying the eggs and the pupae hatching is twenty-one days.'

'So Sunderland had lain there for that long?'

'The body was found on the 29th of June, wasn't it? So, tracking back twenty-one days from 29th June give us the 8th of June. So Tommy Sunderland died on or about June the 8th. And Brook left on . . .'

'The 4th of June and came back on the 11th,' supplied Nicky. 'So it can't have been Brook.'

'He's not your man, Ken.'

Ken sank down on the corner of the desk, his face a mask of disbelief.

'So Brook's got a cast-iron alibi and it's a maggot! It's a maggot!'

Keith Lardner showed Sean Brook out of the station.

'Good luck, Mr Brook. Hope everything works out for you.'

Brook gave him a sardonic smile.

'Yeah. Cheers, mate.'

As Keith watched, Lucy Sunderland, who had been waiting in the shade of a plane tree across the street, ran forward to meet him, calling his name. Ken had told Lardner that Sean had cut his hand when he had swept a shelf of her glass ornaments to the ground, when he had felt that she believed, just as the police did, that he had killed Tommy Sunderland. Ignoring her now, Sean Brook kept on walking, down to the end of the street. Lucy ran alongside him, pleading with him.

'You just don't get it, do you?' she cried. 'This is what Tommy wanted. Me and you, suspicious of each other, not trusting each other. He knew exactly how to get to each one of us, you his mate and me his wife. He thought he knew us that well.'

Sean Brook stopped briefly to face her, but only to snap: 'Yeah, well I can sympathize with him. I thought I knew you pretty well too.'

Turning from her, he walked another few steps, but Lucy tugged at his arm, shouting now.

'Sean, let's just stop this, shall we? Let's just leave Tommy out of this. It's just you and me now.'

Sean Brook shook her off and carried on walking. Lucy's shouts had become sobs.

'If you walk away,' she cried, bending forward as if in pain, her fists clenched on her thighs, 'he'll have won!'

Sean Brook stopped in his tracks. Slowly he turned around. Lucy's sobbing stopped as she tried to gauge his reaction. Was he going to shout back, or . . . but she could see from his face that he was not going to shout. There was something very moving, Keith Lardner thought, about seeing a tough nut like Sean Brook display some emotion. His face seemed to crumple, as if he was going to cry and he held his arms open wide. Lucy flung herself at him and buried her face in his shoulder. One arm went round her, the other hand came up to cradle her head protectively as she sobbed again, in relief this time.

Still standing on the step in the warm sunshine, Keith Lardner smiled to himself. If there was one thing he was a sucker for, it was a happy ending.

The picnic had been Joanna's idea. She'd phoned Al after breakfast and suggested it, with the idea of giving Al some reason for getting through the day. She knew that Al was still feeling bruised and tender, her grief a sore place which would suddenly throb without warning. Al had gone back to university as she had wished, but it had not been a success. On the first night back, she had got extremely drunk and maudlin with Simon, who had had the sense to ring Paul and tell him. Paul and Joanna had driven over and found Al in Simon's room, her teeth chattering over the rim of a mug of black coffee, her face blotched with crying. Gently they had gathered her up, led her downstairs and had driven her home, putting her to bed with her old teddy bear in her old room. Paul had blamed himself for letting her go back, for not being able to help her more, but, as Joanna had said, there wasn't a handy manual giving advice on 'How To Console Your Daughter When Her Boyfriend Dies'. You just had to follow your instincts.

'Yes, well, mine let me down – and her,' said Paul.

Joanna put her arms round him.

'Well, I don't think she'd want to swap you.' She kissed his ear. 'And I wouldn't either.'

They'd arranged to meet on the riverbank, by the weir, at six-thirty. Joanna and Al arrived together, though from different directions. Al was lugging a hamper; Joanna had a picnic rug and a bottle of Chardonnay and a wine cooler. She kissed Al on the cheek and they laid out the rug in the last of the sun. Al unpacked olive ciabatta and Brie and goat's cheese and a quiche and some salad. Joanna uncorked the wine and poured them each a glass. Then they lay back, feeling the sun warm and cherish them. At seven there was still no sign of Paul, so Joanna refilled their glasses.

'It's his turn to drive anyway,' she said in justification.

Al turned her glass so that the evening sunlight, bouncing off the river, refracted and sparkled within it. She gave a visible and audible sigh.

'If Ben was still here,' she said, 'who could say what would have happened. I just can't stop thinking about that. What nobody realized, not even him, was how badly I was falling for him. I was really serious about him.'

Joanna put out a hand and took Al's in hers.

'You can't live your life by ifs,' she said gently. 'You've just got to get on with it.'

The moment was broken by Boozie, who ran up, barking, and nosed between them.

'This looks good.' Paul strolled to join them, Boozie's lead in his hand. 'Any left for me?'

In reply, Joanna held up the three-quarters empty bottle.

' 'Fraid not,' she grinned.

Paul crouched down between the two of them. He rested his hand on Joanna's bare shoulder.

'How are you?'

She lifted her shoulder and tilted her head slightly so

that he could feel the pressure of her warm cheek on his hand.

'Fine.'

Paul eased himself down on to the rug.

'Al? Feeling better?'

'A bit better,' said Al bravely.

'Just a bit? No more than that?' asked Paul lightly. He reached out and broke off a couple of grapes. 'Ah, well, a bit better's good enough for me.'

Both Al and Marty seemed to be slowly sorting themselves out. Early that morning, when he'd been feeding Mr Harris, Marty had come and found him in the aviary. Joanna had warned him that Marty had something to say which concerned his future, but she hadn't gone into any details.

'The thing is . . .' Marty had begun, 'um, well . . . you know I've not really been happy in the job at the hospital and it's . . . er . . . not just 'cos I had a Hitler for a boss, but, well, it wasn't going anywhere, so . . . I've decided to quit.'

Paul continued feeding Mr Harris scraps of chicken liver.

'Um, yeah,' continued Marty. 'So I'm out of work. So I'm going to go back to school and have another crack at my A-levels, and hopefully go on and train and become a physio.'

Paul thought he'd made him suffer enough. Turning with a smile, he said: 'That sounds great.'

'Yeah?' Marty sounded amazed to be getting off so lightly.

'Yeah,' Paul confirmed.

'Oh, right. Good.'

Paul looked out over the river where it tumbled over the weir. One minute it was so smooth, the next, everything was turned upside down. But with Al and Marty back on course, maybe there would be time for himself and Joanna. As if reading his thoughts, she smiled broadly.

'OK, let's eat,' she said.

13

Paul had known Mary Blanchard for years, ever since he had moved to Warwick. She was a local GP who seemed to have an interest in everything. If you wanted someone to sit on a committee, raise funds for a scanner, or raise awareness for enuresis sufferers, Mary was your woman. She had once, before Joanna, before Kate, had an interest in Paul, but it had been only about eighteen months after Celia's death, and he had felt too raw to do anything about it, though the signals had penetrated even the depths of his grief. After a couple of polite refusals on his part, Mary had backed off; nothing had been said but she had contrived things so that they saw less and less of each other. Nowadays Paul met her from time to time at functions to do with the hospital, where she was active in maternity provision, but he hadn't seen her for six months when she phoned him late one evening out of the blue and asked him to go round.

When he got there, Mary told him a story which, if you'd asked him, Paul would have said simply did not happen, or certainly not to him. But Mary had made it happen. And now she wanted Paul to play a part.

She led him upstairs and into a darkened bedroom. Paul could hear the sound of measured breathing, the breathing of a child.

'I have to take medical supplies back to Peschkoveta tomorrow,' explained Mary. 'I want you to look after Adriana for me.'

Downstairs, she made them both coffee. She looked tired and drawn, the result not just of her present predicament but of the preceding six months, which she had spent, it transpired, doing relief work in Bosnia.

'I was working in a makeshift hospital in a safe area,' she explained, tucking her feet underneath her on the sofa and curling her fingers round her coffee mug. 'The building next door was hit. We rushed over to see if there were any survivors. We found the bodies of a family – father, mother, infant – and a voice calling. It was Adriana. I smuggled her into Britain on my passport. I couldn't leave her there. Her wounds are healing but I have to go back and she needs to be looked after by someone I can trust.'

It was the last thing Paul needed. Though much better, Al was still stumbling her way through her grief over Ben. Marty was looking for a summer job to tide him over till he went back to school in September. And Joanna . . . well, Joanna had waited long enough for a share of his attention. He wanted to make things work with her. He needed to make things work. Yet beside little Adriana's pressing need, none of these seemed to have much of a claim. What could he say but yes?

'You're still the master of emotional blackmail, Mary,' he smiled, remembering how she had always been able to get money, time and commitment out of people.

'I'm hoping you're still an easy touch,' she said, relief spreading across her features as she sensed his capitulation. 'It won't be for long, Paul. I'll be back in a few weeks.'

She wanted him to take Adriana then, under cover of darkness. Paul objected, saying it would make things much more confusing for the little girl.

'Have you explained to her what's going to happen?' he asked.

'Well, as best I can,' said Mary. 'She can't really take it in. And she doesn't actually speak much English. How's your Serbo-Croat?'

The situation was so bizarre anyway, thought Paul, as he scooped up the sleeping child and placed her in the back of the Discovery, that snatching her from her bed in the middle of the night seemed quite fitting. And anyway, she had had so much disruption, so much loss, that maybe nothing seemed strange to her any longer. Maybe she had got beyond the stage of needing to know. Driving through the deserted streets of Warwick with her, and along the empty lanes, it did occur to him that this probably compromised every professional oath he had ever sworn and totally undermined his position of trust in the community. Harbouring an illegal immigrant . . . he'd surely be struck off the police surgeon register for that. It wasn't exactly riding a bicycle without lights.

Back at Church House, he led the sleepy child upstairs and indicated that she should wait in his bedroom. He felt that the least he could do, rather than put her in the spare room, was to share his room with her for this first night, or the few hours of it that remained. He crept into Al's room and unearthed her sleeping bag from the bottom of her wardrobe. Fetching a pillow from the airing cupboard, he made up a makeshift bed at the foot of his own, and helped Adriana into it. The wound Mary had referred to was a flesh wound to her thigh, and when her nightie rode up he could see that it was still oozing through the gauze pad which Mary had applied. There was obviously a secondary infection there. He could have a good look at it in the morning, maybe prescribe her some antibiotics. He stroked the little girl's hair back as she snuggled down on the pillow.

'Goodnight,' he said softly. 'Sleep well.'

Leaving his clothes where they fell, and pulling on some tracksuit bottoms for decency, Paul dragged back his duvet and climbed into bed. He shivered as the cool sheet made contact with his flesh, and shivered again when he thought of what he had taken on. Paul closed his eyes, his mind whirring, expecting to lie awake till the alarm went off, but he fell immediately into an enveloping darkness and was roused only by Marty's stunned call of 'Dad!'

Paul sat bolt upright in bed, blinking himself awake, his heart pounding. Then he remembered what he had done. A glance at the foot of the bed confirmed that Adriana had gone walkabout and explained Marty's startled reaction. He arrived in Marty's room to find his son cowering under the duvet and Adriana standing at the side of his bed, her head on one side, considering.

'Dad?'

Paul wondered where to begin.

It was Al's reaction which surprised him most, but then perhaps he took Al too much for granted. While Marty seemed to take Adriana's arrival in his stride – and was not slow to negotiate his pay per hour to act as child-minder while Paul was at work – Al was monosyllabic and unhelpful. Not at all like herself. But then grief did that to you, and there was no doubt she was still suffering for Ben. Not only did you not know who you were, you no longer knew who you wanted to be.

When Paul got to work, he found a message to ring Ken.

'We were chasing around trying to find you last night,' was Ken's greeting when he was put through. 'I had to get Dr Betts in.'

'Sorry, Ken.' Paul smiled his thanks at Julia, who had deposited a mug of coffee in front of him. 'I had to do someone a favour.' He had switched his mobile through to the answering machine when he had been moving Adriana from Mary's, and he had been too shattered to remember to check it for messages.

'Well, it'd be useful to know how we can get hold of you.' Ken paused. 'I don't think your colleague was too amused when we rang her at a quarter to one.'

'My colleague?'

'Joanna,' Ken explained, adding innocently and not

too convincingly, 'I hope I haven't dropped you in it.'

'Thanks, Ken,' said Paul, putting his coffee, which he had lifted to his lips, untasted back on the desk. 'I'll see you.'

Most importantly, he had to see Joanna. If he wasn't at home and he wasn't with her and he wasn't out with the police, she would have to be very incurious indeed not to wonder where he was at a quarter to one in the morning. Paul asked Julia to hold his patients for two minutes and went down the corridor. He listened at Joanna's door to establish whether she'd got a patient with her and, hearing no voices, tapped on the door and went in.

'Come in,' said Joanna sarcastically, since he already was in.

'You're cross,' said Paul.

'Why should I be cross?'

'Lack of sleep?' hazarded Paul.

'Look, Paul, you don't have to account for your movements to me, honestly.' Joanna slit open a letter with a savage finger. 'It's just that I don't like secrets.'

Paul nodded in agreement. He knew exactly what sort of secret Joanna was suspecting.

'Right, well, come for dinner tonight.'

'What for?' Joanna sounded suspicious.

'No secrets. I want you to meet her,' said Paul ingenuously. 'Seven o'clock.'

And he left before she could ask him any more.

He made sure that he was home on time for once, speeding through his evening patients, glad that Nick was on call. At home, everything was under control. Between them, Marty and Adriana had made the supper, laid the table and polished the glasses. Adriana greeted him shyly, though she seemed at ease in the house and had struck up a special relationship with Suki, normally the most antisocial of cats. Marty's day with Adriana seemed to have gone well: they had played in the garden, been for a walk to the village, fished for minnows in the brook and, by the sound of it, consumed their own body weights in ice-cream. Marty actually seemed to have enjoyed it. Paul braced himself for the announcement that he had changed his mind again, and was set on becoming a children's nanny.

'Where's Al?' Paul asked, taking the baked potatoes from the oven.

'In her room. She's not hungry,' replied Marty.

At that moment, the doorbell rang and Paul went to answer it. Joanna stood on the step, looking slightly flushed, in a coral-coloured T-shirt and cream trousers.

'I'm sure this is a big mistake,' she said at once.

'Come in,' said Paul.

Joanna hesitated, then stepped into the hall.

'You look beautiful.' Paul kissed her on the cheek – just to keep her guessing – and led her towards the dining room. 'Come and meet Adriana.'

Unsure of what to expect, Joanna followed Paul into the dining room. They never used the dining room except on special occasions. Still, this Adriana must be special. She had obviously captivated Paul.

The dining room was empty. Paul looked around, as puzzled as she was, and called: 'Adriana?'

Joanna saw the curtains shake as badly-stifled giggles emanated from behind them. Then Marty appeared, pushing a small girl in front of him.

'This is Adriana,' explained Paul, 'my secret friend from Peschkoveta. Adriana is going to be staying with us for a while. Adriana, meet Joanna.'

'My dad's not-so-secret friend,' supplied Marty.

Joanna, still bemused, took the little girl's hand and shook it.

'Pleased to meet you, Adriana,' she said.

'I'll explain later,' said Paul. 'Time to eat!'

After supper he went up to find Al. He knew it was

asking a lot of her, expecting her to accept another change to the established pattern, when the pieces had hardly settled back after the last upheaval, but he knew she could do it.

'Look, she's a little girl, with no family, right?' He held Al against his chest, just as he had done when she was a little girl herself. 'And I thought that maybe we could be her family for a few weeks. You remember how you felt when Mum died?' He felt Al nod. 'Well, think how she's feeling now. You need to find that kind of strength again for her sake. And I'd be so proud of you.'

He felt almost bad about saying it: who was he to accuse Mary Blanchard of emotional blackmail? But Al wiped her eyes and washed her face and came down. She ate a bit of bread and chicken and then she joined them in the garden, where Adriana was teaching Marty her version of 'Eeny Meeny Miney Mo' and 'Round and Round the Garden'.

Quietly, Paul explained to Joanna how the arrangement had come about.

'Mary's afraid that if the authorities find out they'll deport her, so I said I'd look after her for a few weeks.'

If Joanna had been, or looked, fed up at this new intrusion into their lives and their precious time together, Paul would not have been surprised. She would have been perfectly justified. But she didn't seem to mind at all. When it was Adriana's bedtime, it was Joanna who coaxed her out of the bushes where she'd been playing hide and seek, and Joanna who examined her leg wound and insisted that Adriana had a wash and cleaned her teeth.

'I'll do it,' said Paul. 'Come on, Adriana.'

But Adriana pointed towards Joanna.

'Wash, wash,' she said.

Afterwards Joanna sat with Adriana until she fell asleep, stroking her hair and humming a lullaby. She was mesmerized by the rhythmic activity, captivated by the little girl's vulnerability and trust. She wouldn't have believed she could feel so close to another human being in so short a time. As she watched, Adriana's breathing steadied, and her thumb fell from her mouth to lie damply on the pillow. When Joanna had not reappeared after half an hour, Paul came up to find her. Standing in the doorway, seeing Joanna crouched by the bed, just watching the sleeping child, he almost felt as if he was intruding. He touched Joanna on the shoulder and she jumped.

'You can leave her now, she's asleep,' he whispered.

'I know,' Joanna whispered back. 'But I don't want to.'

Next day she took Adriana shopping.

'She needs some clothes,' she explained to Paul.

Really it was just an excuse to treat her.

Joanna wasn't stupid; she knew that the shopping trip was as much for her own benefit as Adriana's. She had never had a little girl to treat. She had two nephews, and a godson, but to go out shopping with a girl, like mother and daughter . . . All the shop assistants would assume they were mother and daughter, she was sure. Adriana didn't look like her, her hair was mid-brown and the shape of her face was different, but plenty of children didn't take after their mothers. What did it matter?

She took her to Leamington, which had a big modern shopping mall on two levels. Adriana looked around her in wonder as they descended the escalator from the rooftop car park. After the grimness which she had been used to for most of her life, Joanna could well understand that all this abundance must seem like something from a fairytale. Surely Mary couldn't be serious about taking her back to Bosnia? It was her homeland, of course, but, as far as Mary knew, there was no close family, or so she had told Paul. Adriana would be parcelled off to some distant relative who didn't really want her, to go back to a life of dodging shells and queuing for food, when there was any, possibly sustaining even worse injuries, maybe even being killed. Joanna had to swallow very hard to stop the tears which were welling up, and she grasped Adriana's hand tightly.

She made for a big department store where she could get everything in one fell swoop. Adriana's leg must be painful: the antibiotics were just starting to work on the infection, and she mustn't expect her to walk too far.

Adriana, it appeared, had firm ideas about what she would and wouldn't wear. Joanna held up leggings and a matching T-shirt. Adriana shook her head. A denim pinafore. Again, no.

'You choose, then,' said Joanna.

Adriana made straight for a rack of dresses, pretty, smocked dresses in sugar-almond colours, sailor dresses in navy and white, floral patterns in the colours of a summer flowerbed.

'Oh, I see. You're an old-fashioned girl,' smiled Joanna. 'OK, let's try them on.'

They brought three dresses and a cardigan, some lace-trimmed ankle socks, a little handbag which Adriana had been eyeing covetously and two hairbands. As Joanna paid, she saw Adriana fingering a brightly-coloured necklace of glass beads by the till.

'Yes, very pretty,' she said, thinking how hideous it was, and wondering why children the world over liked such things. Then added, 'Now put it back!'

'She likes you,' said Paul later, when he and Joanna were curled up on the sofa together, a Rodriguez guitar concerto playing in the background. Adriana was in bed; Al was on the phone; Marty had gone bowling with some friends.

'And you,' said Joanna.

'Me? Oh, come on, what's there not to like?'

Joanna cuddled up against him, smiling. Paul absent-mindedly stroked her hair. She sat like that for a moment, just enjoying the sensation, relishing the feeling of belonging.

'D'you know,' she said, leaning her head back against his shoulder, 'I'd forgotten how comfortable moments like this are. Just sitting.' She paused. 'And now I've got to go.'

'Stay.'

Joanna swivelled round to look at him.

'Do you think we're all ready for this?' she asked.

'Well, I'm ready.'

'Yeah, well, it's not just you, is it? I mean, there's Marty and Al to consider.'

'They've given you their seal of approval,' Paul assured her.

'Oh, passed British Standards, have I?' asked Joanna wryly.

'They like you,' Paul assured her.

He didn't add that he had been on the receiving end of lobbying from both Al and Marty to 'get on with it'.

'What's there not to like?' Joanna echoed his own phrase, and he smiled.

'It's a great house, isn't it?' asked Paul. 'Everybody likes everybody.' Then, as he looked at her, his flippancy faded. 'Stay,' he said again.

'I've forgotten my toothbrush,' said Joanna, still fighting it.

'No,' said Paul. 'I don't just mean tonight.'

Joanna looked at him. His stare back was even and honest. She didn't know if this was the right time or not – maybe there never was a right time – but she did know that Paul wouldn't have asked her to move in if he didn't mean it. Maybe she just had to trust him to take the decision for once.

'OK,' she smiled. 'You lend me a toothbrush and I'll stay tonight. And I'll move my things in tomorrow.'

Paul didn't say anything, just smiled and indicated to her to get up. Then he took her hand and led her upstairs.

Afterwards, when they lay wrapped around each other, Paul said softly: 'Don't get too attached.'

'To you?'

'To Adriana. It's only for a few weeks.'

'I won't.'

But Joanna knew that she already had.

Next day she brought two suitcases and a holdall to work in the boot of her car.

'Tonight?' she asked Paul when she met him in the corridor between patients.

'Can't wait.' She knew that his longing matched her own and she was glad they'd decided to go for it. It felt right.

That evening, Paul carried her cases up to his room. She unzipped them and began unpacking while he lay on the bed, watching her and flicking through a leaflet which he'd found on the table downstairs. Occasionally, as she passed to fetch a hanger, or to put something on the chest of drawers, he reached out for her and pulled her to him, kissing her as if he had to make the most of each moment, as if he had to do it to prove to himself that she was here.

Joanna looked down into the garden, where, prompted by Adriana, Marty and Al had begun work on renovating their old tree-house. Adriana stood on the ground, bossily supervising operations, as Al climbed up and down and with bits of timber and Marty sawed and hammered.

'You know, what she needs is a family . . . a mother and father,' Joanna mused, putting her scarves in a drawer. 'Ones that are married. I mean, there's not really much point in being married any more unless you're going to start a family, is there?'

'No, I suppose not,' replied Paul. 'Did you leave this

out for me?' He waved the leaflet at her. Its cover read: 'Adoption – Some Questions Answered.'

'No, no.' Joanna tried to sound casual. 'I was just trying to learn a bit more about it.'

'Ah, I see,' said Paul knowingly. 'You hadn't really thought beyond that.'

'No, of course not. We really wouldn't be suitable candidates.'

Paul arched an eyebrow, demanding an explanation.

'Well, they're generally married. Not always. But generally. And anyway,' Joanna rambled on, 'even if we were married, we still wouldn't be an ideal couple.'

'In what way wouldn't we be ideal?' enquired Paul.

'We're too old.'

'Ah.'

'And we're not Muslims. There's precedent, however. I mean, we'd have to be vetted by Social Services and providing we didn't get an anally-retentive social worker . . . well, it can take up to a year or maybe even longer, before the High Court will issue a decree . . .'

'Right,' Paul cut in, sounding amused. 'But other than that, you haven't really thought much about it.'

'No.'

'I see.'

'I did run through some names of solicitors,' she added, 'to find one who could help us if we wanted. I just thought it would be good to have a few names in mind.' Joanna grinned sheepishly at Paul. 'Meeting's on Thursday 23rd.'

Paul shook his head in amazement.

'You don't waste much time, do you?' he asked. 'You've barely unpacked your Estée Lauder, and if I'm not very much mistaken there was a sort of proposal in there somewhere!'

'Nonsense!' Joanna crossed to the bed and lay down beside him, sliding her arms round his neck. 'It would be a marriage of convenience, that's all!'

'Oh yes?' Paul nuzzled her neck and began unbuttoning her blouse. 'Whose convenience?'

They were barbecuing that evening. Al was in charge of the barbecue because, Marty said, he had an old score to settle with Adriana who, to his amazement, had beaten him at table tennis earlier.

'So we're having a return match: football, my choice,' he said smugly.

'Marty,' Joanna protested. 'She's only got little legs. And she's got an injury to one of them.'

'Didn't stop her racing me to the ice-cream van in town today,' said Marty. 'Or going on the bouncy castle. Twice.'

Joanna grinned and sipped her drink.

'D'you want any help?' she called through to Paul, who was preparing the salads.

'All under control,' he shouted. 'You relax.'

So Joanna did. She sat on the patio wall and let the sun warm her, as Paul's lovemaking had done. She felt that she should feel swamped, having gone in one swift movement from being on her own to being part of Paul's family, a family which now, possibly, was to be extended to include Adriana as well, but she didn't. She felt comfortable. She could feel herself extend and uncurl, like a plant cosseted by the sun, stretching upwards to take its full place in the world. She closed her eyes. From the kitchen behind her she heard the soaring notes of an opera from Paul's cassette player. She heard Al join Marty and Adriana on the lawn, heard the thud as Marty's foot made convincing contact with the ball and his whoop of delight. Then she heard Al and Adriana shrieking as they chased after it down the garden.

Joanna opened her eyes and smiled at the scene. But as she watched, she saw Adriana fall. She didn't seem to trip, or slip, she just fell, dropped down like a stone. Al and

Marty stood still as they waited for her to get up. But she didn't move.

'Adriana?' Joanna got up and began to move on legs which were stiff with fear towards the body on the lawn. 'Adriana!' she yelled as she suddenly began to run.

Paul was shredding carrots. Through the kitchen window, if he had looked, he would have seen Joanna kneeling by Adriana, turning her over, elevating her throat to clear the windpipe to begin artificial respiration. He would have seen Marty come running towards the house to fetch him while Al, distraught, crouched down, her arm round Joanna's shoulders.

Paul crossed to the fridge to get a pepper. As he did, he glanced through the window. As if in an Old Master painting, it exactly framed the scene: the grieving golden-haired woman, comforted by an equally golden-haired girl, bending over a dark-haired child. As Marty's feet thudded across the terrace, Paul himself ran for the back door.

'Marty's phoning for an ambulance,' Al told him as he arrived at the pathetic little group on the grass.

'I'll do the breathing,' he said to Joanna.

'Come on, baby, come on,' she said desperately, moving aside to give Paul a turn and rubbing Adriana's hands.

'Al, get my bag as fast as you can,' instructed Paul, as he bent over Adriana's open mouth. 'What happened?'

'I don't know!' cried Joanna. 'I don't know! Just do it!'

The ambulance, miraculously, was there in minutes. There had barely been time for Paul to give Adriana a shot of adrenalin before the paramedics were wrapping her in a blanket and putting a drip up before tearing away with the lights flashing.

Paul helped Joanna, who was white and shaking, into the Discovery and drove to Warwick County as fast as he could. All the way she kept saying over and over to herself:

'Come on, darling, please, you can do it, please, baby . . . breathe, breathe . . .'

It was no good. They tried for forty minutes at the hospital to resuscitate Adriana but it was no good. She died shortly after eight-thirty.

Joanna didn't say a word on the journey back. She didn't say a word when they reached home. It seemed she had entered some closed-off place which Paul was not a part of.

Al broke down in tears. Paul couldn't bear it for her, for any of them. Not when they had all been coming to care for Adriana. Not again.

'She was so sweet, Dad,' Al kept saying over and over. 'She was so sweet.'

'I don't understand.' Marty was seated on the piano stool, pressing the keys at random. 'How did it happen?'

'It was Aortic Stenosis – rheumatic heart disease,' said Paul. 'Her heart just stopped beating and there was nothing we could do. Absolutely nothing.'

'Is Joanna all right?' asked Al in a whisper.

'No,' said Paul.

And he had a nasty feeling there was nothing he could do about that, either.

She was out in the back garden, sitting on the wall again. But the warmth had gone from the stone now, and the night was clear. Paul came out of the French door on to the terrace. She knew he was there without having to turn round.

'How do you make sense of something like this?' she asked.

Paul shrugged.

'Well, I don't know that you can.'

'I loved that little girl, you know,' said Joanna fiercely, through tears. 'She was with me such a short time but I loved her like she was part of me, you know, and she loved me back. You could tell.'

'I know.'

'She didn't do anything wrong, Paul. Why did she have to die?'

Paul crossed the terrace and came to crouch in front of her.

'Joanna. Don't torture yourself. There is no explanation. She had a damaged heart.'

'No, no, no,' Joanna keened to herself. 'She had a good heart. A good soul. She was a survivor.'

'And so are you.'

'I can't have children.' She wiped tears away roughly with the flat of her hand. 'I want them desperately but I can't have them and so when I met Adriana on that first night, I thought to myself: "This is why. This is how the puzzle fits together". But now she's gone.'

'Everything happens for a purpose,' said Paul.

She turned on him.

'Oh really? There is no reason that she survived the nightmare of her own country to die here chasing a bloody ball. There is no reason for any of it.'

She broke down. Paul moved instinctively to console her but she jerked away.

'Don't! Don't!'

After a while he left her and went up to bed. He lay there in the dark until he heard her come inside, bolt the french windows and wearily climb the stairs. He watched her undress in the light which shone in from the landing, and when she got into bed he moved to put his arms round her. But she pulled away and hunched over on the other side of the bed without saying a word. Paul rolled back to his own side and lay there, helpless, while she silently shook with sobs. He could do no more for her tonight.

*

Next day, after many false starts, he finally managed to get hold of Mary Blanchard to explain what had happened. Mary sounded distressed, more distressed than he would have expected given the carnage that she had seen on a daily basis.

'It seems such a shame,' she said. 'To be saved from this chaos only to die chasing a ball.'

Exactly what Joanna had said.

'I know.'

Mary was a great help with the practical things, though. She gave him all the names of the people to contact, how to cut through the red tape. She said that Adriana's body could go out on one of the relief flights and that she would supervise the burial. Since her return to Peschkoveta, Mary had established that Adriana had a grandmother still living in the town and two uncles, and cousins. So she did have a family, after all.

Paul dreaded telling Joanna, but she was calm. She said that she'd like to speak to the agencies involved: it would, she said, make her feet better. Paul handed over the scrap of paper on which he'd written the various numbers. Their fingers touched. Paul would have liked to grasp her hand and tell her that he understood – or thought he did – but she pulled it away and stuffed it, along with the piece of paper, in her pocket.

When he got back from surgery that evening, the first thing he saw was her suitcases packed and waiting in the hall.

'Joanna?' he called.

She was in the sitting room, on the little velvet nursing chair, calmly waiting for him, her hands folded in her lap like a Victorian governess.

'What are you doing?' he demanded.

'I'm going, Paul.'

'Why?'

He just didn't understand. Of course she was hurting, they all were, but why did she have to leave?

'You are a kind and gentle man, Paul, and I've been very lucky to have you in my life. But I have to go.'

Paul began to get impatient.

'What are you talking about?'

'I can't just go back to treating hay-fever and colds and wondering if I'm doing enough,' she said simply. 'I don't think there's a reason why these things happen, Paul, you know. There's no master plan and, if there is, I'm not clever enough to understand it. All I can do is what I think is right for me at this moment. You see, it was so close to being perfect. I hurt, Paul. Like never before.'

'Do you think I don't?' Paul demanded. 'Do you think I don't care that she died? Of course I hurt but I'm not going to run out on the people I love – that love me.'

'I can't love you, Paul,' said Joanna sadly, 'and . . . well, there's no good reason for that either, but I can't. Anyway, you have a family to look after.'

'I want you to be part of it.'

'I can't be and you have to understand that.' She stood up and faced him, calm before his anger and confusion. 'I've made arrangements for Adriana's body to go on the weekend flight and I'm going with her. And I'm going to stay and I'm going to work there.'

Paul couldn't take it in. It seemed she was following an impulse when she was clearly too upset to make any rational decision. He gripped her arms just above the elbows and made her look at him.

'Joanna, don't leave. Don't leave me. Look, we have a chance to build a life together. Don't take that chance away.'

'I have to, Paul, and you have to let me.'

There was something about her calmness, about her refusal even to discuss it, which was more effective than any amount of arguing back. Defeated, Paul loosed his grip and took a step backwards to let her pass. She stepped calmly past him out into the hall.

Paul heard the suitcases scrape on the parquet floor, and the front door open and close behind her. Through the window – exactly as before, when he'd been an observer at Adriana's collapse – he saw Joanna leave. Marty and Al came round the side of the house, with Boozie on the lead. Marty helped Joanna to stow the suitcases in the car, while Al hugged her tight. Then she kissed Marty on both cheeks. There were no howls of protest and they didn't seem surprised. Joanna must have told them before she told him. Perhaps they thought it was a perfectly acceptable reaction. Perhaps he was the one who was out of step.

He hadn't meant to go, but when the day came he couldn't stop himself. He had checked the times and he knew that the relief flight left at nine in the morning from the small airport nearby which was usually used for freight. When he got there, the plane was already waiting, its engines screaming, its cargo doors open. As he watched, Joanna emerged from the terminal building, walking alongside a little trolley which carried Adriana's coffin. When they reached the plane, the handlers gently lifted the coffin inside. Joanna stood silently for a moment, her head bowed. Paul came up behind her and said her name.

She turned and he found himself taking her in his arms. He hadn't meant to do that, either: he hadn't come to pressure her. He hugged her close, feeling the contours of her body, at once so familiar and so removed from him, against his own.

'I'll be here for you,' he said. 'When you're ready to come back.'

She smiled faintly and kissed his cheek. She glanced at the hold of the plane, whose doors were firmly closed now, then turned back to look at him. With a sad, knowing look, she kissed him full on the mouth. Then she pulled herself gently away and moved towards the plane.

Paul retreated to the shelter of the terminal building as the screech of the plane's engines whirred higher and higher. Then it started to roll along the runway for take-off. When it reached the end of the runway it turned, then, gathering speed, chased back towards him, lifting off the ground as it came level with him, heading east, into the sun.

Paul watched it go until his eyes hurt. The whole thing suddenly reminded him, absurdly, of the end of *Casablanca*, when Humphrey Bogart sees Ingrid Bergman off on the plane after she chooses to stay with her husband. It was a pity Ken Jackson wasn't with him, thought Paul: he'd have played the Claude Raines figure rather well.

He thought he might give Ken a ring later and see if he was free for a drink tonight. Ken had such a cynical outlook on life that he was, perversely, a very good companion when you were feeling low yourself. It suddenly occurred to Paul that he ought to ring Al to let her know where he was. She'd be awake by now. But as he reached inside his jacket for his mobile, it rang.

'Hello?'

'Paul? It's Ken. I need you over at the reservoir, Paul. Divers went down after some drums of chemicals some lads saw being dumped last evening, and guess what they've come up with? A body . . .'

Grief and loss affected everyone differently. For some, like Joanna, the solution was to try something new. But for Paul, the solution was more of the same. Business as usual. Because life – and death – goes on.

'OK, I'll be there.' Another plane was revving its engines and Paul could hardly hear. 'Where exactly is it?' he shouted.

'I'll put Nicky on to give you the directions,' said Ken, then asked, 'Paul, where are you? It sounds like an airport.'

'That's because it is an airport.'

Ken chuckled.

'You don't half get about. And here was I worrying I might be disturbing your Sunday morning lie-in with Dr Stevens.'

'No, Ken,' said Paul. 'Not today.'